Praise

Kathy's columns have entertained our newspaper readers for years, so it doesn't surprise me she'll now be entertaining the world with a new cozy mystery series.

— KIM LEWICKI, PUBLISHER, HIGHLANDS NEWSPAPER

Astonbury, the fictional Cotswolds village in this new Dickens and Christie series, much like Louise Penny's famous Canadian village Three Pines, will have you longing to visit and even live there. Something is amiss, though, in this vibrant village, and you'll find yourself trying to solve an unexpected murder. Highly recommended for lovers of cozy animal mysteries.

— KATIE WILLS, LIBRARIAN

An author whose books are set to become bestsellers.

— LONGTIME READER

Reader Reviews from Amazon...

What a fun ride

The author has done a wondrous job detailing not only the characters but also the surroundings and backdrop. The way she has developed all of the characters truly makes them come alive. It's as if they are friends of mine that I've known forever! Thank you Kathy Manos Penn for such a fun ride!

Love this Series

I have not always been a fan of the animal detective books but I love this series. I think it is because the dialog is so believable. I can see Dickens and Christie in my mind's eye as I read the story. I love the setting, the warmth of the cozy village, and the themes of these books are believable, fun, and just a pleasure to read. I will be waiting eagerly for the next book to come out.

Refreshing and Entertaining

I hope this series continues. Light and entertaining without being juvenile. Enough mystery to keep you guessing. I admit I love the aspect of the protagonist being able to understand what her fur kids are saying. Great for stress relief, this book is interesting enough to keep you reading and light enough to lift your spirits.

Nancy Drew and Jessica Fletcher (Murder She Wrote), You have met your match

I thoroughly enjoyed this delightful cozy mystery. The narrator has moved from Atlanta, where I live, to a charming English village, which I would love to do also. She tells the story as she would to a friend over a cup of tea or better yet, a glass of wine. It has everything that I like in a mystery: suspense, light-hearted humor, and a cast of interesting human (and animal) characters. And since it's set in England, it's just plain charming. If you've ever read Agatha Christie or enjoyed watching Midsomer Murders, you probably will be happy to find this author.

BELLS, TAILS & MURDER

A Dickens & Christie Mystery
Book I

Kathy Manos Penn

Also by Kathy Manos Penn

Dickens & Christie Series

Bells, Tails & Murder

Pumpkins, Paws & Murder

Whiskers, Wreaths & Murder

Collectors, Cats & Murder

Castles, Catnip & Murder

Bicycles, Barking & Murder (2022)

https://www.amazon.com/gp/product/B085FSHQYW

Would you like to know when the next book is on the way?
Click here to sign up for my newsletter. https://bit.ly/3bEjsfi

To my husband, who took me at
my word when I said I was retiring.
Little did he know.

There are no secrets that time does not reveal.

— JEAN RACINE

CONTENTS

Cast of Characters

Aleta "Leta" Petkas Parker—Retired American banker living in the village of Astonbury in the Cotswolds with Dickens the dog and Christie the cat.

Henry Parker—An avid cyclist, handsome blue-eyed Henry is Leta's husband.

Dickens—Leta's white dog, a dwarf Great Pyrenees, is a tad sensitive about his size.

Christie—Leta's black cat, Christie is sassy, opinionated and uppity.

Anna Metaxas—Leta's youngest sister lives in Atlanta with her husband Andrew, five cats, and a Great Dane.

Sophia Smyth—Leta's younger sister is married to Jeremy and lives in New Orleans.

Alice Johnson—Housekeeper to Leta and her friends in the village.

Martha and Dylan—The donkeys

Libby and Gavin Taylor—Owners of The Olde Mill Inn in Astonbury

Gemma Taylor—A Detective Sergeant at the Stow-on-the-Wold station, she's the daughter of Libby and Gavin and lives in the guest cottage behind the inn.

Paddington—Libby and Gavin's Burmese cat.

Constable James—Constable at Gemma's station.

Beatrix Scott— Owner of the Book Nook in Astonbury, she hosts the monthly Book Club Meeting.

Thom Cook—Graduate of Oxford, Beatrix's assistant at the Book Nook, and nephew of George Evans, who owns Cotswolds Tours

Wendy Davies—A retired English teacher from North Carolina who has returned to Astonbury to look after her mum. She and Leta are good friends.

Peter Davies—Wendy's twin and owner of the local garage, Peter is a cyclist and cricket player.

Belle Davies— Mother to the twins, Wendy and Peter, Belle lives at Sunshine Cottage with Wendy.

Rhiannon Smith—Owner of the Let It Be yoga studio where Leta and Wendy take classes.

Ian and Marilyn Vella—A couple from Malta staying at the inn.

Dave Prentiss—A journalist from the States. He and Leta hit it off when he stayed at the inn.

Toby White—Owner of Toby's Tearoom who gave up his London advertising job to pursue his dream of owning a small business.

Cynthia White—Interior designer and wife of Toby, she spends part of every week in London.

Timmy Watson—The little boy who lives next door to Leta with his parents Deborah and John.

Deborah Watson—Mother to Timmy and wife to Dr. John Watson, the village dentist

Mr. and Mrs. Morgan—Leta's neighbors across the street.

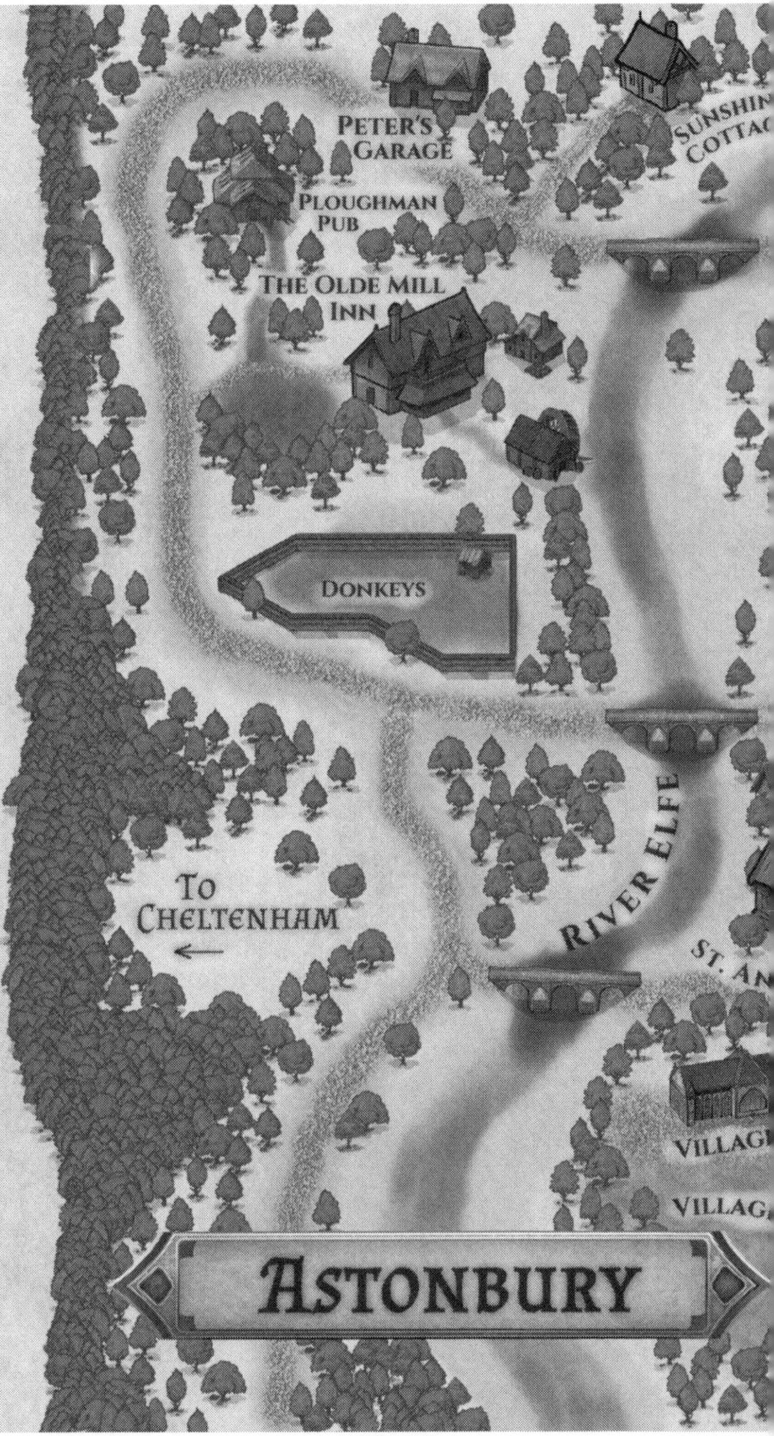
PETER'S GARAGE
SUNSHIN
COTTAG
PLOUGHMAN PUB
THE OLDE MILL INN
DONKEYS
RIVER ELFE
TO CHELTENHAM
ST. AN
VILLAG
VILLAG
ASTONBURY

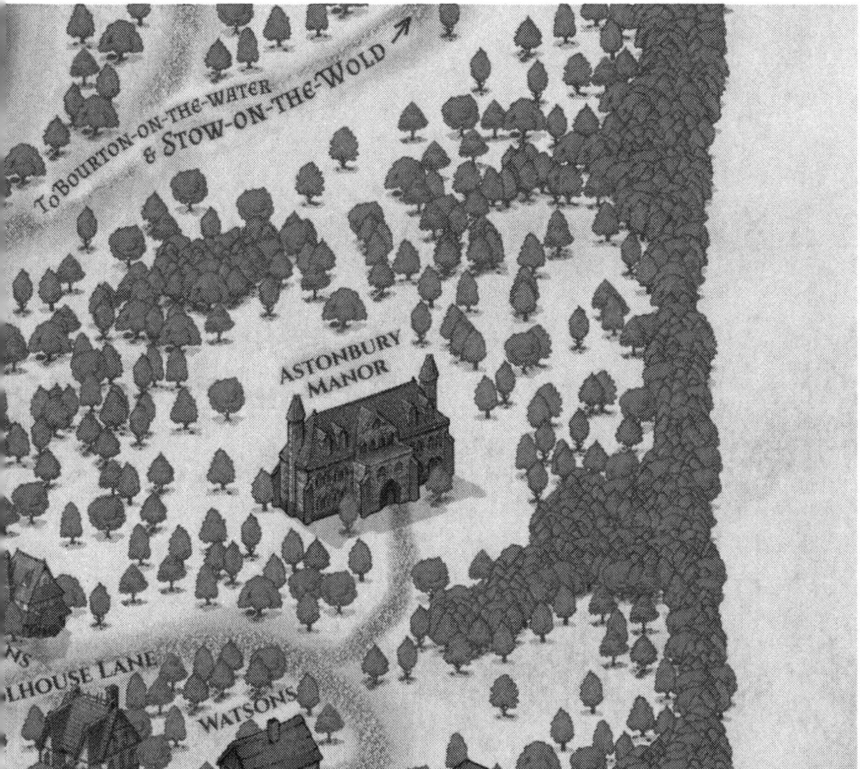

To Bourton-on-the-water
& Stow-on-the-Wold ↗
Astonbury Manor
Watsons
Leta
High Street
Letit Be Yoga
Toby's Tea Room
Book Nook

Chapter One

Early April

I couldn't believe I'd let Henry talk me into cycling up this hill yet another Saturday. Sure, I improved each time I tackled it, but I could barely keep my bicycle upright. I was in the lowest gear and still, the pedals didn't want to go 'round. Thank goodness it was the last leg of the day, and there'd be a cold beer at the end.

I much preferred the first part of our ride, the flat portion along the scenic Chattahoochee River, where I'd glimpse geese, fishermen, and canoes. Often, the Georgia State Rowing Club would be out in force. All would be well until we came to the dreaded stop sign, where we turned left and started uphill.

"I'll see you at the top, but if you don't make it by dark, I'll send out a search party," Henry sang out as he powered past me in his blue cycling jersey. With his slender 6'2" frame and long legs, my husband made the uphill climb look easy.

I stuck my tongue out and replied, "By dark, my foot. I'll be there in 30 minutes, and my chicken wings and ice-cold beer better be on the table." I sometimes thought the promised lunch at Taco Mac was the only thing that kept me coming back every Saturday.

Head down, I was praying I'd soon be at the peak where the road would level out when a car horn blew behind me accompanied by the blaring of a radio. *Lord*, I thought, *I hate horns, and there's plenty of room for whoever it is to pass me on this road without scaring the heck out of me.*

As the red Mercedes convertible shot past, I glanced up in time to see the blonde, pony-tailed driver bebopping to the music. The car took the curve and vanished from sight, and I pedaled on. The next sequence of sounds was one that haunted my dreams—the long blast of a car horn, the squeal of tires, and the screech of rending metal, followed by silence.

Without thinking, I threw down my bike and jogged up the hill. When I reached the top, my worst fears were confirmed. Henry lay unmoving, with another cyclist administering CPR, a jogger checking on the driver of the Mercedes, and another frantically conversing with 911 on her cell phone.

September the following year

Neither my waking nor sleeping dreams ever progressed beyond this point. I came back to the present and realized I was standing on the flower-flanked path to my Cotswolds cottage, its golden stone luminescent in the sunlight. *Shake it off, girl*, I said to myself as I wiped tears from my eyes. *This is your new life, and you know Henry's looking down right now and sending happy wishes.*

I squared my shoulders and pasted a smile on my face. It

was time to head to the airport to pick up Dickens and Christie, who were arriving from the States. I was sure they'd both have plenty to say about riding in the cargo hold of the jet. Dickens would bark and Christie would meow, and the ride to our new home would be filled with complaints at least until we left Heathrow. I was hopeful the new sights, sounds, and smells would quickly distract them and put an end to their grumbling.

As I walked to the garage, my housekeeper, Alice Johnson, pulled up and began unloading cleaning supplies and a basket of goodies from the car. What a comforting sight. Her plump figure, her broad smile, and her head of curly red hair brought a smile to my face.

"Hello, luv. Today's the big day, right?" she asked. "I've brought the usual scones plus an easy dinner for you to pop in the oven later."

"Goodness, Alice," I said, "What a wonderful surprise. You *are* a treasure. Now wish me luck with the traffic, and I'll be on my way."

Driving in the UK was a challenge for me, so I concentrated on keeping my refurbished London taxi on the proper side of the road. I loved my black car. Purchasing a used taxi had never entered my mind until my friend Peter had suggested I try to find one. Only briefly had I entertained the idea of getting one in red before settling on black as more practical.

Seeing my taxi parked in the garage made me think back to happier times visiting London with Henry. Plus, it was roomy and low to the ground, which would make it easy for Dickens to climb in. At forty pounds, my handsome white dog was a bit much for me to boost into an SUV, as I'd done back in the States.

I chuckled as I envisioned Dickens stepping into his new ride and seeing his dog bed on the back seat. *I can hear him now,* I thought. "Whoa, wait a minute," he'll exclaim. "This is seriously cool."

I imagined Christie, my feisty black cat, would not be nearly as polite. Christie didn't care for the car at the best of times, and after a flight across the pond, she'd be even crankier.

How life has changed for the three of us. A new home, a new country . . . and a new life . . . without Henry. I wondered whether the animals missed him as much as I did.

The sound of a horn reminded me to focus on the road. I'd soon be at Heathrow and get to hear firsthand what my four-legged friends thought about their journey.

I ran to the crates in the cargo area. "Shhh, shhh," I cooed. "You can't imagine how much I've missed you two and how glad I am you're here. I want to hear all about your trip, but first, we've got to get you settled in the car."

As I led the porter to the car, I tried to tune out the uproar emanating from my two pets. The barking and meowing were nonstop. When I opened the door to Dickens's crate, he looked at me, cocked his head, and studied his new ride. After I got him comfy and attached his seatbelt harness, I placed Christie's crate on the floor behind the passenger seat.

Dickens peppered me with questions and comments. "Oh my gosh, Leta, I've missed you. Where have you been? Where are we? How could you leave me cooped up in a crate for so long?"

Christie, on the other hand, screeched her complaints. "What on earth were you thinking? Do you realize I've been stuck in here for hours? Hours, I tell you! Let me out now, Aleta Petkas Parker! Wait, why are you putting me in the car . . . still in the crate? Let me out, quick."

Uh-oh, I know she's fit to be tied when she uses my full name. I was finding it difficult to respond to the menagerie and maneuver my way out of Heathrow and onto the road back to Astonbury. "Hush, you two. I'll answer your questions as soon as I can. I've got to pay attention to driving." When I was safely on M40, I breathed a sigh of relief.

"I've missed you both, and I can't wait to show you our new home. Christie, I know you're going to love lying in the garden in the sun. And Dickens—"

"Never mind Dickens," screeched Christie. "How long before you let me out of this crate?"

"Oh, for goodness' sake, Christie," ruffed Dickens. "Calm down. You know you can't be let loose in the car. You'd be all over the place and make us run off the road for sure—right, Leta?"

"Yes, dogs are much better suited for car rides. And just wait until you go on your first walk in the country. You're going to love meeting the sheep and Martha and Dylan, the donkeys."

And so the conversation went, back and forth among the three of us. I reminded myself that I'd have to get back in the habit of speaking to my four-legged friends the way most people speak to their pets, as though they're only surmising what the barks and meows mean. If any of my new friends thought I was talking to my animals à la Dr. Dolittle, well, that would be a problem. Even Henry had thought I was simply super intuitive and had had no idea the animals and I conversed.

Who knows why I have this ability? I'd learned to hide my quirk so people wouldn't think I was crazy. My family thought talking to the animals was cute when I was small and other children spoke to their imaginary pets. But as I got older and continued to carry on these conversations, people began to give me strange looks. It wasn't long before I picked up on their glances and adjusted my behavior accordingly.

My cottage was a welcome sight. I'd been house hunting when the restored 1840s schoolhouse came on the market. When Henry and I'd visited the area, we'd driven by it and admired it, but I'd never dreamed that one day this would be my home. I may have only taught English for a few years right out of college, but I felt an immediate affinity for the place.

As soon as I unlatched his harness, Dickens ran off to explore the garden. Christie, I carried into the house in her crate. She couldn't be trusted outside until she grew used to her new home. True to form, when I opened the door, she darted out and zoomed around the first floor and then up the stairs. I didn't bother to follow her, knowing she'd find a bed to hide beneath until dinner time.

Dickens came to the door ready for a treat followed by food and water. We ate lunch together in the cheery kitchen.

"Oh, Leta," he barked, "It reminds me of our kitchen back home."

"Dickens, this is your *new* home, and I just know you're gonna love it."

I showed Dickens his dog beds, one each in the kitchen, my office, my bedroom, and the sitting room. Once I sat down at my desk, he chose the bed at my feet. When we'd lived in Atlanta, Dickens could always be found snoozing beneath my desk while I wrote my weekly newspaper columns—a side job I'd stumbled onto a few years back. As long as I intermittently rubbed his belly with my foot, he was content. Once Christie adjusted to her new environment, she'd take up her usual position stretched out atop the desk.

It was one of the few pieces of furniture I'd shipped to Astonbury from Atlanta. Henry had made it for me, so it was never an option to leave it behind. Over the years, he'd made sideboards, mantels, tables, and more, but the desk was my favorite piece. He'd joked that everything he made was basically a box, but his friends and I knew better. He'd been a true craftsman.

The desk drawers and legs of the desk were finished in distressed black, and the writing surface was a slab of golden oak. I'm not sure Christie appreciated his craftsmanship, but when she wasn't lying on top of the desk, she was curled up in the right-hand file drawer. Early on, I'd given up trying to use it for files. Thank goodness my talented husband had also built me a matching filing cabinet.

This is my new life, I thought, as I looked around my sitting room and listened to Dickens snoring softly. I desperately missed Henry and imagined him sitting here in his easy chair looking up from his paper to ask, "Have I told you lately that I love you?" as he'd done every day in Atlanta.

Then again, had Henry's life not been cut short, I wouldn't be retired, and I wouldn't be living in the Cotswolds. If I was honest with myself, I knew Henry never would've moved overseas. Yes, we used to talk about retiring to France or England, my preferred location, but all that talk was never more than a pipe dream.

"Think about it, Dickens," I said as I rubbed his belly. "I decided to move us to England. I still can't believe I did that, and I'm sure a few of my friends are waiting for me to come to my senses and return home."

One friend had said, "You're only avoiding dealing with your grief by running off to England."

I'd responded, "Perhaps I am, but I'd be doing the same thing by going back to working sixty-hour weeks and traveling Monday through Friday for the bank. Moving to England will be way more fun, and it seems to me like the opportunity of a lifetime. And, you know what? If I give the Cotswolds a chance and it doesn't seem right, Atlanta will still be here."

The ringing of the phone interrupted my reverie. It was Libby Taylor at the inn.

"How was the reunion with Dickens and Christie?" she asked. "Have they settled in?"

"I bet you can imagine how it's going. Dickens is on his bed beneath my desk, and I haven't seen Christie since she ran upstairs hours ago."

"Right," responded Libby. "Paddington would have been close behind Christie, looking for someplace to hide." Paddington was Libby's Burmese cat. He and I had become fast friends when I stayed at The Olde Mill Inn while house hunting.

"Well, I'm calling to invite you to a cocktail party at the inn Friday night. I have some interesting guests this week, and I thought I'd gather the usual gang and get Alice to prepare some appetizers."

"That sounds like fun. Are you okay if Dickens comes too and checks out your garden?"

"Of course. You know Paddington may give him a talking-to, but he's generally pretty good with dogs. On the other hand, Paddington may choose to hang out in his favorite guest room, the one you stayed in."

That's how Paddington and I had become friends. For reasons unknown to his pet parents Libby and Gavin, he preferred the Green Room to any other, and if the door wasn't properly latched, he'd push his way in to snuggle with whoever had that room. Not all guests were as enchanted with him as I was.

I laughed. "Dickens lives with a feisty black cat, so I'm sure he can handle whatever Paddington throws his way. Thanks for the invitation. We'll see you Friday."

Since Alice had left me a delicious shepherd's pie and salad, dinner was a snap. Dickens had yet to leave my side, and Christie finally put in an appearance as I was finishing the dishes.

"Food," she meowed. "I want food—and not that dry stuff."

"Well, yes, dear," I said.

That meant the princess wanted a dab of wet food in her special dish. She daintily licked it all up, and we three moved to the sitting room. Relaxing in front of the glowing fireplace reading a book was one of my favorite pastimes, and my two friends seemed to be settling in—Dickens on his dog bed and Christie stretched out on the rug in front of the fireplace.

After a night in her new home, Christie was her old self and spent her time exploring every nook and cranny of the cottage while I drank my coffee. When I stepped outside to check on

Dickens, I caught him joyfully rolling on his back in the damp grass.

"Ready to meet Martha and Dylan?" I called.

"Donkeys? I get to meet the donkeys? Yes, yes, yes, let's go," he barked.

We'd just latched the garden gate when Peter Davies stopped out front on his bicycle. Peter owned the local garage and kept my London taxi in tip-top shape.

"This must be the famous Dickens," he called. "I'd ask to come in to meet Christie, but I've got to get back to open the garage." He waved and cycled on.

We didn't have far to go before we saw the two donkeys in the field. I laughed as they spied me with Dickens and jogged to the fence.

"You two are something else," I called as I pulled carrots from my pockets. "Meet Dickens. Lucky for you, he doesn't like carrots."

"Hi guys," barked Dickens as the pair followed us along the fence line. "Leta's told me all about you."

I doled out two more carrots and then turned Dickens towards our cottage, where he romped in the garden as I filled the bird feeders and pulled a few weeds. Pulling weeds was the extent of my gardening expertise. Thank goodness, the cottage came with an idyllic mature garden filled with beautiful plants.

I knew that sooner or later, I'd have to hire a gardener to ensure it didn't die a painful death. My brown thumb had been famous in my Atlanta neighborhood, as had my philosophy— visit Pike's Nursery, buy a plant, stick it in the dirt, and water it. If a flower or a bush required anything beyond that, it was doomed.

Inside, I washed my hands and pulled out my notes for the book club meeting that evening at the Book Nook. Beatrix

Scott, the owner, had asked me to lead this month's meeting when I'd suggested a book by Charlie Lovett as the September selection.

I hadn't read all his books, but I'd read the three literary mysteries whose plots focused on authors and legends of yore. Tonight, we'd be discussing *The Bookman's Tale*, a novel about an antiquarian bookseller from North Carolina who moves to England and stumbles across clues to Shakespeare's identity and possible Shakespeare forgeries. I couldn't wait.

Usually, our group indulged in appetizers and beverages and discussed the evening's selection—what was believable and what wasn't, what we especially liked or didn't, and what we'd change if anything. Tonight, we were not only discussing the book but Thom Cook, Beatrix's assistant, was also providing an overview of the world of book collecting as a tie-in to Charlie Lovett's main character.

I ran into my friend Wendy Davies as I was parking outside the Book Nook. Petite, slim, and almost elfin, she wore her platinum blonde hair in a short spiky do. We'd hit it off as soon as we'd met and were regulars at the bookshop and the yoga studio down the street.

As I was telling Wendy how Dickens and Christie were doing, I saw Alice leaving the shop.

"Hey there," I called. "That shepherd's pie was to die for, and you know I'll be getting a second meal out of it. Did you do tonight's food?"

"Yes, Beatrix asked me to prepare a few things. And, I'm very glad you enjoyed your dinner. How are the pets?" asked Alice.

"Oh, I was just explaining to Wendy that they're settling in pretty well. Dickens slightly better than Christie, but that's typical of cats and dogs, I think."

"Ha," she exclaimed. "My Tigger took almost a week to adjust when we moved here, so Christie's doing pretty well. Now, I'm off to start baking for Libby's do tomorrow night. Will you two be there?" she asked me and Wendy.

"Yes, and Dickens too." We waved goodbye and went into the bookshop. We were early, and only about five others had arrived. Tommy and Tuppence, the resident cats, were perched on the shelf behind the register, and Beatrix had arranged books by tonight's author on the counter. I was pretty sure our discussion would result in lots of sales.

Rhiannon Smith was the last one in the door. She owned the Let It Be yoga studio and had just finished teaching a class. When Beatrix flipped the sign from Open to Closed and locked the door, we had fifteen members present, a good number. In addition to Thom, we had one more man—Gavin Taylor, Libby's husband. I always wondered why book clubs consisted mostly of women, but that seemed to be the way. Being in the minority never seemed to bother Gavin, though, and he rarely missed a meeting.

Beatrix kicked off the evening by inviting us to fill our plates while Thom poured wine and tea. The usual suspects— Rhiannon, Wendy, Gavin, Beatrix, and I—were the only ones drinking wine. When Beatrix introduced me, a formality, as we all knew each other, I set my food and wine down and pulled out my notes and my red reading glasses.

I started with some background on the author and opined that given the rich literary history of Astonbury and the surrounding villages, I saw *The Bookman's Tale* as appropriate for our book club. We had an energetic dialogue, and we talked about being avid readers without ever having been collectors. That was a natural lead-in to Thom's part of the talk.

I thought he did a lovely job explaining the lure of collecting. He referenced the author's passion for collecting copies of *Alice in Wonderland* and explained that some enthusiasts searched only for copies of one particular book while others collected anything written by a particular author—even letters and diaries. Still others collected anything deemed rare.

His favorite professor at Oxford collected works by J. M. Barrie, the author of *Peter Pan*. Until then, I hadn't realized Barrie had written much else.

When Thom gave us examples of what rare books could go for, I had to interject. "Well, I haunted many a used bookstore in my younger days because I couldn't support my three-book-a-week habit with full-price books, not because I was searching for rare ones. Imagine if I'd known what to look for! I 'coulda been a contender, I mean, collector.'"

Gavin weighed in too. "You know, Libby and I went to estate sales to find books for the bookshelves at the inn. That was ten years ago, and I'm somewhat embarrassed to admit we chose books based on the covers looking old. Who knows? There could be a hidden treasure buried in the midst of all those antique-looking books."

By now, everyone was laughing, and we all said we could see why we read books but didn't collect them. Beatrix brought the talk to a close and reminded us that Rhiannon would be leading the October discussion of *Wicked Autumn*.

Rhiannon grinned. "I'm especially enchanted with this book because one of the characters owns a New Age shop and rents space to a yoga teacher. Maybe I should add a shop in my studio."

"With crystals and incense?" asked Wendy. "Or maybe yoga pants and tops?"

While Wendy and Rhiannon chatted, I approached Thom. "I enjoyed your presentation, and I'm curious. Did your professor ever show his collection to his students or did he keep it under wraps?"

"I think because I spent summers here as Barrie did, he showed me one book, but only one and only once. He wouldn't even let me hold it, just placed it on his desk and turned the pages," said Thom.

"Wow. Which book was it? Or was it a copy of the play, *Peter Pan*?"

"No, it was *Peter and Wendy*, a book published after the play in 1911."

"How interesting. I'd love to sit down with you one day and hear more. Thanks again for an engaging talk, Thom."

I picked up my notes and waved goodbye to Beatrix and the others. I was eager to get home to Dickens and Christie, change into my nightgown, and read a bit. It didn't matter how late or early I went to bed, I was a dyed-in-the-wool bookworm and had to read at least a few pages before turning out the light.

Dickens had only a short walk the next morning as I had work to do. Though I'd retired from my corporate job and moved to England, I'd continued to write weekly newspaper columns for two papers in the States. I loved that my editors allowed me to write about whatever struck my fancy, though the topics no longer included the deer in my Atlanta yard, the local library sale, or the annual arts festival.

Instead, I wrote about house hunting in the Cotswolds, finding a new yoga studio, meeting Martha and Dylan, and ideas triggered by reading newspaper articles. I'd worried my audience might be turned off by this shift, but I was pleasantly surprised at their reactions. Judging from the emails I received from readers, these columns were as well-received as my earlier ones.

I edited some drafts and spent another hour at my desk checking emails and Facebook. My computer pinged with a Facebook message, and I saw it was my friend Bev. We'd met as teachers years ago and been friends ever since, and she'd taken care of Dickens and Christie when I'd been house hunting in England.

She'd sent me a picture of her latest foster dog. "Conway is a mess," she wrote. "I'm trying to break him of nipping at other dogs when we walk. I wish I had Dickens here to help train him. He's such a little gentleman."

I chuckled at the description of my young man. "I have to agree he's well-behaved," I wrote back. "He's my date to a cocktail party tonight, and your comment makes me think he needs a bowtie. I wish I still had a few of Henry's, or at least the black one he wore with his tux. Wouldn't Dickens look dapper in a black bow tie? Or maybe a red one? Against his white fur, either would be perfect."

I signed off and considered running out to shop for a bow tie, but I gave in to my lazy side instead. I ate lunch and then stretched out on the couch to read until my eyes got heavy. I considered reading the perfect prelude to napping. Christie did too, so she hopped up on my chest and positioned herself between me and my book.

Eventually, we both napped, as did Dickens on his bed by

the couch. When it was time to get dressed for the party, my two friends followed me upstairs.

I knew drinks at the inn didn't require anything fancy, but I didn't get many chances to dress up, so I pulled out a long-sleeved red dress, black boots, and a necklace of jet and crystal beads. Red was my favorite color, and it complemented my brunette hair and dark brown eyes. I was fond of saying the only colors I needed were black, white, red and purple, and that preference would be obvious to anyone who glanced in my closet.

Henry, on the other hand, had joked that he was going through the khaki phase of life. It had taken me several years to liven up his look with the addition of coral, yellow, and red shirts instead of white, beige, and the occasional blue.

The weather seemed mild enough that the food would be served in the garden with the outdoor fireplace going, so I added a patterned wrap to the mix. Dickens and Christie watched as I twirled in front of the mirror.

"Awww, we haven't seen you dress up in a while," said Christie. "You look beautiful."

"I agree," barked Dickens. "What's the occasion?"

"Thanks, guys. It's a party with some of my new friends, and Dickens, you get to be my date. Are you up for another ride in my taxi?"

Chapter Two

As we pulled up to the inn, the sun was low in the sky and the hundred-year-old waterwheel on the River Elfe was visible in the background. The Taylors, Libby and Gavin, had bought and refurbished the early 1900s buildings ten years ago, and it was a popular tourist destination. The flour mill had been a going concern from WWI until it ceased operations in the late 1950s, and Libby and Gavin had transformed the adjoining smaller mill building into a guest cottage. The larger building was now the inn proper.

Paddington greeted us outside the front door and seemed none too pleased to see Dickens. "Who are *you?*" he meowed. "Leta is *my* special friend."

"Hey, she was my special friend first, so you'd best step aside," growled Dickens. "And she also has a beautiful cat named Christie. I'd suggest you change your tune if you'd like us all to be friends."

"Enough, you two. I have room for lots of friends in my life, so get over it." With that, I opened the door and called out, "Libby, Gavin, company."

I followed the sound of voices through the sitting room out to the garden and found Gavin pouring wine. With his graying goatee and a cloth napkin draped over his arm, he looked the spitting image of a London maître d. The scene was complete when Alice came through the door dressed in a black dress with a white collar. Carrying a silver tray of cheese puffs, she seemed like something out of Downton Abbey.

"Looks like I'm just in time, and yes, I'd love a glass of red," I responded to Gavin's gesture with the bottle. "And, oh my gosh, Alice, the cheese puffs look divine."

Wendy and Beatrix were already ensconced in cushioned wrought iron chairs. Wendy's twin Peter stood with his back to the fire, a beer in his hand. The two had similar facial features and coloring but were otherwise almost complete opposites. Unlike his sister, Peter was tall and lanky with greying blonde hair.

The group greeted me, but Dickens was clearly the star attraction. Adjectives like adorable, well-behaved, and cute abounded. They couldn't get over his long lustrous white hair, and he was loving the attention.

"Leta, we missed you at yoga today," said Wendy.

"I know, I know, I've gotten a little lazy since Dickens and Christie got here, but I'll make it Sunday or Monday for sure."

I turned to Beatrix and commented, "Now if that isn't a perfect outfit for you, a skirt with a collage of book covers. That reminds me, I meant to call and ask if the latest Louise Penny novel had arrived."

"Not yet, but it should be here soon. How many books have you read this week—your usual two to three?" Beatrix asked. "You've even got Wendy beat with your habit."

Wendy, blue-rimmed reading glasses perched on her nose, laughed. "The problem for you, Beatrix, is that if Leta and I read the same kinds of books, your sales numbers would plummet. She claims she went through her romance phase in college. Me? I never got over it."

"Admit it, though, I've introduced you to a few mystery authors you've liked. And you enjoyed this month's book club selection too."

Just then, a young couple and an attractive dark-haired man, who looked to be in his fifties, followed Libby outside. "Everyone, let me introduce our guests at the inn this week. We have Dave Prentiss from the States and Ian and Marilyn Vella from Malta."

The three shook hands all around as the locals introduced themselves. Ian and Marilyn went straight for Dickens and oohed and aahed at his white fur. Dickens preened as they petted him and then rolled over for belly rubs. "Things are good over here," he barked.

"He looks like a Great Pyrenees," commented Ian, "but he's so small."

Dickens barked, "Who you calling small? I'm the perfect size."

"He's a dwarf Great Pyrenees," I explained, "so he's thankfully much smaller than a full-sized Pyr, but that's the only difference. At forty pounds, he can still be a handful. By the way, he's quite sensitive about being called small. That's what the bark meant." Ian, of course, thought I was joking.

Dave looked at Wendy and me and expressed his surprise at hearing American accents in the mix. "Are you ladies visiting too?"

We both responded with a chuckle. Wendy said, "I was born here, and I've just returned to live with my mum now that I've retired from teaching in North Carolina."

"And I'm also fortunate enough to have retired to the

Cotswolds. It's been a dream of mine to live in England, and I'm finally here, complete with my dog and cat, who've just arrived from Atlanta."

"Now, what brings you to Astonbury?" Wendy inquired. "I hope it's vacation since there's so much to see."

"Well, as a journalist, I manage to make every trip a combo of work and vacation. And I'm in luck here. Every time I turn around, I hear another great story," replied Dave.

"A journalist!" exclaimed Beatrix. "What types of articles do you write?"

"I started as a reporter on the crime beat after I got my journalism degree, but I switched to freelancing years ago. Lately, I've been focusing on stories for *The New York Book Review* and occasionally for *The Strand*—stories about authors, their books, their inspiration, that kind of thing.

"I was in London doing research for an article on Arthur Conan Doyle when someone mentioned the literary connections to be found in the Cotswolds. Hearing that Doyle, J. M. Barrie, and A. A. Milne all vacationed in this area back in the day was intriguing, so I decided to check it out. Today, when I toured the Stanway House, I heard the story of J. M. Barrie donating a cricket pavilion."

"Ah yes," interjected Peter. "By all accounts, Barrie was an awful player, but what he lacked in talent, he made up for in enthusiasm and the pleasure he took in playing. I'm on the local cricket team, and we still use that pavilion.

"You know, he even formed a cricket team named the Allahakbarries, and lots of authors like H. G. Wells, Rudyard Kipling, and Arthur Conan Doyle played on it. And I guess if you're researching Conan Doyle, you already know he formed a cricket team before that—the Authors Cricket Club. Seems those writers were mad for cricket."

"You probably don't play cricket," said Gavin to Dave, "but if you're a walker, you can get a good look at the pavilion near the Cotswolds Way, and you'll see plenty of sheep too."

"Funny," I said, "I have fond memories of seeing Mary Martin in *Peter Pan* on television but don't know much more about Barrie. Oops, I guess I just dated myself."

"Leta, Peter and I can go you one better," interjected Wendy. "Not only did we see the play in London as children, but our Gran actually knew J. M. Barrie."

"Are you kidding? How?" asked Dave.

Peter rolled his eyes and replied, "Our gran was a maid at the Stanway House where he and his friends vacationed. She never tired of telling those stories."

"Wow, I wish I could hear them. They could turn into a great article. Did she talk about the other authors too?" asked Dave.

Wendy laughed. "No, just endless stories about Barrie. Too bad you couldn't have heard Gran talk about him. She said he had awful insomnia and kept the other guests awake. They were grateful when she took to sitting up with him and listening to his stories. That let everyone else off the hook, and the two of them became friends in the process."

"If that's the case, I bet there's plenty of Peter Pan memorabilia at your mom's house," commented Dave.

"All I remember is the Disney book with the colorful illustrations. I think I liked the movie even better than the play. If there's anything else, I don't recall seeing it. What do you think, Peter?"

Peter thought for a moment. "I think she has another book written by Barrie, but that's about it. What I know for sure is she still has her ancient *Winnie-the-Pooh* books from when she was a girl. They're on the bookshelf in the sitting room, right next to the mysteries she gets from Beatrix."

"I bet we all had copies of *Winnie-the-Pooh*, right?" asked Gavin as he poured more wine.

"Uh-oh," I responded. "I hope that's not a prerequisite for being friends with you guys. I have to admit my younger sisters loved *Winnie-the-Pooh*—my sister Sophia even named her two cats Pooh and Piglet—but somehow I never read the A. A. Milne stories. On the other hand, I *have* read lots of the Sherlock Holmes stories and most of the modern variations. I'm addicted to mysteries, especially British mysteries. Does that count?"

Before Gavin could respond, Rhiannon, Thom, and Toby White wandered into the garden, and another round of introductions ensued. Alice nodded a greeting to the trio as she passed a tray of veggies with spinach dip.

"Thank goodness you three are here," said Libby. "This was fast turning into a book club meeting."

"Toby, is Cynthia coming later?" asked Wendy.

"No, she usually wraps up work on Thursday or Friday at the latest, but not this week. She has some important clients to entertain over the weekend." Toby owned the Tearoom in the village, and his wife Cynthia was a partner in an interior design firm in London. She only spent weekends at home in Astonbury.

The couple seemed to take their long-distance living arrangement in stride, and I assumed it was much like when I'd traveled for my career. Most weeks, I'd leave for the airport on Monday mornings and come home exhausted Thursday or Friday night, but Henry and I made it work.

"I assured him all we single women would look after him,"

said Rhiannon with a laugh. She was dressed in a flowing green and rust ensemble that suited her tall yoga-toned body and long wavy blonde hair. She reminded me of the singer Stevie Nicks, only taller.

"Honestly, Rhiannon," I said, "When I look at you in that ensemble, I think wood nymph, and I mean that as a compliment. I could never pull off those colors."

"Oh stop," said Rhiannon. "You look stunning tonight; red is your color."

Toby had to chime in. "What? No comments about my jeans and corduroy shirt and how they complement my graying hair?"

That prompted the men to joke about each other's attire for a second or two, and then the conversation turned to plans for the next day. Thom, with the day off from the Book Nook, was leading a group of Americans on a bicycle tour. Henry and I had met Thom on our Cotswolds trip when he'd taken the two of us on a tour. He'd been a knowledgeable guide and taken good care of us. I'd never forgotten his comical comment that I was like a tortoise on the uphills, slow and steady.

What I wouldn't give to be sharing that memory with Henry now. I was sure he'd be laughing.

Dave was headed to Bourton-on-the-Water, and Marilyn was excited about visiting Blenheim Palace on the way to stay in Oxford. "I'm a Churchill fan," she explained, "and I want to see the exhibit at Blenheim and the War Room in London too."

"She also wants to tour the Bodleian Library in Oxford," Ian said, "which I may let her do on her own. I'm sure there's a pub I can visit while she gets her library fix."

Wendy and I chimed in at the same time to say we had tickets to tour the library the following week. We had plans to drive over, do the tour, take in a play, and spend the night. "Of course, Leta and I think you've made a great choice, Marilyn," said Wendy. "She and I were both English majors and think it's a must-see. Can you imagine the treasures it holds?"

Catching a glimpse of Dickens's tail disappearing into the inn, I chased after him to be sure he wasn't headed to the kitchen. He would be like a kid in a candy store if he found hors d'oeuvres on the kitchen table. He wasn't tall enough to counter surf, but he was adept at jumping onto a kitchen chair to reach the table.

I passed Alice in the hall, another tray of goodies in hand. "Alice, I thought the food at book club was delicious, but you've outdone yourself tonight."

She grinned and shook her red curls. "Why thank you. You know I love to cook, and I'd watch those cooking shows all day long if I could. You can tell that from my shape, can't you?"

We both laughed. She nodded in the direction she'd come from and told me to hurry before Dickens discovered the tray of cheese and crackers she'd just set out.

I caught up to him in the kitchen with his nose held high in the air. He looked as though he were trying to decide which delicacy to sample first, and I was just in time to intercept him as he placed his front paws on the nearest chair. "No way, you little Dickens," I said as I grabbed his collar.

Thom had followed me to the kitchen to get a beer, and he chuckled at the sight of Dickens caught in the act. "Dickens, you'll have to be stealthier if you're going to score any snacks."

The two of us chatted about his years at Oxford where he'd read English, and I asked him how it felt to have graduated.

"It's great to be out, but I'm a bit at loose ends. As you can imagine, I'm pretty heavily in debt so I feel like I need to find a full-time job, but doing what?"

"Sounds like the stories I hear back home," I said. "I owed money when I graduated, but nothing like what I hear about today. For me, getting a teaching job was my top priority."

"I love books, so reading English at Oxford was for sure the right thing for me, but I don't think I want to teach. For now, I can't decide whether to look for some kind of full-time job or to keep on working for Beatrix at the bookshop and leading tours for my uncle George. Maybe I should view this year as a break—a chance to stick with work I enjoy while I decide what I want to do long-term."

"Could be taking a year to clear your mind will lead to a better decision. Going right to work as I did and then taking night classes to get a Masters was no walk in the park. I wonder whether I'd have done things differently if I'd had some time to think."

"I'm trying to save as much as I can so I'll have the option to pursue an advanced degree if I want to. Immersing myself in literature again would be awesome, but the social environment? Not so much."

"What was the issue with the social part?" I asked.

"I grew up poor and lived in council housing in Manchester. I know I was lucky to go to Oxford, but I never really fit in with the toffs who'd gone to the best schools. That part? Feeling left out and being made fun of? Not good.

"What's good for now is Uncle George letting me live rent-free in the flat over his shop and making good tips leading tours. I enjoy chatting with the tourists too," he said.

"I'm not sure I realized George Evans was your uncle.

Maybe I knew and I've forgotten. We took a driving tour with him the same year we cycled with you. It was with George that I learned about the authors who summered at the Stanway House. Between the two of you, Henry and I learned a lot."

"Yes, Uncle George has always been keen on history, and spending summers with him, I couldn't help but learn plenty. Every summer, Mum made sure I escaped Manchester, as she put it, to breathe the country air. With Dad disabled and on the dole, money was tight, so summers with Uncle George were a blessing."

"Is your mum on her own now?" I asked.

"Yes, Dad passed away before I went to Oxford," said Thom. "Uncle George keeps trying to get her to move here, but she says Manchester's her home. She's that attached to her council flat and her neighbors, I guess."

We continued our conversation as we returned to the garden with my rogue dog. Everyone had a laugh about Dickens's failed attempt to scarf people food while breathing a sigh of relief that the nibbles were safe. The wine flowed freely, and the lively conversation continued.

The party began to wrap up as those who had to start early the next day made moves towards the gravel drive where the cars were parked. Toby had to open the Tearoom, Rhiannon had an early morning class, and Peter would be up early to ride his bike before he opened the garage.

Just then, Gemma arrived, still in her dark navy suit and crisp white blouse. Libby gave her daughter a kiss on the cheek and introduced her to Dave and Marilyn and Ian. "Sit awhile, luv, and tell us about your day. Is all well in the kingdom, all ne'er-do-wells and criminal masterminds apprehended and locked away?"

Gemma was Detective Sergeant at the Stow-on-the-Wold police station and lived in the guest house in the back corner of the garden. She'd only recently transferred back home from the Thames Valley force.

Gemma laughed. "Not quite, Mum, but good enough. Did you lot leave me any of Alice's cheese puffs or cucumber sandwiches? And, Dad, a glass of wine wouldn't be half bad."

She asked after Wendy's mother. "How's Belle doing? She must be happy to have you at home."

"Oh yes," replied Wendy, "although Alice has taken excellent care of her the last year or so, keeping the house straight and cooking a few meals. She even found time to take Mum to the library."

The mention of Belle seemed to give Dave an idea. "Wendy, do you think your mum would let me come by to speak with her about her memories of your Gran and her stories about Stanway House and J. M. Barrie?"

"I can't think of anything she'd enjoy more than reminiscing about Gran. Let's plan on Sunday," said Wendy. "Leta, you might enjoy the stories too, and I know Mum wants to meet Dickens."

"That would be great," I replied. "I always enjoy time with your mum, and I can't believe I haven't heard the Gran stories yet. As for Dickens, as long as someone rubs his belly, he's in."

Dickens barked and looked at me. "Belly rub? Did I hear belly rub?"

I laughed and commented, "Gee, you'd think he understood me."

Christie was talkative the next morning. She was quite set in her ways and had me well trained. She expected a small puddle of milk in her bowl first thing every morning. I was allowed to start the coffee, but then I had to turn my attention to milk duty.

If something about her dish of milk wasn't to her liking, she'd sit and stare at me until I somehow changed it. For some reason, she refused to provide direction. She clearly thought her indignant looks were sufficient.

This morning, she deigned to drink her milk right off, allowing me to sip my first cup of coffee in peace and read the Saturday edition of the *Wall Street Journal*. I considered a leisurely read of the weekend paper one of life's great pleasures, right up there with afternoon naps.

Dickens looked at me expectantly as I opened the door to the garden. It was part of our routine that I'd toss him a treat as he ran outside. When he returned, he'd gulp water and eat a bit of dry food while he waited for me to glance at the paper and play a few games of Words with Friends. Some mornings, that activity took only thirty minutes. Saturdays it stretched to an hour or so. Fortunately for me, Dickens was a patient soul.

When I returned to the kitchen dressed in jeans and a long-sleeved T-shirt and grabbed my ball cap and the leash, he knew the game was afoot. I called, "Dickens, shake a leg, you lazy thing! After hearing Peter mention the Cotswolds Way and the cricket pavilion, I've decided we'll take our walk there today. You used to get a kick from seeing the goats at home; now, you'll get to see sheep."

"Sheep? Sheep? Oh boy, let's go," he barked.

Christie stretched out full length in a sunspot on the

kitchen floor and gave a big yawn. "You know I have no interest in a walk, but when do I at least get to investigate our garden?"

"A few more days, Christie," I said. "I want to be sure you're acclimated and not likely to take off and get lost. Dickens and I'll be back in a few hours for lunch."

In the car, Dickens shared his impressions of the friends he'd met the night before. "I wish that couple from Malta wasn't leaving today. They have a dog at home, so they were expert at belly rubs. And I bet you didn't notice Peter sneaking me a few crackers. We need to see him more often. Rhiannon tried giving me a celery stick—yuck."

"You know, Dickens, I don't judge my friends by how well they choose snacks for you. What did you think of Beatrix and Wendy?"

"I especially like Wendy 'cause she's so tiny. I can't believe you found a friend even shorter than you are."

I laughed. "As sensitive as you are about being called small, I can't believe you just made a short comment." I think he harbored a secret wish to be a full-sized Pyr, though Henry and I had chosen him because he wasn't.

"Yeah, but you're not bothered by being short. It's not like I joked about your nose."

Ah, he had me there. When I was a child, my sister Sophia had commented that my nose was big, like my father's, and I'd been sensitive about it ever since. Heaven forbid anyone were to take a photo of me in profile.

"So, am I wrong?" he continued. "Or is Beatrix not used to dogs?"

"You're right, Beatrix has two cats at the Book Nook. She doesn't dislike dogs; she's just not around them all that much."

"Speaking of cats, Paddington and I came to an understanding that he can be your special friend when you visit the Inn, as long as he understands he's not 'top cat.' That honor belongs to Christie."

"It's sweet that you're looking out for your feline sister, Dickens. Keep going. I want to hear your perspective on the others."

"Well, Dave was a bit standoffish with me, but he was awfully friendly with you and Wendy. In fact, I wouldn't be surprised if he had a thing for you."

"You're too funny. I bet Dave's at least five to ten years younger than me."

"So what if you're in your fifties, Leta? You look younger, and I think you're beautiful."

I laughed at my sweet boy. He hadn't used that dreaded phrase, 'young for your age,' nor mentioned my hair beginning to turn grey. "Thank you. Well, you're on a roll. What about Rhiannon and Toby and Thom?"

"Ha!" he barked. "Rhiannon is maybe a little too airy-fairy for me, but Toby seemed nice enough, if a bit preoccupied. Now, Gavin and Libby are my kind of people, even if they only have a cat. And I'd like to spend more time with Gemma too."

"Thom?"

"Nice young man. He said I should be stealthy, so I'd like some tips on how to do that."

"Uh-uh, I don't think so. You get away with filching enough treats as it is. And Alice? Did she slip you a snack too?"

"Not only did she give me a cheese puff, but she also told me she'd bring me home-baked dog treats next time she cleans our cottage."

Processing all that, I slowed as I saw the cricket pavilion. A light morning mist was rising above the grass, and I could see sheep in the distance. It was hard to believe this brown wooden building had been built close to a hundred years ago and was still in regular use. I pulled to the side of the road where I could access the Cotswolds Way. There was another car parked up ahead, and it looked like Alice's, which was odd because no one had ever mistaken Alice for a walker.

Dickens started barking nonstop and was barely free of his seatbelt before he took off towards the cricket pavilion. "It's bad, it's bad," he barked.

That's his alert bark, I thought. *Something's wrong.* I jogged after him as he disappeared behind the building. His barking got more frantic as he darted in front of the wooden structure and then raced behind it again.

Rounding the corner of the pavilion, I saw the scene in flashes—Dickens licking an outstretched hand, a black dress, a white collar, red curly hair, a person sprawled facedown in the grass. *Oh, no, no,* I thought. *Don't let that be what I think it is. A body? Please, not a body. Oh my God, can it be Alice?*

I called Dickens to my side and coaxed him to sit before I moved closer. I'd watched enough BBC murder mysteries to know I shouldn't disturb the scene, but I had to check for a pulse. I pressed my fingers to her wrist. Her skin was cold, and I couldn't find a pulse.

Take a breath, calm down, what do you do now? I thought. My first inclination was to call Libby in the hope that Gemma was still at home. I stood staring at the body as I dialed the inn. "Libby, Libby, Libby," I gasped. "Please tell me Gemma's there."

"Leta? What's wrong? You sound frantic. And, yes, she's here. This is her day off. She was on her way out for a run."

When Gemma came to the phone, I sobbed out the story.

Gemma told me to go back to my car and wait. As she was handing the phone back to her mum, I heard her say, "She was crying so she was hard to understand, but she's found a body by the cricket pavilion and she thinks it's Alice. Oh, hell, I shouldn't have told you that. It'll be all over Astonbury before I crank the car."

Chapter Three

I tried to do what Gemma had told me, but Dickens wouldn't budge. "We can't leave her alone," he growled as he trotted over to the nearest large mushroom-shaped stone. I recalled reading that these stone supports were used for granaries but for some reason had been part of the design for the cricket pavilion.

Why on earth did that bit of trivia pop into my mind? I wondered. I noticed Dickens was now sniffing around the stone. "What is it, Dickens?"

"It's blood, Leta. Look here on the stone."

I pressed my knuckles against my mouth as I muttered, "Oh my God, oh my God," over and over. I looked at the body again and saw that Alice had something small and blue clutched in her hand.

To keep Dickens from disturbing the scene, I walked him to my car and then on an impulse continued on to the other car. "Oh, this *is* Alice's car, Dickens. I can see her box of cleaning supplies on the back seat and there's a tray of leftovers in plastic wrap on the front seat. She must have come here straight from the party. But why?"

I was standing between the two cars when Gemma arrived, followed by a young male constable in a separate car. Dressed in her black suit with her blonde hair pulled back in a ponytail, Gemma looked completely pulled together despite having been on her way out to run. *Just like on TV,* I thought. *No matter what the detective is doing when the call comes in, they look professional when they arrive at the scene.*

Gemma guided me away from the cars, sat me down on the front steps of the pavilion, and gave me a sip from a bottle of water. "Leta, stay here and keep Dickens with you while we check this out. Constable James will be back with you shortly."

The constable and Gemma moved to the back of the pavilion. I couldn't hear their conversation, but Dickens could, and he repeated it for me seemingly verbatim. This was one time I was thankful for his keen sense of hearing.

He started with Gemma's words. "No pulse. Definitely dead and already cold to the touch. I guess she could have stumbled out here in the dark. And it must have been dark given there's a flashlight next to her. I'm afraid we're going to need the SOCOs to confirm it was accidental. I wonder what she was doing out here in the dark. Hustle back to the car and contact the SOCOs and let's hope they can get here quickly from Quedgeley."

After Constable James checked on me and made the call, he returned to Gemma. "What do we do now?" I was able to hear him ask.

Dickens picked up with Gemma's response. "Well, this is not something we often get called out on from Stow-on-the-Wold. Our crimes run more to the snatch and grab variety, maybe a break-in, or a car theft. I think this is likely your first dead body, so tell me what you see."

The constable's voice carried better than Gemma's and I could hear him answer, "You're half right, Gemma. I was once first on the scene of an auto accident where two people died, but I've never been to this kind of crime scene.

"I see a middle-aged woman on the ground. She's dressed in a black dress, a bit like a uniform. Her hands are flung out as though she may have been trying to brace herself. There's a flashlight near one hand, which makes me think she came here last night, and her other hand is closed in a fist. Is there something in that hand?"

Good grief, I thought as I sat sniffling. *I'm witnessing an investigation or, more accurately, I'm overhearing one.*

With Dickens's help, I got the next bit from Gemma. "It looks as though she's clutching something, maybe a purse strap, but I can't tell from here. Could be she was holding on to her purse as someone tried to grab it. But why would a purse-snatcher be out here? For that matter, what was she doing out here? What else do you see?"

Constable James paused. "Well, I don't see any obvious signs of an assault, no blood on the body that we can see. Could be there's a wound or something more on the front side. But look, just by the stone. Is that a tube of lipstick? Oh, and I see a few coins on the ground. And it's hard to tell from here, but it looks as though there's a stain on the top of the stone. You know, the part that looks like a mushroom top?"

As Dickens continued sharing Gemma's words, I realized she and I were in sync about what the scene revealed. "I think you're right on both counts. I can't quite suss out what happened here. I suppose she could have tripped and fallen and hit her head. Or perhaps she had some sort of seizure that made her fall. And, since I saw her last night working at my mum and dad's, I'm pretty sure she came here after she left the inn. But why?

"When I left Thames Valley, I'd hoped never to deal with a suspicious death again, but that's what we've got here. Or at least we've got a puzzle I can't readily solve. Let's talk to Leta —um, I mean the witness—while we wait for the SOCOs."

They returned to me and Dickens. I felt calmer and sat with my hand on Dickens's head as he sat by my feet. Gemma asked Constable James to take me back through the events of the morning.

"We were out for a walk. I'd been by here any number of times in my car and thought it would be interesting to see the pavilion and the sheep up close after one of the guests at your mum's party mentioned it. I noticed the car when we drove up and it passed through my mind that it looked like Alice's, but really, I'm not all that good about cars, so the thought didn't stick."

"Right, ma'am, then what?" prompted Constable James.

"Well, almost right away, Dickens barked his worried bark, his alert or danger bark, and ran behind the pavilion where I couldn't see him. He kept barking, so I ran too." I took a deep breath as I recalled the images from earlier. "It was almost like I couldn't see it all at once. I saw a hand, and I saw that familiar red hair. Oh my gosh, it was the hair. And then the black dress. I somehow knew it had to be Alice even if I couldn't see her face. She only recently got that dress for when she serves at parties, and she's so proud of it. It is Alice, isn't it?"

Gemma answered, "Yes, Leta, I'm afraid it is. Did you see anyone else around?"

"No, only the sheep off in the field."

"Did you touch anything?" asked the Constable.

"I did . . . I did take her hand and touch her wrist to feel for a pulse, but I couldn't feel one, so I backed away. But Dickens didn't want to leave. He kept sniffing that big stone support beneath the building. I know I should have dialed 999, but I couldn't think of calling anyone but you, Gemma."

"That's understandable," Gemma replied. Just then, two SOCOs hustled up and she directed them to the back of the pavilion. Dickens stood up as though to follow them, but I grabbed his collar.

"Ma'am," asked the constable, "did you see anything else at all, whether you think it would be helpful or not?"

"No," I replied. "The walking paths are usually pretty deserted this early in the morning, so it was just me . . . and Dickens, of course. While we were waiting, I looked in the car and could tell it's definitely Alice's." I began to tear up. "Will I have to go to the station, or can I go home now?"

"Can you hold on just a bit longer, Leta?" asked Gemma as the SOCOs came to the front steps.

"We've strung the yellow crime scene tape around back and we'll check the car next," said the one who seemed to be in charge. The group moved a little away from me, but their voices carried in the crisp morning air.

"Ma'am, you were right to call us. There's a wound on the victim's forehead, and it appears she may have struck her head on one of the stones. The simple explanation would be she fell on her own, though I guess you two think it's suspicious she was out here at night. We won't know until we get the lab results, but it's likely her blood on the stone."

"Can you tell whether the lipstick and coins have been here a while or are new? Could someone have been running off with her purse and the coins fell out?" Constable James asked.

"It's hard not to speculate, but let's see what we can learn from her car," said Gemma. "And we need to call in the license and get an address for our victim so we can go there before the day's out."

"We'll give the car a quick going-over for you and then call to have it towed to Quedgeley. We can be more thorough there if need be," was the reply.

"You can go on now, Leta," said Gemma. "Is there anyone we can call to sit with you so you don't have to be alone with this? Maybe Mum or Wendy?"

I shook my head. "No, I just want to hold Dickens and forget what I saw. Come on, boy, let's go home."

I started toward my cottage and then I realized Gemma was right. I didn't want to be alone, so I called Wendy. She and I had become fast friends in the few months we'd known each other. "I've got to see you. Something awful's happened."

When I pulled up to Sunshine Cottage, Wendy was waiting outside. "What on earth?" said Wendy as I stumbled from the car. "Lord, you look upset, and you're forgetting Dickens."

I turned back to the car, opened the back door, and fumbled with the seatbelt as Dickens licked my face. "It will be okay, Leta," he said, trying to get me to calm down.

I sat in the homey kitchen while Wendy made tea, Dickens glued to my side. Belle had decorated the kitchen in cheery reds—chair cushions with a cherry pattern and coordinating red and white checked curtains. A hooked rug was on the floor. "I know you like your coffee in the morning, but a good strong cup of tea is what you need right now," said Wendy. "Mum's in her room watching her morning program. She's not up and dressed yet. Now tell me what's going on. Is it bad news from home? What is it?"

As Wendy looked on astonished, I poured out my story. Dickens, sensing my agitation, laid his head on my lap.

"Alice? It can't have been Alice," said Wendy. "What was she doing out there early in the morning? Did she fall? Did she trip?"

I was sobbing now. "No, she had to have gone there last night. She still had on her black dress, the one she wears when she serves cocktails or dinner at the Inn. She would have been dressed in something else if she'd been out for a walk this morning."

"Shhh," said Wendy as she poured us both another cup of tea. "And when have we ever known Alice to take a walk? Drink this while I take care of Mum. She's going to want to hear this."

After Wendy helped her mum into the kitchen, she asked me to tell the story again. Every time I repeated it, I found the telling got a bit easier. I almost made it through this time without tears. Belle braced herself on her cane and leaned over to give me a hug.

"My goodness, girl, I can't believe you had to see that," said Belle. "What an awful sight it must have been. Did Gemma think Alice had fallen and hit her head? I mean, what else could have happened?"

"Well, Gemma and the others seemed to think she might have tripped, but they weren't sure. But what was she doing at the cricket pavilion in the first place? Why would she go there?"

"Goodness knows," said Belle. "Could she have been meeting someone out there? I mean we all know her as Alice, who cleans our houses and bakes amazing sweets, but we don't really *know* her. She's only lived here a few years, so she's not really one of us."

Wendy sighed. "You know what that means, right, Leta? You'll be a newbie forever. You're not 'one of us' unless you were born here or possibly 'married into' the area. Peter and I are only accepted because Mum's lived here all her life."

I couldn't quite muster a chuckle. "Guess I'm fortunate to have fallen in with you, then. Between you and Libby, I seem to be getting along fine."

My thoughts returned to the comments about Alice. "Even if Alice isn't one of us, as you say, we *must* know something about her. Belle, you may know her the best because she not only cleaned and cooked for you, but Wendy says she also took you to the grocery store and even the library in Moreton-on-Marsh before Wendy came home from the States."

"She was always polite and pleasant and good-natured with me," said Belle, "but when I think about it, she wasn't one for sharing much about her personal life. I did sometimes hear her having some strained conversations on her cellphone. She'd help me into my bedroom so I could read a bit before my afternoon nap and then come sit here in the kitchen and get on the phone. Everyone thinks I can't hear because I wear hearing aids, but I *can hear* when I have them in my ears."

"What do you mean by strained, Mum?" asked Wendy.

"It was a mix of things, luv. I once heard her say, 'Everyone has secrets.' And another time, she said 'This is the last time I'm going to ask' in kind of an angry way. It was like hearing one of those shows on the telly. I guess she could have been talking about something completely innocent, but some of the things she said made me wonder. And, oh, one time she even said, 'You know where to put it, the usual place, and it better be there.' Don't you think those are strange comments?"

Wendy and I looked at each other. "Good grief, Wendy," I said, "What could she have been talking about . . . and who could she have been talking to?"

Belle didn't hesitate. "I'm sick over what happened to Alice, but if she was out at the cricket pavilion at night, she had to be up to something, right? Maybe that something got her killed. Oh my, I can't believe I just said that word—*killed*. But that's what happened, isn't it? The way you described it, Leta, it didn't sound like an accident . . ."

"Up to something! That's awfully harsh, isn't it?" I said.

"Now, Mum, take a breath and slow down," cautioned Wendy. "We can't have you getting overexcited. And I think we're jumping to conclusions without having all the facts."

"But Belle, you could be on to something. Did Alice ever say anything like that directly to you?" I asked. "Or was it just one side of a conversation you heard her having with others?"

Belle frowned and thought for a moment. "You know, one afternoon, we were watching telly while she made my tea, and she said something about folks not always being what they seem. I think there was a news report on about some politician getting caught running around on his wife. Yes, that was it, and Alice said, 'There's a bit of that going 'round, you know.' When I questioned her, that's when she said something like, 'Belle, everyone has secrets. Some are just better at hiding them than others.'"

I couldn't help myself. "Oh for goodness' sake, are we talking about Astonbury? This sounds like a soap opera."

Wendy looked at me. "Alice cleaned your house too. Have you noticed any changes in her behavior lately?"

"Well, you know I've only been here a few months, so I may not be the best person to ask. You've been back living with your mum a year. What would you say?"

Wendy leaned forward and said, "Now that I think about it, in just the last few months, I've noticed Alice wearing a bit of jewelry when she never did before, and she just got that new black dress and got a new car last month. I mean, it was used, but it was new to her."

"I hadn't thought about it, Wendy," I responded, "but I've noticed Alice wearing several new outfits lately, not just the black dress. In fact, I complimented her on them. You know I tend to notice clothes, and I even asked her where she shopped, since I don't yet know all the places to go. But, does any of that really mean anything?"

"She wears nice perfume," Dickens mentioned to me.

The perfume comment prompted me to ask, "By the way, Belle, has Alice always worn perfume?"

"Funny you should mention that," mused Belle. "Not until recently."

"What? Do you think she has a secret boyfriend?" said Wendy. "Listen to us. What do we think we're doing?"

"Oh my gosh," I said, "While we've been acting like amateur detectives, I forgot Alice's cat Tigger has been home by himself all this time. I guess that's one of the few things I *do* know about her. When I told her how much I missed Christie, she showed me a photo of Tigger. Someone needs to check on the poor thing, but, but I don't even know where Alice lives . . . lived . . . in a flat in Bourton-on-the-Water, I think."

"Good grief, Leta, Christie would be fit to be tied if she missed a meal, much less two," said Dickens. "Let's hope Tigger's okay."

"Mum, if you think you'll be all right by yourself, I'll go with Leta. She doesn't need to be on her own after her experience this morning," said Wendy.

"Wendy, do you even know where the flat is?" asked Belle in exasperation. "I've been there a few times with Alice when we were close by shopping. I think you'd best take me with you."

"Oh, for goodness' sake, this is turning in to an expedition," groaned Wendy. "OK, Mum, let's get your cane and get a move on."

When we pulled up to Alice's home, it was Belle who asked the logical question. "And just how are we going to get in since none of us has a key?"

"I hear plenty of folks around here don't lock their doors. Let's hope Alice is one of them," I said as I let Dickens out the car. "Belle, why don't you and Dickens wait out here until we're sure?"

We were in luck. The door was not only unlocked, it was also slightly ajar—and we could hear Tigger mewing loudly. The front door opened to a tiny sitting area to the right and the kitchen off to the left. I stopped in my tracks, and Wendy piled into me. The sitting area was in disarray—not quite a shambles, but close. Books and papers littered the floor, and cushions had been thrown off the couch. In the kitchen, the freezer and fridge doors were standing open. Even the oven door was open. I guess the good news was there was no smashed crockery or knickknacks. It seemed to be controlled chaos.

"Oh my gosh, oh my gosh" said Wendy and then she called, "Is anyone here?"

We could hear Tigger meowing from the back of the flat but no other sounds, so I carefully stepped through the mess to the bedroom, which looked much like the front area, with the mattress pulled off the bed frame, and the drawers of the dresser and the small desk hanging open, their contents strewn across the room. The cat was backed against the wall beneath the bed and had to be coaxed out.

"Do you need help?" shouted Wendy.

"No, I've got him, poor thing. He's scared to death." I backtracked to the kitchen and found a water dish and food bowl in one corner and canned food in a cabinet. Taking care of Tigger gave me time to collect my thoughts, but Tigger seemed too traumatized to bother with food or water.

"What do we do now?" I wondered aloud. "We've landed smack-dab in the middle of something, and given this mess, I can't see how Alice could have accidentally fallen and hit her head."

"Girls," Belle said from the doorway where she stood with Dickens, "don't you think we need to call Gemma?"

"Ummm, not yet," I said. "I mean, we had to come over to tend to the cat, and since we're here, what's the harm in looking around—before we make the call?"

"Right," said Wendy, "Because Alice is—I mean was—a constant in our lives, we may pick up on something the police wouldn't. But we need to move quickly . . . and carefully. Gemma's gonna have a fit if she thinks we did anything more than take care of Tigger. It can't look like we've been digging around."

"Isn't that exactly what you two are doing?" asked Belle. "But, hey, I'll be the lookout, so have at it."

"Wouldn't it be lovely," I said, "if it were like what we see on TV, a big muddy footprint on the floor that points to an obvious suspect? Oh, but speaking of TV gives me an idea. We need to take photos so we can study this later. I'll start in the bedroom."

"I wish we had gloves," said Wendy. "All we need is for the police to find our fingerprints and think we're the cause of this mess."

"Try wrapping your sleeve around your hand. I'm wrapping my sweater around mine, and I'm trying not to touch much. That's the best we can do," I said. "That makes the photos all the more important. Wait, I can't believe this, I see one of my Frog Prince figurines on the dresser. What's it doing here?" I was about to snatch it up but thought better of that move. I'd have to get it from Gemma later.

Dickens started towards the kitchen and Wendy hollered, "Oh no, Dickens, don't go in there! Gemma will have our heads if she finds pawprints on the floor."

"Dickens, is that your name?" called Tigger. "It was a man, it was a man who did all this. I was scared almost to death."

"Yes, I'm Leta's dog. Try not to worry; she'll take good care of you. Do you think the man found something while he was here?"

"Once I hid beneath the bed, I couldn't tell you what he did, but he was cursing the whole time he was here, so I don't think he found what he came for."

"I see Alice's big blue purse tossed in the corner," said Wendy. "And it looks to be missing its strap."

I popped my head out of the bedroom. "That's it! That's what didn't seem right. Why didn't Alice have her purse with her?"

Wendy tiptoed to the corner, picked up the purse, and opened it wide. A tiny spiral notepad was tucked in an inside pocket. "Whatever they were looking for, they must have missed this pad," murmured Wendy. "It seems to be Alice's schedule of clients, all of us whose houses she cleaned.

"Leta, you're down for Tuesdays, Mum and I are on Mondays and Thursdays, and Libby's listed for mornings daily at the inn, and so on. It looks like she did the rooms at the inn late morning after breakfast and then visited the rest of us when she finished there. I didn't know she cleaned for so many people. Peter, Rhiannon, Toby, Beatrix at home and at the Book Nook, and those are just the ones I know. She was one busy lady."

"Let me get pics of the pages before you put it back," I said. "I didn't see anything else suspicious in the bedroom— besides the mess and my figurine, that is."

"What figurine?" asked Wendy.

I'm sure my indignation was evident. "Well, I can hardly believe it, but it's one of the Frog Prince figurines Henry gave me. I don't know how it could have wound up here, and I've a mind to take it back right this minute, but I guess it's evidence of some sort."

Wendy looked shocked. "What? Something from your cottage is here, in Alice's flat? What can that mean?"

I was just about to say it was time to call Gemma when I heard Belle say, "Why, good afternoon, Gemma. Is this handsome young man your partner?"

Too late, I thought as I walked to the door to explain about the cat.

Constable James seemed speechless at the sight of me, my dog, and two strange women at the victim's house. It was clear Gemma was furious.

"What on earth . . ." she spluttered. "I thought you were going home, Leta. Why are you here? And why are Wendy and Belle here with you?"

It was Belle who jumped in to explain in her best little old lady voice. "We were beside ourselves with worry over the poor cat, and none of us wanted to come here alone, so we piled in Leta's car without another thought and came to Tigger's rescue. We didn't mean any harm."

Gemma looked flummoxed. I could tell she was finding it difficult to be angry with Belle. Besides, she had to know the idea for this excursion had come from me or Wendy or both of us—not Belle. In a reasonably calm voice, Gemma said, "Just tell me what you've touched."

I went into great detail about hearing poor Tigger crying, pulling him out from under the bed, and giving him water and food. Then I glossed over the rest while Wendy stood by nodding her head. "We were just getting ready to leave and take Tigger with us. He obviously can't stay here."

Gemma gritted her teeth, muttered something about meddling old fools, and ushered us all out with a stern warning to go home and stay out of the way.

Chapter Four

On the drive back to Sunshine Cottage, we went back and forth between vowing not to interfere any further in the police investigation and rationalizing why we couldn't let it go.

"Ladies, this isn't practical," I said.

"But we three have the best chance of figuring this out," argued Wendy.

"What do you mean?" asked Belle. "We've all said we didn't really know her that well."

"Think about it, Mum. Maybe we don't, but I bet you're the only one of her clients who'd ever been to her flat. She only cleaned for everyone else; she cooked for you and drove you around to run errands. You two had more of a relationship.

"And Leta had enough of a relationship with her to know she had a cat named Tigger, and we three are awfully observant. I can assure you neither Peter nor Toby noticed she suddenly had new outfits and new jewelry. And forget Rhiannon," scoffed Wendy. "The only thing she might've noticed would be Alice's aura. A lot of help that would be."

Belle nodded her head in agreement and added, "Peter may have noticed the new car. He owns a garage, after all. But Toby, I think he's too focused on keeping his business and his marriage alive."

I gave Belle a sidelong glance at that comment and wondered what she was hinting at before I said, "We know her best because she cleans for everyone else when they're at work. Even when she cleans the rooms at the Inn, Gavin and Libby are either in their office or dealing with guests or attending to all the million other things they have to do. We're the only ones who're at home when she visits our houses.

"Oh, for goodness' sake," I groaned. "It's sounding more and more as though it's up to us to figure this out."

Belle wasn't convinced. "Why isn't it up to Gemma? Why would she need us?"

"Nuances," I said. "It's nuances and connections we can pick up on because Alice worked for us and so many of our friends. Some of those subtleties might get by the police."

Wendy nodded in agreement, and Belle threw up her hands. "That's it, then. In for a penny, in for a pound, but not without my afternoon nap."

That remark made us all chuckle as we pulled up to Sunshine Cottage. Wendy carried Tigger inside, and I helped Belle out of the car and to the door. *I could use a nap too,* I thought as I drove off.

I couldn't help second-guessing myself all afternoon. "Dickens, I can't believe what I've gotten myself into. You know I always look before I leap, and I'm practical to a fault. Henry used to complain that I overthought and over-planned everything. He couldn't even get me to spontaneously have a cookout. And now look at me."

"Oh my gosh, Dickens," Christie meowed, "What have you let her get herself into?"

"Don't look at me," barked Dickens. "I thought it was only a morning walk, and before I knew it, there was a dead body, police, and a surprise cat rescue. This is a never-before-seen Leta."

Dickens and I rehashed the tale for Christie, ate a snack, and tried to set the morning's adventure aside. I was exhausted. They, whoever they are, say stress will wear you out. Guess this morning qualified as stressful.

Dickens was already taking a nap, and I desperately wanted to take one too but needed to finish another column before the day was over. At least working on "Parker's Pen" would take my mind off the immediate problem. Just recalling how Henry and I together had come up with the name as a play on my name, Aleta Petkas Parker, brought a smile to my face.

"You know, Christie, my columns are always lighthearted reads, and I'm not feeling particularly lighthearted at the moment," I said.

"I bet you're not," meowed Christie. "I have an idea. Why don't you write about me and Dickens arriving at Heathrow and getting to ride to Astonbury in your London taxi? You've already written about your decision to move here and how you found a schoolhouse to live in. Don't you think they'll be happy to hear that we're here too?"

"Brilliant! I can describe the racket you two made, and you can remind me of the sights we saw on the drive."

Huffed Christie, "Must I remind you that my carrier was on the floorboard, and I saw absolutely no sights once we left the airport?"

My little princess never minced her words. Christie offered input on the sights and sounds at Heathrow, and I took it from there. The column came together easily and was a happy distraction. We two moved to the bedroom, and Christie took up her usual nap position curled against my side. To my surprise, I was able to drop off to sleep right away and awake rested.

My first thought was to call Wendy. "Would you and Belle like to come over for a light dinner so we can look at the photos we took at Alice's flat? I can upload them to my computer so we can see them more easily."

"Ooh, will you make one of your Greek salads?" asked Wendy. "You know Mum and I both love them."

"Well, if that's what it takes to get you over here, that's what I'll do. I'll run to the bakery to get some bread, and we'll be set."

I opened a bottle of red wine and prepped the salad. I'd just set out a bowl of almonds when Belle and Wendy pulled up.

I'd had Wendy over to my cottage several times, but not Belle. As she admired my cozy kitchen, I explained that my Atlanta kitchen had been decorated much the same—in reds and golds with a hint of green. She agreed the colorful chair cushions, curtains, and rugs combined to make the kitchen warm and inviting.

I took her on the rest of the tour. In slightly different patterns, I'd continued the same color scheme in the sitting room. I thought of the fireplace and the large window looking out to the back garden as the highlights of that room.

"I feel so fortunate that Cynthia took me on as a client when I needed help decorating this place. It had good bones, as they say, but you should have seen it. The previous owners were strangely enamored of dull browns, almost as though they didn't want anything to stand out. With my love of jewel tones, that was never going to do."

Wendy added, "Lord, I remember coming over right after you bought it. Who knew what a difference a coat of gleaming off-white could make? And Cynthia is a whiz with fabric and furnishings."

"I think my favorite updates are the bookcases we added around the fireplace and the rugs that reveal the flagstone floor but also warm up the rooms. And I loved her idea of removing the shelves from the office bookcase to paint the back wall red. With the shelves back in place, it's just the right touch."

"Ha," said Wendy. "Of course you love it—it's red, isn't it? Have you noticed, Mum, how much Leta likes red?"

"About as much as you like pale blue?" said Belle.

I could tell it was time to move to the sitting room so Belle could sit down. Christie was quick to jump in her lap and start purring.

"A new friend, little girl?" I asked.

"Two cats in one day," said Belle as she stroked Christie. "I'm already getting used to Tigger. He crawled up in bed with me when I took my nap, and his purr was a delight."

"I had the same experience here with Christie," I said. "Purring cats may be the secret ingredient for keeping us calm and focused as we sort things out."

"Hey," barked Dickens, "what about your dog, Detective Dickens? I was by your side finding important clues."

I chuckled and shared what Dickens had said, except I made it sound as though the funny line had just popped into my head. No way I was letting on to my friends that Dickens spoke to me.

"I see your Frog Prince collection. Have you checked to see if any others are missing?" asked Wendy. "Oh, and tell Mum how you came to collect them."

"I don't think any others are missing, but I have so many, it's hard to be sure. When I met Henry, I'd about given up hope of ever meeting the right man, and when we got engaged, a friend joked about how many frogs I'd had to kiss to find my prince. When Henry heard that, he brought me the stuffed Frog Prince you see on the top shelf. I fell in love with his little velvet outfit and crown, and every anniversary, Henry presented me with a Frog Prince figurine or toy or another illustrated version of the fairytale.

"When I packed up to move here, I left most of my furniture and knickknacks behind, but the Frog Prince collection from Henry had to come with me. I can't believe Alice took it. And, I mean, she must have taken it, right? How else did it come to be in her cottage?"

Wendy looked thoughtful. "I don't see any other way, but why would she take it? And, if she filched your little figurine, did she also take things from her other clients? Could Mum be right, that Alice was up to something that could have gotten her killed?"

"I think so, so we need to get to work, but not before we have dinner," I replied.

Wendy and Belle asked for my salad recipe, and as always, I had to explain there was no recipe. I can list the basic ingredients, which I change from time to time, but there have never been any measurements. My sisters and I had watched my father make it all his life and had continued the tradition.

I topped off our wine glasses and said, "We're going to need a plan. We know the goal is to solve Alice's murder. We *are* positive it was murder, right?"

"Yes, we are," Wendy and Belle said in unison.

"Great, I typed up what I saw this morning and even what I remember of our conversation before we went to Alice's flat. I printed us all copies, and I think we should look at the notes and then review the photos we took and see where all that leads us."

Belle smiled and said, "I love a take-charge girl. Reminds me of myself in my nursing days."

I quietly read my bullet points about the scene at the cricket pavilion and the subsequent conversation we'd had in Belle's kitchen and was happy to see my fellow sleuths doing the same and jotting down ideas.

"Are we ready to talk about this, ladies?"

Belle started, "I can't understand why Alice didn't have her purse with her. You said you didn't see it in the car, right? I know we found one at her flat, but could she have more than one?"

"Well, I know I have several, but don't you think the one at the flat looked to be the big blue purse she usually has with her?" said Wendy.

"Yes, it did. So, maybe she had it with her but somehow it wound up back at her cottage? How did that happen?" I wondered.

"Let's play this out," said Wendy. "Whoever met her at the pavilion, maybe they had a row, and he or she tried to grab her purse. Maybe that's how the strap ended up in her hand. It broke off. And, for the record, I can't imagine it was a she."

I encouraged her to go on.

"Maybe they wanted something from Alice, and she wouldn't give it up, so they grabbed her purse thinking what they wanted was in it."

I added, "And then maybe they checked the car to see if

the missing whatever was in there. Nothing was disturbed in the car, except the glovebox was open. And they probably checked the trunk but closed it back."

Belle asked, "Do you think this mysterious someone meant to kill Alice, or could it have been an accident? If they were having a row and they jerked the purse away, could that have caused Alice to fall and hit her head?"

"Anything's possible," said Wendy.

"Gee," I said, "I'd like to think we aren't dealing with a stone-cold killer and that it scared them no end when they realized Alice was dead—assuming she died instantly, that is. It'd be even more awful if she wasn't dead, and they could have saved her if only they'd call 999."

"OK," said Wendy. "Regardless of how that part went, they must have checked the car and then driven their own vehicle to Alice's place. Again, to look for whatever Alice didn't seem to have with her. At least, I think that could be how it happened. Do we think they found what they were looking for?"

"Tigger thinks not," Dickens reminded me. "He says the man cursed the entire time and seemed awfully upset."

That was a good tip from Dickens, but of course, only I understood him. "Um, no," I said. "Or if they did, it had to be in the last place they looked. Otherwise, why ransack every inch? If it were me, I would've stopped as soon as I found what I was looking for."

"That makes sense," Belle murmured.

"Soon," I continued, "we need to look at the photos we took, but first, Belle, let's think about the things you remember Alice saying on the phone and while watching TV. I found those one-liners pretty disturbing." I read them aloud:

"This is the last time I'm going to ask."

"You know where to put it, the usual place, and it better be there."

"Everyone has secrets. Some are just better at hiding them than others."

"There's a bit of that going 'round, you know."

Belle interjected, "And that last comment was about someone on the telly having an affair."

"Wow," Wendy said, "When you list them out like that, the words sound pretty threatening. So, 'Last time I'm going to ask?' Ask for what?"

"Money," I blurted. That was the first thing that came to mind.

"And," Belle said, "was there someplace someone had to deliver the money or hide it?"

"I think someone or some two were having an affair and Alice found out about it," said Wendy.

I was furiously jotting down everything we were saying. "This whole thing is mind-boggling," I said. "Could she have been pilfering things from all of our cottages? Not just mine? Maybe the photos we took will show us something."

I pulled two more chairs up to my desk so we could view the photos on my monitor, and we all gathered around. Once we could see beyond the mess, we began to see intact items here and there. It seemed that whoever did this wasn't necessarily interested in wanton destruction.

"Isn't that a lovely teapot?" said Belle, pointing to a porcelain teapot with a delicate picture of Alice in Wonderland. "There are quite a few porcelain pieces scattered around, and surprisingly, they weren't broken by whoever made the mess."

"Look," said Wendy, "Is that a picture of Rhiannon with . . . Toby? He's standing behind her with his hands on her shoulders. What's with that?" She hesitated and then blurted out, "Are they having an affair?"

"Uh-huh," said Belle. "I'd been wondering about them. You know how you just sense things sometimes? Maybe that's what Alice meant by her comment 'There's a lot of that going around.' She was talking about those two, and they have the perfect setup with Toby's wife Cynthia gone all week every week!"

"Can you read what it says on that piece of paper on the floor?" asked Wendy. "The one with the teacup image across the top?"

"Let me zoom in," I responded. "Can you read it now?"

"We should be able to get together this weekend without any interruptions. Cynthia has a big job in Spain and will be overseeing the renovation for a week. Her boss is partnering with her on this project, so she won't be after me to join her. Besides, she knows I can't leave for much more than a day or two. With a whole weekend available, the White Knight and the White Witch should be able to work out a partnership."

"Now what's that about? And who's the White Knight?" asked Belle.

"Wait a sec, let me think," said Wendy. "Is it only because we saw that photo that I'm thinking this, or could the White Knight be Toby White? And is the note to Rhiannon? You know her name means witch."

"If I'm not mistaken, it means white witch. I'm beginning to have a sick feeling about this," I said. "This is more than I want to know about our friends. Are we making a mistake getting involved in this?"

Belle looked at me sternly. "We're already involved, and I don't see how we can stop now."

I may have been hesitant, but Wendy hadn't missed a beat.

"Look. There's another photo of a couple on the refrigerator door, but I can't see it all that well."

"Let me see if I can make it a bit bigger," I murmured.

"Oh my gosh," blurted Wendy, "that's Peter with his arm around Alice. Alice? And Peter? I had no idea. Did you, Mum?"

"No, dear. I can't remember the last time your brother had a girlfriend. I'm sure he's dated here and there, but nothing too serious. Not like he's brought anyone around to meet me."

"Oh, Mum, look at the time," said Wendy. "We certainly need to talk more about Peter, but it's past time for us to be in bed. Maybe Leta will invite us back to look at the photos again. There's bound to be more to see if we look closely. And we haven't even looked at the notebook pages yet."

"Sure I will," I replied. "It's going to take all three of us to figure this out."

Wendy tapped her forehead and said, "Oh my goodness, with all that's happened, I almost forgot about Dave Prentiss, the journalist, coming over tomorrow. You're still coming, right?"

"I'll be there. And I should have plenty of time before then to go to yoga class, have coffee at Toby's, and even pop by the Book Nook. That way I can let you know what I've found out once the journalist leaves."

"Well, we've got lots to think about and plenty to keep us busy for at least a day or two," said Wendy. "We'll see you tomorrow."

I let Dickens out for a brief garden visit and then sat down at my desk. I couldn't believe I'd started my day by finding a body. If I'd been at home, my first call would have been to my youngest sister Anna. I decided instead to write an email to both my sisters. Maybe trying to explain it in an email in some coherent fashion would help me sort through it all yet another time.

Like me, Anna was fond of murder mysteries, though she leaned more toward serial killer fiction than I did. Still, she was going to find this tale pretty unbelievable. She might even think I was pulling her leg. Most likely, she was going to react by reading me the riot act.

I was betting my sister Sophia's reply would be more measured and philosophical. When I hit send, I was already anticipating two very different responses.

By morning, I was once again questioning my involvement in a murder investigation, but nonetheless, I set out to follow the plan. I took a moment to check my email while drinking my coffee. I was right. Anna had sent me a blistering email that started with, "What the heck do you think you're doing? Have you lost your mind?" Ah yes, I knew I could depend on my practical, matter-of-fact sister to cut right to the chase. I'd respond to her later.

I planned to start the day with a calming yoga class. Surely, that would help to clear my mind before I started snooping. Boy, was I ever wrong.

My discovery of Alice's body had spread through Astonbury's grapevine, and I was greeted by a group of women wanting the details. No matter that Rhiannon quieted the chattering women long enough to hold class, I couldn't quiet the chattering inside my head. I kept my gaze down as I rolled up my mat and looped the strap around it, hoping to avoid any more questions.

Rhiannon pulled me aside once the others had left. She

was not her usual calm self this morning—she seemed anxious. I sensed it wasn't so much grief over Alice's death as it was some kind of personal worry. She grew increasingly anxious when I told her about the visit to Alice's flat, a detail I hadn't revealed to the other class participants.

"You went to her home?" Rhiannon said. "Umm, did you find anything that shouldn't have been there?"

"Well, for starters, it had been ransacked," I replied. "But what do you mean by 'something that shouldn't have been there?' What are you asking?"

"Oh, nothing. It's just I've missed the odd item now and then from my flat, and I keep thinking either Alice moved it, or . . . maybe took it. I know, I know, I'm speaking ill of the dead. I'm sorry, never mind."

"Seriously, what kind of odd item?" What was Rhiannon hinting at?

"Oh, a favorite photo I planned to frame and a thank you note from a friend—things like that. I probably misplaced them. You know how disorganized I can be. Forget I even mentioned it. Let's go have our usual tea at Toby's."

As we walked up the street, my mind was racing. Was she talking about the photo of her and Toby I'd seen in Alice's cottage? Was a thank you note Rhiannon's euphemism for the note from the White Knight?

Why would Alice take Rhiannon's photo and note? Why would she take my Frog Prince? Unpacking the boxes that had arrived from the States had left my cottage in disarray for several months, and it was no wonder I hadn't missed my figurine until I saw it in Alice's cottage.

I should have realized Toby's Tearoom would be abuzz this morning too. The village grapevine not only worked in the old-fashioned way by telephone, but also via the *Astonbury Aha*, a website where villagers could post news, items for sale, and messages about missing dogs and cats. Apparently today, all the news had been about Alice's death, and the Tearoom was packed.

Toby greeted me with concern. "How are you doing after your ordeal? It must have been quite a shock. I recommend you skip your usual coffee and have a strong sugary cup of black tea instead."

I gave a weak smile and said I'd stick with coffee. All the concern was wearing on me. I much preferred to hear others' concerns rather than share mine. It was my ability to listen and observe that had made me an effective manager and coach in my banking days, and I'd always believed it was my genuine interest in people that made them open up to me. Me open up to others? Uh-uh.

Rhiannon seemed preoccupied, and I was content to sip my coffee in silence and pick up fragments of other conversations as they floated my way. The villagers were mostly complimentary of the service Alice provided and of her scones and biscuits, but there were also a few unkind comments:

"She was an outsider, plain and simple."

"I heard she moved here to get away from something."

"She was cagey about where she came from."

"I'm not sure I trusted her."

As I paid at the counter, Toby leaned in and said, "May I call you later?"

"Sure," I replied. I left with a puzzled expression on my face and walked across the street to the Book Nook. Tommy and Tuppence were in the window, Thom was on a ladder hanging cobwebs and spiders on the ceiling, and Beatrix was arranging a display of Halloween mysteries in preparation for the upcoming holiday. She was also sporting a witch's hat today, and with her ash blonde hair, she reminded me of Samantha in *Bewitched*.

"You're here right on cue," she exclaimed as she gave me a hug. "The Louise Penny books arrived yesterday afternoon, but when I heard the news about Alice, I didn't want to bother you with a call."

"Thanks, a new book is just what I need. I'm having visions of shutting out the world and sitting in the garden to read. Honestly, one more question about what I saw yesterday and how I feel will send me over the edge."

"Funny, isn't it?" mused Beatrix. "Alice was a constant in all our lives, but I hardly ever saw her except occasionally at Libby and Gavin's gatherings. She'd leave me scones or short-bread when she cleaned my cottage, and I'd leave her cash in an envelope, but I rarely saw her. Even when she cleaned this place every week, it was after hours."

"She didn't come in to buy books like everyone else in the village?" I asked.

"You know, not really, not until late last year. First, she found a Sherlock Holmes anthology among the used books. Then she bought a biography of J. M. Barrie. I always have those on hand. She briefly shifted to American authors when she asked if I could recommend an Edgar Allan Poe biography. And just lately, it was *Winnie-the-Pooh*—not the children's book but the biography, *The Extraordinary Life of A. A. Milne*. I had to order the Poe biography, but I keep the Milne bio in stock."

"Hmmm, with the exception of Poe, it sounds like she was interested in the authors who summered here in the last century. Maybe after living here a few years, she developed a natural curiosity about the history of the area. I know the literary associations have fascinated me."

"And you know who else is curious?" said Beatrix. "Dave

Prentiss, the journalist staying at The Olde Mill. He came by yesterday asking for a copy of *Peter and Wendy*. Not many people know Barrie wrote that book after he wrote the play, and of course, I stock copies of it and several Barrie biographies. I think he's going to see Belle today. Now, there's a story."

"Then I'm in luck, because Wendy invited me to join them. Who knows? I may be back for a Barrie biography too after that visit."

Not only was I eager to hear Belle's tales, but after Dickens's comment about the journalist being interested in me, I was also a tiny bit curious to see whether he might be right. Not that *I* was interested or anything.

Chapter Five

Dickens and I arrived at the cottage before Dave. We found Wendy puttering around making tea and Belle in the sitting room with Tigger in her lap.

"He's settling in," said Belle, "and you can see who his favorite is."

I laughed. "Does that mean he has a new home? He certainly looks comfy."

Just then, Wendy brought Dave Prentiss into the room, and Tigger bolted from Belle's lap.

"Whoa!" I exclaimed. "I wonder if he's not used to men or he's just still skittish from his experience."

"Huh," said Dave. "Is he all right?"

"It's a long story," said Belle.

"Never mind," said Wendy. "Mum, this is Dave Prentiss from the States, the gentleman Leta and I met the other night at the inn. So, now you have a captive audience of two, or I guess three if you count Dickens. I'm going to leave you lot to it, as I've heard these stories many times over. I'll be in the kitchen, though, so let me know if you need anything."

Dave and I listened intently as Belle told the tale of how her mother knew J. M. Barrie and how he had taken care of her when she was pregnant with Belle. Dickens lay at Belle's feet.

"Oh my gosh, I can't believe Barrie set your gran up in this cottage and you were born here. Did her mother really turn her out, an unwed mother with no place to go? And Barrie gave her this cottage? From the bits I've read about him, he was a caring man, but your story is amazing," I exclaimed.

"Can it really be because she sat up listening to his stories when he couldn't sleep? Don't you ever wonder if there was something else to it? It would have been a substantial gift, even in those days," said Dave.

"Oh piffle," huffed Belle. "I suppose you think there was something more going on between them, just like others through the years who've suggested he must have been my father. Mum would have set you straight in no time.

"When Uncle Jim's wife took up with a younger man and divorced him, she let it be known that their marriage had never been a *real* one—if you know what I mean. The supposition was that he was impotent. Not that he was gay, another rumor that used to go around. He was just a big kid—well, not so big. He was quite short."

"Belle," I said. "I'm sitting here in awe of the fact that you knew the author of *Peter Pan* so well that you called him Uncle Jim. What a story."

"Mum told me that's what the three Llewelyn Davies boys called him—you know, the family that inspired his play?" said Belle. "Uncle Jim was a kind and generous man, plain and simple. You know he supported those boys after their parents died, right?"

"Yes," said Dave. "You see reference to the Llewelyn Davies

boys everywhere, but I've never seen anything about this other part of his life. He must have been an amazing man."

"Oh," I said. "I remember their story from the movie *Neverland*, the one with Johnny Depp and Kate Winslet."

"Belle, if I may be so bold, who *was* your father?" Dave asked.

"Mum never ever said. I suppose it could have been one of the cricket players or authors or someone else otherwise unsuitable, but suffice it to say that I was born out of wedlock. Of course, she was no longer welcome at the Stanway House, but we had our cottage and until Uncle Jim died, he sent Mum money so she wouldn't have to go back to housekeeping work until I went to school. He was a generous man, though I don't have too many memories of him. He died in 1937 when I was only seven and hadn't visited in a few years."

"He visited you?" I asked.

"Yes, and he brought the most marvelous gifts," said Belle. "For my first birthday, he brought me all four *Winnie-the-Pooh* books. Of course, I don't remember my first birthday, but Mum read me the books, and I still have them. A. A. Milne was one of the authors who summered at the Stanway House with Uncle Jim, and they both played cricket. Would you like to see the books? They're a bit worn, as I read them to my twins too."

"Oh yes, I'd love to see them," I said, "especially as I seem to be the only person around here who didn't read them as a child."

"Belle, this just gets better and better. You have *Winnie-the-Pooh* books from the 1930s? What treasures," exclaimed Dave.

"Oh, I loved my books, but not as much as the dog. It was Uncle Jim who brought me my first dog the very next year. Mum named her Tinker after you-know-who in *Peter Pan*. That little thing lived to the ripe old age of fifteen and is buried in the garden. One year, Uncle Jim sent me *Peter and Wendy,* the book he wrote after the play. It's similar in many ways but has more detail in it. I almost know it by heart, as Mum read it to me, and I read it to the twins. I guess now you know who they're named after."

She chuckled. "He didn't visit many more times, I don't think, though he wrote Mum quite regularly. He was a fascinating man.

"Leta, can you reach over and get the *Winnie-the-Pooh* books from the bookcase, please, there on the bottom shelf?" asked Belle. "I can't manage them and my cane."

"No problem," I said as I retrieved the books. "Shall we look through them together?"

"Yes, but please be careful; they're in decent shape for being over eighty years old, but still they're a bit fragile," said Belle.

Dave moved to the couch next to me as I opened the first book, *When We Were Very Young.* He gasped as I opened it, and I looked at him not understanding his reaction.

"It's a first edition," he explained. "And it's signed. There can't be very many of these around. Could they all be signed first editions?"

"I never really thought about it," said Belle. "To me, they're storybooks that Uncle Jim gave me. Leta, what do you think?"

"Well, for starters, they're all signed," I said. "But I don't know how to identify whether or not they're first editions. I guess I'll have to defer to Dave."

"Oh, they are, and this is an amazing find, even though they're not in pristine condition. Is there any chance you also have the letters your Uncle Jim wrote to your mum?" asked Dave.

"Oh yes, I've saved them all. I don't read them much anymore, but I've kept them," said Belle.

"Wow. Has anyone ever approached you about buying them? They'd be a major asset at any of the universities that house Barrie collections," said Dave. "Is it possible for me to see them?"

"Not today, young man. As much as I've enjoyed reminiscing with you, it's past time for my nap. Besides, I keep my mum's letters tied with a lace ribbon and tucked away in a special box. I'd have to get Wendy to get the box down for me."

I knew Belle rested daily, but it wasn't quite time yet, and I sensed something else in her dismissal of Dave. Dave was effusive in his thanks. "I can't tell you how much I enjoyed your story. Thanks to you both for inviting me," he said as he turned from Belle to Wendy.

"Well, thank you for listening. I must admit," said Belle, "I *do* love an appreciative audience. As of late, Alice was the only person who'd listen to me prattle on. There's something about sitting in the kitchen with a pot of tea that leads to reminiscing, don't you think?"

"Alice?" asked Dave. "From The Olde Mill Inn? The one who died?"

"Yes," said Wendy, "the woman who served all that delicious food at the party. And she made it all, too. She was the housekeeper for many of us—Leta, Beatrix from the bookshop, me and Mum. She really was a treasure."

Dave looked somber and a little uncomfortable. He told us all he was sorry for our loss and said goodbye.

"Gee, Belle, I can't believe I've been here for months and am only now hearing your story," I said. "Does everybody in Astonbury know about this?"

Belle laughed and said, "Unless they're newbies like you, they know. For those who were born and raised here, it's just part of the local lore and not anything special. Frankly, I get a bit put out with folks like Dave Prentiss who seem a little overly curious. I mean, what makes him think I'd share my mum's personal letters with him?"

Wendy stuck her head in the door and said, "I heard him ask you, Mum, and I couldn't believe it. Up until then, he'd been attentive and polite, but I thought that was quite forward of him."

Funny, I hadn't thought a thing about his request. "Now, now, ladies, you're not going to start in with stereotypes like 'Americans are brash and rude and all that,' are you? I don't think he meant to be insulting. Is he the first person to ask, or have there been others?"

"I can't recall anyone ever asking for the letters," said Belle. "Younger villagers sometimes ask if it's true that Uncle Jim gave my mum this cottage, but that's about it. They hear the story from their grandparents or parents and think it's all made up, you know."

"I can see where they'd see it as some kind of exaggerated tale, but it sure is a heartwarming story," I said.

"Oh, and that nice George Evans sat with me one day to take notes about the tales I'd heard from my mum about Stanway House, Uncle Jim, and the other authors. I hear George does a nice job entertaining the tourists with the highlights."

I laughed. "Well, Henry and I certainly enjoyed George's tour. I'm glad you helped him out. Now, Belle, I know you want to get to your nap, but do you two have time for me to share what I learned this morning in the village? After that, I'll be ready for a nap too."

Belle and Wendy were eager to hear my news, so I outlined my impressions from speaking with Rhiannon, Toby, and Beatrix. We were now convinced that Toby was the White Knight and that he and Rhiannon were the ones having an affair. What we couldn't figure out was what the pilfered items like my figurine had to do with things like photos and notes.

I thought we needed to see what Libby had to say, since Alice had spent more time at The Olde Mill Inn than anywhere else, and Wendy was chomping at the bit to speak with her twin about his relationship with her. She was flabbergasted that she hadn't known a thing about it, and also a bit hurt, I thought. I got her to agree to hold off, as I was concerned they'd wind up having an argument instead of a productive conversation.

We agreed I'd find a way to tackle Libby, and Wendy would spend her time trying to see whether anything was missing from Sunshine Cottage. The little cottage was packed to the gills, so that would be no easy task.

"Okay, Detective Dickens," I said as I drove us home, "What did you discover while we listened to Belle's story?"

"Hmmm. Tigger is sad. He understands Alice isn't coming back and feels safe with Belle and Wendy, but he's grieving. I think it will take him a while to get back to normal."

"Why did he bolt from Belle's lap when Dave came in?"

"Well, Tigger isn't sure. He said a bad feeling came over

him, but he thinks it's because he has a thing about men after whoever ransacked Alice's flat scared him half to death."

"Could be," I said. "How 'bout we go home and give Libby a call? Maybe we can see her this afternoon."

I was pulling into my gravel drive when the phone rang. It was my sister Anna, who was none too pleased with me. "Who are you and what have you done with my big sister? What on earth is going on over there? My cautious, risk-averse big sister moves to a picture-perfect English village and suddenly gets involved in a murder? A murder?"

"Now, now, you make it sound like I'm sneaking around alleyways with a gun drawn. I went out for a nice walk—"

"And you found a body, and then you went to the victim's house? Are you nuts?"

"Does it make you feel any better to hear that Wendy and Belle and Dickens were with me? I mean Belle is close to ninety, for goodness' sake."

"Then I think you're all crazy. Please tell me you've come to your senses after a good night's sleep."

"We're only asking a few innocent questions here and there, no big deal."

"You need to get this out of your system and run—don't walk—to the nearest police station. Tell that Gemma girl what you think you know and let her handle it."

"So nice to hear from you, Anna, and how have you been?" I said sweetly.

"Okay, if we're going to play that game, then tell me how my niece and nephew are doing," she said. "Let me guess, Dickens is good and Christie is paying you back for mistreating her, right?" Anna knew how it was because she had five cats and a Great Dane—*and* a husband. I always added that last bit when describing her to folks who didn't know her, lest they think she was a crazy cat lady.

"You guessed it," I said. "She takes it in spells, but she's settling in. Dickens even got to go to a cocktail party."

"Typical." Anna laughed. "And beyond getting involved in a murder case, how's my big sis doing? Have you got the cottage just the way you want it? Or is there some retail therapy in your future?"

"You know me too well," I said. "But the big things are mostly done. That means I can take my time and shop at flea markets and pottery shops for just the right accent items. Oh, and garden shops too. You know how Henry used to tease me about my need for yard art. I'm visiting Oxford this week, and I'm sure to find something I can't live without."

Anna chuckled at that. Though my youngest sister despised shopping for clothes—a trait I found quite bizarre—she *did* enjoy decorating her Atlanta home and her vacation home on the coast of Georgia. She and I had spent many an enjoyable day searching for the perfect lamp or quintessential seaside painting, and occasionally I managed to drag her into a clothing shop along the way.

"Gee, you sound almost like my *real* big sister. I suggest you go to Oxford now and make a week of it. Maybe that would keep you out of trouble."

"Enough. I'm glad you called, but I've got to run. I'll give you a holler this week. Say hello to Andrew. Love you."

As I was finishing off the leftover Greek salad, Christie came in the kitchen and stretched. "Where've you two been?" she meowed.

"Doing important detective work," said Dickens. "And you? I bet you've been napping the whole time we were gone, right?"

"Well, yes, a girl's got to get her beauty sleep," she meowed.

I was smiling at their discussion when the phone rang. It was Toby asking if I'd be up for an early dinner at the Ploughman Pub. This was a first, and if my curiosity hadn't gotten the better of me, I might have begged off. Maybe this was my chance to get the scoop on what was going on with him and Rhiannon.

I'd postpone calling Libby until later tonight and try to get by the inn tomorrow. I chuckled and pictured Nancy Drew as I imagined needing a sleuthing calendar to keep my appointments straight—except, I reminded myself, this was no laughing matter.

"That sounds nice," I said. "It's time Dickens got to see the inside of a pub. And he'll get a special kick out of this one because of the dog beds scattered around. You know, in the States, dogs can sit on the patios at restaurants and bars, but not inside." I told him I'd walk there with Dickens, and he offered to drive us home afterward. Maybe by then, I'd have answers to some of my questions.

Chapter Six

I was happy to have some time to myself, and I stretched out on the couch with my new Louise Penny book. As engrossing as it was, I couldn't keep my eyes open and, with Christie tucked against my side and Dickens on the rug, I took a short nap. I *do* love a good nap.

When the school bell clanged, I jerked awake and Christie took flight. The bell was attached to the left of the front door, and my next-door neighbor Timmy liked nothing better than to clamber onto the stone bench beneath it and grab the rope pull. The four-year-old had been eagerly anticipating the arrival of my pets, and I was sure he'd badgered his mum to let him visit.

"Well, hello, Timmy," I said as I opened the front door with Dickens at my side.

Timmy jumped down from the bench and laughed at Dickens. "He's my size," he said. "Can I pet him?"

"Yes, and he'd love a hug too."

As Timmy giggled and threw his arms around his neck, Dickens sat still and asked, "Who's this little fella?"

"Dickens, meet my neighbor Timmy Watson. He's heard all about you and wants to be your friend."

I invited Timmy to join us in the sitting room, hoping Christie might come out, but no such luck. She'd have to get used to the ringing of the school bell. Fortunately for my feline friend, tow-headed Timmy was the only one to use it. When I heard a knock at the door, I knew it was Timmy's mum come to take him home.

"Come in, Deborah," I said. "Meet Dickens. I think he and Timmy are going to be great friends."

Deborah exclaimed over the petite proportions of Dickens and his calm demeanor. "He's the perfect dog for Timmy. So many of the pups around here are either tiny terrors or intimidating giants." As Dickens rolled over, she reached down to give him a belly rub, and Timmy grabbed a handful of long white fur. Deborah was impressed that Dickens didn't flinch. "Yes, a perfect pup," she said.

"Hey, I like her. Imagine realizing right away that I'm perfect," barked Dickens.

"Well, not totally perfect. He has a tendency to bark, so I hope you'll let me know if it gets to be too much. My sister says her dog barks at everything—walkers, birds, squirrels, an ant crawling on a blade of grass—you get the picture. Well, that's Dickens to a tee. Sometimes I see what he's barking at. Other times? Let's just say he sees things I don't."

Deborah laughed. "I see, but if you can take Timmy ringing the school bell, I think we can deal with a bit of barking. When John's free, I'll bring him by to be properly introduced to the new four-legged neighbors. For some reason, weekend dental emergencies have been the norm for the past month, and he never seems to get a break."

John Watson was the local dentist, and we were all very

happy to have him conveniently located in Astonbury. As soon as Timmy and Deborah left, Christie padded down the stairs. "What was that godawful noise?" she screeched.

"A school bell that hangs by the front door. It was left behind when the school closed. I especially like the bench below it with its carving of an open book and the inscription that reads 'In Memory of Miss Peters.' I've been told she was a favorite schoolmistress."

Christie jumped in my lap and looked me in the eyes. "That thing has got to go. I'm pretty sure I lost one of my nine lives when it rang."

"Well, aren't you demanding?" I said. "The bell isn't going anywhere."

Dickens gave his sister an affectionate pat with his paw. "Get over it. I like the bell, and I like Timmy."

"Harrumph," was all Christie had to say.

As I was brewing a cup of tea, the phone rang. "Hello, sistah," said my sister Sophia. "Now tell me true, did you find a body or was your message some kind of elaborate joke?"

I never knew which one of Sophia's personas would greet me when I picked up the phone. Sometimes she took on a British accent. Sometimes it was pure New Orleans. Other times, she spoke like a Brooklyn native, and she had more in her repertoire. She'd been entertaining us with her various accents ever since she'd studied drama in college. Today, she'd greeted me with her New Orleans version of sister, but there was no telling where she'd end up. She often shifted personas in a brief conversation.

"Oh, I found a body, alright."

Now it was her upper crust persona that emerged. "Well, I do hope you aren't getting unduly distressed."

I laughed. "Right, Sophia, like you wouldn't be *unduly*

distressed if you stumbled upon a dead body—the body of someone you knew. I'd say I'm pretty darned calm considering the circumstances."

"Well, Jeremy says you should let the authorities handle this unpleasantness and stay out of it. He is, however, prepared to fly over should you need him." Jeremy was Sophia's very proper British husband and always the voice of reason. As the CEO of an insurance firm in New Orleans, he was good at crisis management.

"Please tell him I appreciate his concern, but I'll be fine. Besides, aren't you two off to Italy next week?"

"Yes, we've rented our usual villa in Tuscany, and Jeremy is especially looking forward to leaving work behind for a few weeks. Still, we'll both come if you need us."

"No, no. Enjoy your trip and don't worry about me. I know I'll get to see you both when Jeremy takes his next business trip to London. By then, I'll probably have a tale to tell about the *unpleasantness* in Astonbury."

"Okay then. I'll let you know our London schedule once it's firmed up. Ta-ta." Had it been an email, she would have signed off TTFN.

I chuckled as I reflected on how different yet true to form my sisters' reactions had been. We three may have looked alike, but our personalities were quite distinct.

I hurried to change into jeans, walking shoes, and a purple sweater, or *jumper*, as my neighbors say. *I suppose I'm destined to be labeled a newbie, at least until I can start using the proper terms for my apparel*, I thought. As I grabbed his leash and my new hat, Dickens gave me a questioning look.

"That's not a ball cap," he said. "I mean, I guess it's a *hat*, but what is it?"

"You'll get used to it. It's called a cloche, and I found it at the Mad Hatter in Burford. It's one of my favorite shops because it's a combo hat shop *and* book shop. What more could a girl ask for?"

"As long as it goes with a walk, it works for me," he barked. "Where are we going tonight?"

I explained he was getting to meet a new friend at a new place, and we set off. The weather had turned cooler, and I was glad I'd thrown on a jacket and worn my new wool hat.

Toby was already seated near one of the several fireplaces when we arrived, and there was an available dog bed by the hearth for Dickens. He made a fuss over Dickens's thick coat of long white hair and his diminutive size as compared to full-grown Pyrs and then went to the bar to get us ciders. I was never sure about all the beer choices, but I'd grown to like cider.

"Wow, Leta," said Dickens. "Dog beds? How cool is this?"

"I knew you'd like that," I said as I thought back to when I'd been house hunting and first met Toby at one of Libby's cocktail parties. There was something special about him, and we'd hit it off right away. Realizing I was in the process of making a major life change, he was eager to tell me his story—how he'd walked away from a successful career in advertising to get back to his roots, as he called it.

He'd grown up working in his parents' small grocery in Cornwall before going to university and longed to return to a simpler way of life where he'd know his customers and his neighbors. He'd made that dream come true in Astonbury.

"I just couldn't face trying to throw something together for dinner after being run ragged all day," said Toby as we sipped our drinks. "Even for a Sunday, the crowds were amazing."

"I know how hard it is to get excited about fixing dinner

for one," I said. "I don't starve, but there are nights I eat cheese and crackers or popcorn or even grits."

"Grits?"

"Ah yes, I forget you guys don't do grits. It's a breakfast staple in the South, kind of a warm cereal. I guess the closest you'd come is porridge, except we don't put yogurt or honey in our grits. I like mine with butter, cheese, and lots of salt and pepper."

"I might have to give them a try one of these nights when Cynthia's in London or elsewhere," he replied. "And on that note, I need to explain my ulterior motive for asking you to join me this evening. I felt a need to get some things out in the open."

I leaned forward and nodded as he haltingly told me that he and Cynthia had been struggling for some time. When they'd made the decision to move to Astonbury, Cynthia had been on board, but her enthusiasm had waned as her design career began to take off.

Initially, she'd been able to work remotely and spend only Sunday to Wednesday nights in the city, but that had changed a year ago. Her business had taken off and she'd been pushing for them to move back to London, a shift that meant Toby would have to abandon his dream, just as the tearoom was beginning to turn a profit. Profitable, but not for long if he had to hire a manager to run it in his absence.

"I'm sorry to hear that, Toby," I said. "Not just for you but for Astonbury as well. It seems such a vital part of the community. I suppose you've considered other options like refinancing?"

"Oh, I've been running all kinds of scenarios through my head, and for a time, Cynthia was willing to indulge me. I approached Rhiannon about becoming a partner. I know she seems like a space cadet at times, but she's a savvy business-woman. We spent a while running the numbers, but in the end, we couldn't make it work.

"Believe it or not, I even toyed with the idea of approaching you as an investor, but before I could, Cynthia hit me with a double whammy. First, she said our marriage had been in a death spiral for a while, and before I could absorb that, she said she wanted to sell the tearoom outright so she could invest the money in her business. And she owns half of Toby's Tearoom so where does that leave me?"

I was trying to figure out why Toby was confiding in me. I was a customer, and we saw each other at social functions, but this seemed a bit like TMI for him to be sharing with me. Then again, before I retired, my co-workers had always brought me their problems.

"As if that wasn't enough," Toby blurted out, "Alice started blackmailing me."

"What?" I cried. "Blackmailing you over what?"

"It's complicated. Bloody hell, I hate to speak ill of the dead, but somehow Alice got it into her head that Rhiannon and I were more than potential business partners. She texted a photo of me and Rhiannon and threatened to send it to Cynthia if I didn't pay up. When I told her the photo was innocent, she claimed she had something more incriminating than the photo, but I couldn't imagine what it was. So I came up with the money."

"You mean you paid her?" I asked.

"Of course, I paid her. I'm not explaining myself well, I know. She's in and out of our flat above the tearoom all the time. She'd seen the draft divorce papers on Cynthia's desk and knew, probably before I did, that Cynthia was getting ready to file. As my wife so kindly put it when she finally showed me the papers, 'our marriage is dead.' I was already going to be fighting for my livelihood, and if Alice had something Cynthia could use in the divorce, I could lose everything."

"How long has this been going on?"

"A few months. Rhiannon tried to help out, but really she didn't have to. She had nothing to lose. Oh, I mean I guess she had a bit of reputational risk—being painted as the scarlet woman, but in this day and age, what does that matter? It's all about me losing everything, and I didn't even do anything!" he cried.

"OK, so I've got to ask, Toby, why are you telling me all this?"

"Well, because I know you found Alice's body at the cricket pavilion, and Rhiannon tells me you went to Alice's flat too. I was wondering whether you saw anything in either place that could get me in trouble with the police?"

"What? Like what?"

"I don't know, do I?" he shouted.

Patrons at nearby tables looked at us as Toby's voice rose. Dickens left the dog bed, moved to my side, and growled. I could see Toby trying to get himself under control. "The photo is nothing," he whispered, "but I don't *know* what the 'other thing' is. If Rhiannon and I are innocent, what could Alice possibly have?"

By now, my mind was operating on two separate tracks. First, I was thinking, *what on earth have I gotten myself tangled up in? No way I'm smart enough to figure any of this out.* At the same time, a lightbulb had gone off and I now knew what Rhiannon was so worried about.

I figured the more incriminating something Alice had referred to was the strange note I'd seen, but for some reason, I didn't want to tell Toby about that. Based on what he'd said,

I could see it as an innocent message about he and Rhiannon —the White Knight and the White Witch—discussing going into business.

I stuck with the photo. "Yes, I saw the photo of you and Rhiannon, and you're right, it looked fairly innocent, but I can't think of anything else." I wasn't exactly lying, as I couldn't be positive what the note meant. "I think you should be prepared, though, for Gemma to come see you. She may want to know about the photo. And, Toby—" I groaned. "All my mystery book plots are swirling in my brain now. You know the police always look at motive *and* opportunity, so Gemma will be looking for your alibi."

"Like I have an alibi," he said. "When Cynthia's in London, I sleep alone. I don't even have a dog or cat to vouch for me. I better hope Gemma makes fast work of finding the real culprit so she doesn't focus her energy on me."

With all that in the open, we finally got around to ordering. Without fail, the food at the Ploughman was amazingly good. I ordered the fish special and Toby went with a burger. I could see Dickens eyeing the burger and warned Toby not to give him anything.

I was trying to resist Toby's pleas for us to split a dessert when Thom stopped by our table to say hello and pet Dickens.

"I see Dickens is making the rounds," said Thom. "What does he think of the Ploughman?"

I laughed and said, "He can't believe all the dog beds, and I'm pretty sure he approves. Did you finish hanging cobwebs for Beatrix?"

Thom chuckled. "Beatrix won't be done decorating until Halloween is over. There's no telling what she'll come up with next. She was looking online at skeletons when I left."

Toby asked, "Are you here for dinner?"

"No, just meeting a mate for a pint," he replied. "And I'd recommend the brownies if you two are going for dessert," he said as he moved to the bar.

That cinched it. Toby had to get the brownies, and I couldn't resist eating my share. I'd need to take an extra-long walk tomorrow to make up for that indulgence.

We agreed we'd stay in touch, not difficult since I visited the tearoom several mornings a week, and Toby drove me and Dickens home. I could tell Dickens was chomping at the bit to tell me what he thought, but I hushed him until we were inside the cottage.

"What do you think, Leta? Do you think he had something to do with Alice's death?" Dickens barked.

"My gut tells me he didn't, but he certainly has a motive," I said. "It's easier to believe he had something to do with it if I imagine the scene as an accident. No way Toby could deliberately kill someone. I just don't know."

"I'd have to agree that he lacks the killer instinct. I can't imagine him hurting anyone. He's not like the villains on the shows you watch—just plain evil."

"Ah, Dickens, something tells me that in real life, it's not that obvious."

Toby's emotionally charged outpouring had exhausted me, but I wanted to call Libby before I turned in. She answered the phone sounding harried, and I dove right in. "Libby, how would you like some help getting the guest rooms in shape? You must be at your wits' end without Alice."

I could tell Libby had started crying. "I'm sorry, just hearing her name . . . it's too much. And I can't believe you found her."

"It's OK, Libby. We're all upset. But hey, let me help. It's hard enough for you to do all the work on top of being upset."

"Oh, Leta, it's kind of you to offer, but I can't let you do that. I can't have you scrubbing floors or doing the laundry."

"Don't be silly. How 'bout I make beds and straighten the rooms? Someone has to change out the used towels for fresh ones, empty trash cans, and collect dishes from nightstands. I can do that while you do the heavy lifting, so to speak."

"Oh my, you're a lifesaver. I'm saying 'yes' before you change your mind. Can you come tomorrow morning after breakfast? All but Dave Prentiss are checking out, and it would be a big help if you could straighten his room and strip the other beds."

And so it was that Dickens and I got to snoop around the Inn Monday morning.

Chapter Seven

I was rinsing the breakfast dishes the next day when Christie flopped and rolled on the kitchen floor. That was Henry's term for the way she stretched out full length, exposing her cute tummy, and whenever she did, neither of us could resist rubbing her belly. Funny how both my animals were into belly rubs.

"And how are you doing this morning, little girl?" I asked.

"Very well, thank you. I'm liking our new digs better and better, and I think I'm over my jet lag," she replied.

"Leta, can you believe her?" asked Dickens. "She's claiming jet lag when she's been sleeping eighteen hours a day as long as I've known her."

Christie yawned and made a pronouncement. "Whatever. Now that I'm well-rested, I have an idea about how I can help you two with this detective business. Leta, if you set the photos up so I can see them on your computer, I can take a look. You know, we felines are not only highly intelligent, we also have extraordinary eyesight. You ladies may have missed something, and if it's at all visible, I'm bound to find it."

Even Dickens thought that was a grand idea, so I put the photos in slideshow mode. I chuckled as Christie stood on her hind legs in my desk chair, paws perched on the desk, eyes intent on the monitor. *A different perspective can't hurt*, I thought.

Dickens hadn't had a good long walk in several days and I'd told myself the night before I needed to walk off the brownies, so I decided to walk the two miles to and from the Inn to help Libby, and to feed Martha and Dylan on the way back. There was a chill in the air, so I put on my ball cap, a jacket, and gloves, grabbed the leash, and off we went.

Gavin greeted me as I came up the drive. "Morning. Do you have any idea how ecstatic you've made my wife? She's actually smiling for the first time in days."

"Happy to help," I said. "We're all of us missing Alice, but you two also have a business to run." I chuckled as I added, "I can't bake scones and tarts, but with a little direction, I can function quite well as unskilled labor."

Libby threw her arms around me and gave Dickens a hug too when we walked in the kitchen. "Do you mind if I set you to work first? And then we can have tea when the guestrooms are straight and the linens are in the washer."

With six rooms and a suite, I had my work cut out for me. I first tackled the rooms of the folks who'd already checked out, knowing they'd need a more thorough cleaning than Dave's room. Libby said he was out for the day, so I knew I could save his room for last without inconveniencing him. It was kind of mindless work, giving me a chance to mull over what I'd heard the past few days. It was hard to believe it was just over forty-eight hours since I'd found Alice's body.

Paddington greeted us as we made our way to the Green Room. "Hi, Leta. Hi, Dickens. Things are topsy-turvy around here. Gavin's been running around like a madman doing the indoor and outdoor chores, and Libby bursts into tears at the drop of a hat."

"I can only imagine," I said. "I've done a bit of crying myself. You must miss Alice terribly since she was here every day."

Dickens piped up, "She was nice to me at the party, and she promised me treats. Did she make cat treats too?"

"Yes," meowed Paddington. "And hers were much better than the ones in the box from Sainsbury's. I followed her from room to room as she worked, and I loved diving in the linens when she took them off the beds. It was always a party when Alice was around."

I had a huge pile of sheets and towels piled in the hallway and two bags of garbage all ready to go downstairs when I finally made it to Dave's room. The six rooms were named for colors—green, rose, blue, white, yellow, and lavender—and Dave was in the Yellow Room overlooking the roof of the conservatory.

His room was fairly tidy, with the wet towels folded and hung over the towel bar and his clothes put away rather than strewn around the room. His laptop was on the dressing table with a notebook and file folders, and I smiled at the thought of him writing at the feminine doily-covered table, his brief-case propped beside the lace-covered stool.

On the bedside table sat the copy of *Peter and Wendy* Beatrix had mentioned, a biography of A. A. Milne, and a book I'd never heard of, *Rare Books Uncovered: True Stories of Fantastic Finds*. Given that he freelanced for *The New York Review of Books* and *The Strand*, I supposed it made sense he'd have an interest in rare books. I wondered whether he was a collector.

As I straightened the pile on the dressing table, I noticed a sticky note I couldn't help but glance at. The words "Poe book, one of 50 copies, sold for $600,000" and "*Winnie-the-Pooh* signed first edition—$6500" were scribbled on it. *Hmmm*, I thought, *he is into rare books. Fascinating.* I pulled my phone out of my pocket and snapped a photo.

Good grief, I thought, *what made me snap a pic of that? I'm turning into a regular Nancy Drew.* I shooed Dickens out of the room and added the wet towels to the pile in the hallway. Paddington took that opportunity to poke his head out from the middle of the sheets and meow, prompting Dickens to bark and dive into the pile with him. "Paddington, you funny thing," I said. "Have you missed me?"

"But of course, Leta," he replied. "You're the only human who's ever been able to understand me. Libby and Gavin try, but they can't manage it. I suffer endless questions like 'What does my Paddington want today?' when I've been perfectly clear that I want milk or wet food or a head scratch," he grumbled. "But they *do* love me and treat me well, so I make allowances for their shortcomings."

After depositing the linens in the laundry room, I found Libby in the kitchen making a grocery list. "Give me a minute," she said. "I've got to get Gavin off to the store so I have the ingredients for finger sandwiches for the guests arriving this afternoon. And we'll have to make do with store-bought scones for tomorrow's breakfast. Without Alice, I'll have to find someone else to make them on a regular basis." She teared up at the thought of Alice, and I gave her a quick hug and went to sit in the sun in the conservatory. Even after several months, I still wanted to call it a sunroom as we did in the States.

Libby came in with two cups of tea and said Gemma

would be joining us for a quick cup before going to work. I wondered whether Gemma had gotten over her irritation with me. If so, maybe she'd give me an update on the investigation.

"Morning, all," said Gemma as she gave Dickens a scratch behind his ears. "Leta, are you recovering from your experience at the cricket pavilion?"

"Thank you for asking. Yes, I am," I replied. "I keep trying to tell myself Alice had some kind of accident so I won't be scared, but—"

Gemma interrupted me. "No, it wasn't an accident, or at least she didn't trip on her own, we don't think. Someone else was there with her, and, as you know, someone was at her flat."

"Um, yes, I hope our worry over the cat didn't mess up anything for you. I do have a request, though. I noticed one of my Frog Prince figurines in Alice's bedroom, and I was afraid to take it and disturb the crime scene, as they say on TV. Is there any way I'll be able to get it back?"

"Eventually, yes," replied Gemma. "I think there are quite a few things that will need to be returned to their rightful owners if we can figure out what belongs to who."

Libby's mouth fell open. "What are you on about? You were in Alice's flat? And you saw something of yours? Clearly, I've been out of the loop."

"Yes and yes. Funny, in all the disarray, I had a feeling some things didn't belong, but I couldn't quite put my finger on why," I said. "Just the odd item here and there maybe. By the way, have you been able to locate Alice's family?"

"We've found she had an elderly aunt in a Manchester nursing home. She seems to be the only family Alice had, and we've established Alice moved here from Manchester."

"Oh. It always amazes me how the police figure these

things out. I guess nothing much stays hidden in this day and age. I wonder what brought Alice to the Cotswolds."

Libby piped up. "Well, I could have told you she was from Manchester. She told me when I hired her that she wanted a change and didn't have any ties there. Funny, she didn't mention her aunt. She kept seeing the Cotswolds on the telly as an ideal place to live, so she packed up and moved."

"Mum, you checked her references, right?" asked Gemma.

"Of course. What do you take me for? They were all part-time jobs. She'd worked at a bakery, which must be why she was a genius at scones, and she'd had the odd housekeeping job here and there. Glowing, those references were all glowing," said Libby. "And she had a booth at a flea market too."

"No offense, Mum," soothed Gemma. "It's just that she'd been arrested in Manchester though never charged."

"What?" spluttered Libby. "Arrested for what?"

"Nicking the odd item here and there from homes where she worked as a housekeeper. It seemed to be mostly books and bric-a-brac, occasionally a silver piece. In the end, there wasn't enough evidence to proceed with charging her, especially as none of her clients wanted to press charges. It was suspected she was selling the things she pinched at her flea market stall."

Libby was speechless. I, on the other hand, was eager to get as much information as I could from Gemma. "That story fits with her having my figurine and whatever else you found in her flat. So, it seems she was more than a simple kleptomaniac and she was looking to make money off what she took?"

"Yes, the flea market angle makes it seem that way. First, we've got to speak with her clients to see what they may be missing from their homes or businesses; then we'll try to match that list with what's in her flat. It's a slow process, and at the moment we're most concerned with evidence that can help identify her killer. I can't see missing bric-a-brac leading to murder, can you?"

"No," I said. "By the way, did you find a computer or a cell phone anywhere?"

"You're a curious one, aren't you?" said Gemma. "But, no, we didn't find either, which just makes this whole case more complex. I have to think that whoever ransacked her flat took her computer and phone, but why?"

Libby was close to sobbing. "I can't fathom all this. Do I need to check to see what may be missing from the Olde Mill?"

"Yes, Mum, sooner or later, but it's not urgent. And you too, Leta. There could be more missing from your cottage, and I guess since Belle and Wendy were with you when you rescued Tigger, you might as well suggest the same to them. There may be a more sinister aspect to all this, but I've already shared more than I should with you two, so let's leave it at that. Thanks for the tea, Mum. Gotta run."

"Libby," I said, "it's time Dickens and I headed home. I'm happy to return later this week to change linens again if that helps. Dickens and Paddington put on quite a show for me this morning. Maybe I can get a repeat performance."

"Let me check the schedule, and I'll let you know what might be the best day. I think the lot that's checking into the inn today are only staying two nights, and then I'll get a new batch of guests Friday night."

I was fastening Dickens's harness in the back seat when Dave Prentiss drove up. He greeted me and said he'd forgotten something in his haste to set off after breakfast.

"I'm glad I've run into you," he said. "I was going to ask Libby for your phone number so I could invite you to dinner."

"Me?" I exclaimed, somewhat unartfully. I could have kicked myself for reacting as though no one would want to take me out. Honestly, an invitation from Toby and now one from an almost-stranger in the same week . . . I was floored, even if Toby was a friend with an ulterior motive for the dinner.

"Yes, you," Dave responded with a chuckle. "Don't act so surprised. Two Americans in the Cotswolds seems like a grand opportunity to get better acquainted. I'd love to hear more about how you decided to relocate here and what your experience has been. Who knows? It could even turn into a travel article—one featuring an attractive brunette and her sidekick, Dickens the dog. Would Tuesday evening suit?"

"Sounds delightful," I said. "Let me warn you, though, if you write an article, you'll have to mention Christie too, or there'll be hell to pay. She's quite the sensitive little thing."

"And Christie is . . . ?"

"My black cat. I'm betting you know who my four-legged companions are named for, right?"

Dave frowned and paused before his face broke into a smile. "Charles Dickens and Agatha Christie, of course!"

"Got it in one," I said.

"It's a date, then. I'll get some suggestions from Gavin as to a good place for dinner, and I'll pick you up at six. That way, I can meet Christie. If I'm going to write about her, I'll need some background."

Dickens and I stopped to see Martha and Dylan on our walk home. As I rubbed Dylan's nose, I heard the jingle of a bicycle bell and looked up to see Peter stopping on the grass. "What a glorious morning for a ride," he said. "I rode over to the Broadway Tower, and the views are gorgeous today."

"I bet. I've only climbed it once, back when Henry and I visited. He was taken with its World War Two history, especially the story of the British bomber that crashed nearby during a training mission. Maybe Dickens and I will take the car one day and do another bit of the Cotswolds Way."

"Maybe one of these days, I'll manage to get you on your bicycle, and we can visit it that way, though we'll have to leave Dickens behind for that," said Peter.

"I know, I know, I keep threatening to ride again. I see you on your bicycle so many mornings and ask myself when I'm going to get up the courage, but it hasn't happened yet. I wonder if getting my bicycle tuned up would give me the push I need," I said.

"That could do it," Peter replied. "Your bicycle shined up, ready to roll, and parked up front in the garage instead of tucked away out of sight. How 'bout I come by and pick it up and take it to the bicycle shop in Bourton-on-the-Water?"

I hesitated. "That might be too much pressure for me, but what the heck? If you're free this evening, why don't you come by for dinner and you can get it then? Nothing fancy, but I'll throw something together. What do you think?"

"You're on. Don't you know a confirmed bachelor never turns down an offer of food?"

Dickens looked at me as Peter rode off. "Confirmed bachelor, but we suspect Alice was his girlfriend? What's he trying to hide, Leta?"

"Perhaps we'll find out tonight, Dickens. Now, what shall we make for dinner? The usual Greek salad. Just like at home, everyone wants me to make my salad, but what else? Maybe some simple baked chicken."

We popped into the kitchen to get the car keys and drove to the grocery. Dickens reminded me we also needed cat and dog treats and more carrots, and I had a yearning for cheese grits after telling Toby about them, so I picked up some cheddar cheese too.

I was ready to sit a while when we got back to the cottage, but as I was putting away the groceries, Christie strolled into the kitchen. "I found two interesting things in your photos before I took my nap," she meowed.

"Right," barked Dickens. "How much time did you spend studying the slideshow versus napping?"

"Enough to discover one of Leta's Frog Prince fairytale books in one of the bedroom pics," she said. "The one with the mustard-gold cover."

"Seriously?" I said. "What on earth would trigger an interest in the Frog Prince? Maybe she's *just* a thief, plain and simple, though the things she took from me aren't especially valuable. And, of course, a simple thief wouldn't have been blackmailing Toby."

"Do you want me to show you what else I found?" asked Christie as she hopped up on my desk.

Christie stared at the computer until a photo of the bedroom came up. "There," she meowed, pointing her paw at a tiny black and white photo visible on a side table in the corner of the screen. "It's an old photo and looks like a little girl with a short mustached man. They both have big smiles."

I zoomed in so I could see it more clearly. It was in a tarnished gold metal frame like we used to get at Woolworth's when I was a child. I couldn't be sure, but the man looked like the photos I'd seen of J. M. Barrie. Could the little girl be Belle when she was young? I would have to show this to Belle and Wendy. That reminded me—I wondered whether Wendy had been able to determine if anything was missing from their cottage. I'd give her a call after Peter left. That way, we could compare notes from our day.

"Blimey," Peter said as he pushed back from the table. "I think I could eat one of your salads every day. They're that good."

"Why, thank you. When I was growing up, my dad fixed one for every Sunday dinner. It was a staple at our house, much like scones are around here. I have ice cream for dessert—no cookies or tarts, though. Goodness, how I miss Alice and her baking."

"Yes, she was the best with sweets, that's for sure," said Peter. "It's only been two days, and I already miss seeing her come up the drive with her cloth-covered basket filled with whatever she'd decided to bake that week."

"How often did she clean for you, Peter?" I asked.

"Twice a week, a few hours in my flat and a few in my office. My flat didn't get all that messy, but it always looked better after she'd been . . . aw, give me a sec," he said as he wiped his eyes on the napkin. "Now, my office at the garage was another thing entirely. I can hear her now fussing at the greasy fingerprints everywhere." And then big tears rolled down his face.

"Oh gosh, Peter, I didn't mean to upset you."

"It's just that . . . she was more than a housekeeper to me, Leta. I don't think many people knew, and for sure Wendy and Mum didn't, but we'd been seeing each other for about six months, and we'd just broken up. She was going down a path I couldn't deal with, and I couldn't get her to listen to reason."

"What do you mean, Peter?"

"I knew I should have spoken to Gemma, but I couldn't face it."

"What? Well, maybe you should go to Gemma now, whatever it is," I said.

Peter didn't seem to hear me as he stumbled on. "It took me a while to see she was pinching the odd thing here and there, and I was shocked. We weren't often at her place, so I didn't notice at first—until the night I saw a funny little teapot in her kitchen. It was an Alice in Wonderland teapot, and it looked strangely familiar. When I commented on it, she said, 'Oh that; it was at the book shop.' I waited for her to say she'd bought it, but instead she said, 'I fancied it, so I took it.'"

"Just like that?" I exclaimed.

"Yes. She said she took things from time to time, and she either sold them to a flea market friend she had in Manchester or she pawned them. Or she'd send them on to her aunt in Manchester. She was in a nursing home, and a little something here and there cheered her up."

This all lined up with what Gemma had told me.

Peter looked miserable. "I couldn't believe what she was telling me. And the worst part was she didn't see any real harm in it. She only took from people who had more than they needed, she said."

"Well, I have to admit when I went to her flat to see to Tigger, I saw one of my figurines," I said. "And yes, perhaps in her book I have more than I need, but that little crystal Frog Prince was given to me by Henry and it means a lot to me. Could be she thought it would cheer up her aunt, but still."

"Could be," he said. "She never had much money and was always worried about fixing her car or paying the rent, and she seemed to think it was okay to make ends meet by helping herself to what others had."

"I wonder how much of it was the thrill of getting away with something?" I said. "I've heard that's why some people shoplift. But the way you explain it, I guess this was more a case of Alice feeling she was in need and that her clients weren't. I wonder whether it bothered her at all to steal from us—people she knew and liked. Well, at least I felt like she liked us."

"I don't know, Leta. I guess it could've been a combination of needing money plus getting a kick out of putting one over on folks. I really cared about her, and I wanted to help her. I thought if I could get her on her feet financially, she might stop. And she *did* stop for a bit when I gave her that used car."

"You *gave* her the car?"

"Um, yes. I'd gotten it for a song as I sometimes do from customers who are upgrading, and I thought if she didn't have to worry about the constant repairs on the old one, she could catch up on her bills. She was surprised and grateful, but it wasn't long before she was back at it. I knew because I saw a small Peter Rabbit piggy bank in her bedroom. It looked suspiciously like the one Mum had given me when I was a boy—the one I'd left in my bedroom when I moved out. That's when we had our first real row."

"Gosh, Peter, she stole from your mum? And here you were, doing everything you could to help her. Short of turning her in, that is."

"I guess I should've, because it didn't stop there. We had an even bigger row when I figured out she was blackmailing Toby. Blackmail, can you believe it? She told me he was the only one, but I couldn't believe her anymore."

"Did she say what she was blackmailing Toby about?" I asked.

"That was the worst of it. She said he was having an affair

with Rhiannon. No way I believed that, but there was no convincing Alice of anything once she'd made up her mind. I guess the fact Toby paid her means she was right and I was wrong, but somehow I still don't believe it."

By now I was just nodding as Peter poured out his story. I suspected he'd never told anyone about all this and was relieved to get it off his chest. I pointed to the tea kettle and he nodded yes. Christie, sensing his distress, climbed into his lap, and he seemed to take some comfort from stroking her.

"Fool that I was, I offered to pay her rent for a month or two if she'd stop. She seemed genuinely contrite and touched and said she'd think about it. I should have known better."

"Why, Peter?" I asked. "What happened?"

"The last time she cleaned my office, she told me she could make do without the rent money, that she'd soon be quitting the blackmail altogether as she had a new scheme to get all the money she needed. She was right chuffed. That was it for me, and I told her I was at my rope's end, that I wouldn't stand for her doing anything else illegal.

"She laughed at me! I couldn't believe she *laughed* at me. She told me straight I had no say in what she did or didn't do. She called me a fool and a few other choice things and walked out. I'd never felt so humiliated in my life."

"Oh, Peter," I said. "I'm so sorry."

"I tried to talk to her at the party, but she made a point of ignoring me. I just can't believe she's dead," he said. "And I can't help but think it had something to do with this latest moneymaking scheme, or maybe she was blackmailing lots of folks. Who knows?"

"You know you need to go to Gemma, right?" I said.

"I know, I know. But don't they always suspect the husband or boyfriend in the movies? I'm that afraid Gemma will think I had something to do with her death, and I'm not sure I won't be in trouble because I knew about the knickknacks she took and then the blackmail and didn't speak up. What's the wording they use? 'Accomplice after the fact?'"

"Yes, I think that's right, and I can see why you're hesitant. They're bound to ask you about an alibi for the night Alice died too." He had good reason to be worried, and I wasn't sure what to tell him. Deep in thought, I poured us both more tea.

Staring into his cup, Peter said, "Thank you for listening. Somehow, I couldn't tell Wendy or Mum. They'd think me a complete idiot; well, I guess I am, actually. I've never been any good with girls. I was always awkward and shy, but somehow I could talk to Alice. Guess I was just plain naïve. What a fool."

"Umm, Peter," I said, "You know I'm good friends with Wendy. Do I need to keep this conversation a secret?"

"In some ways, it'd make it easier if you told her about my relationship with Alice. Then by the time I speak with her, she'll be over her shock. She might only call me an idiot once or twice instead of going on and on." He smiled as he said the last bit and stood up.

"Anyway, let's at least get your bicycle on the back of my car. Maybe something good will come out of my unloading on you, and we'll get you back on your bike before long."

After Peter loaded up my bicycle, I took Dickens for a quick walk, hoping the exercise would clear my mind. No such luck. My brain was packed way too full with distressing information. It reminded me of the old adage from the few years I worked in Human Resources: "Once you've heard the two sides of the story, you'll find the truth somewhere in the middle."

Except now, I felt like I was hearing several sides of Alice's story, and I couldn't figure out the truth or what any of it had to do with her death at the cricket pavilion. I even shushed Dickens because I couldn't deal with his questions.

Peter seemed like such a soft-hearted guy, but people aren't always what they seem. Could he have killed Alice in a rage over their breakup or at being humiliated at giving her a car and realizing how he'd been taken advantage of? He hadn't responded when I mentioned an alibi, and since he lived at home, I'm sure he wouldn't have one. I didn't want to believe the man I'd eaten dinner with alone at my cottage could be a killer.

When we returned to the cottage, both Christie and Dickens wanted to rehash the dinner conversation and grumbled when I nixed that idea. Emotionally exhausted, I couldn't even face a phone call with Wendy. Instead, before trudging upstairs with my book, I shot off a short email inviting her to come over for lunch to compare notes. Tomorrow would be soon enough to find out what she'd discovered in her snooping.

Chapter Eight

I woke up early with the niggling thought that I'd missed something vital in the photos of Alice's flat. Still in my robe and slippers, I sat down at my desk with my first cup of coffee. It wasn't until the caffeine kicked in that I thought to study the pics of the notebook pages.

"That's it," I said to the four-legged sleuths who'd joined me. "Each client has a page, but not all clients are alike."

Christie hopped on the desk and positioned herself smack dab in front of the computer screen and meowed indignantly when I nudged her aside. Not wanting to miss out, Dickens placed his paws on my desk chair, craning his neck to see what I was talking about.

"Look, for most clients, like me, Wendy, Gavin and Libby, for example, the notes are pretty straightforward—our rates and our regular days plus an occasional mention of lunch or dinner and a charge for that. Alice has only prepared one meal for me so far but quite often cooks light meals for Belle and Wendy and others. And I bet 'party' on the page for Gavin and

Libby means the times she prepared snacks at the Inn like the other night."

"That seems innocent enough, Leta," meowed Christie.

"Yes, it does, until you look at other pages like Toby's," I pointed out. Beneath his rate and days are additional lines of dates and amounts like £100, £50, £75, etc. Those must be the amounts she demanded to keep quiet about Rhiannon. And the checkmarks after the amounts must mean Alice received her payment."

"But Toby said there was nothing going on between him and Rhiannon," barked Dickens.

"Doesn't matter. As long as Alice was threatening to tell Cynthia the two were having an affair and to show her some kind of evidence to that effect, Toby was going to pay. And, uh-oh, the information on Beatrix's page is similar; only the amounts are different. What could Alice have had on Beatrix?"

"Blimey," responded Dickens, "guess this calls for Detectives Parker and Dickens to visit the Book Nook."

"Would you listen to him," meowed Christie. "We've barely been here a week, and he's going all British on us."

As upsetting as the morning's information was, I had to laugh at that comment. A glance at my email told me Wendy had accepted my lunch invitation, so I decided I'd kill two birds with one stone—tackle Beatrix and pick up sandwiches in the village.

I'd wanted to speak with Beatrix ever since I'd learned about Alice's flea market business in Manchester. I was curious as to what she might know about that, and I also wanted to know whether she'd missed the Alice in Wonderland teapot. Given the amounts listed on her page in Alice's notebook, that conversation now seemed even more critical.

The bell tinkled as I opened the door into the Book Nook. This was Dickens's first visit, and Tommy and Tuppence gave him a wide berth as he set about sniffing every inch. "Good mornin', Beatrix," I greeted her as she came hustling out from the backroom.

"Mornin' yourself, and mornin' to you, Dickens," she replied with a smile. "Just browsing today or looking for something in particular?"

"I came by to pick your brain, but as long as I'm here, I think I'll pick up a biography of J. M. Barrie. No matter where I turn, his name keeps coming up, so it's high time I learned more about him. What would you recommend, Beatrix?"

"Oh, *Hide-and-Seek with Angels* for sure. I've always found it to be the most informative. You'll find it on the table of biographies, but if you're interested, I just got in a flawless copy of a first edition."

"Wow, I knew you sold used books but didn't expect you had rare or collectible books. How does one come by something like that?"

"I keep my feelers out," said Beatrix. "And I visit estate sales. Plus a few of the flea market vendors I know will contact me if they get something special in. You have to know people and know what you're looking for."

"I've never owned a first edition of any book, but now that I've made my home in Astonbury, it seems only appropriate my first one be a Barrie biography. Not if it's priced anything like the examples Thom gave us the other night, though. Still, I'd love to see it."

As Beatrix went to the backroom, Dickens settled on a

snoozing spot. He turned around several times and stretched out.

The book Beatrix brought me was in pristine condition. "I'd love to have it, Beatrix. So, break it to me gently, what does something like this go for?"

She explained that it would probably go for as high as £60, but for a friend and for cash, she'd take £50. I pulled out five £10 notes, and she tucked them in her pocket.

As she wrapped my purchase, I eased my way into what I hoped would sound like innocuous questions about Alice. "I'm curious. I've heard Alice once had a flea market stall in Manchester and that she sold books among other things. Since you deal in used books and collectibles like this Barrie biography, it occurred to me you might have known Alice before she moved here."

Beatrix didn't reply right away. She busied herself with tying a bow around my package and then looked up. "Yes, I'd met her before on my occasional flea market foray."

"Did you ever purchase anything from her?" I asked.

"Yes, a used book here and there, and once, if I recall correctly, an unusual Alice in Wonderland teapot. Why do you ask?"

"Honestly? When I went to her flat to get Tigger, I saw some things that made me uncomfortable. For starters, I saw one of my Frog Prince figurines, which means Alice took it from my cottage. And the teapot you just mentioned was there too. If you bought it from her, what was it doing back with her?"

"Ah well, she wanted it back, so I let her have it; that's all."

"That was kind of you, Beatrix. There's also something else that's worrying me."

She gave me an anxious look. "Like what?"

"Alice kept a notebook with client names and notations on when she cleaned for us and what she charged us. For example, next to my name, it said £50/Tu for my rate and my day of the week. And for a few clients, she listed extra charges for meals she prepared. But next to your name and the names of one or two others, it showed the rate and day and then a series of amounts like £50, £30, £40, and on and on with no explanation. Here's a photo I took of the page so you can see for yourself. Was she charging you extra for some reason?"

Beatrix hesitated before answering, "Perhaps, now and then."

"I guess that's a yes, then," I said. "Beatrix, you're a dear friend, and I'm concerned you may be tangled up in something. You must know that the police will be asking the same questions."

"What does it matter that she charged me extra from time to time?"

"It matters because I've discovered Alice was blackmailing at least one of her clients, and I think she was blackmailing you too. If she was, the police will see you as having a motive for murder."

"Murder? Are they saying it was murder?" she exclaimed.

"Yes, and now they're looking for suspects," I said.

"Look," she said. "Alice and I had business dealings in the past, always on a cash basis. When she started cleaning the Book Nook, she nosed around and put two and two together."

Beatrix sounded exasperated rather than alarmed. "She figured out I was keeping some of my business—mostly the rare collectibles—off the books by dealing in cash. She'd done it herself, so she knew exactly what I was doing. She threatened to call the tax hotline on me if I didn't pay her. It was just easier to pay her now and then than it would have been to have to get a lawyer and fight the taxman."

How could she be so nonchalant about breaking the law? Clearly, she and I had a different sense of what was acceptable behavior. It dawned on me that was what I'd just witnessed when she put my £50 in her pocket rather than in the cash register. And here I was thinking the cash price was less because she wouldn't have to pay a credit card fee. How naïve of me. "Beatrix, please tell me Thom isn't involved in this somehow."

"That one?" she scoffed. "He's fairly knowledgeable about rare books, which is helpful. I think he picked up some of that from one of his professors, but no way I'd knowingly let him or anyone else in on the cash business. Besides, I've known him since he was a lad, and he's pure as the driven snow."

It was nice to hear *someone* was innocent, but I was dismayed, no that wasn't strong enough—I was horrified—that Beatrix was doing something illegal. "Well, I'm glad to hear Thom isn't caught up in this. So how did Alice approach you? Did she just intermittently ask for money?"

"Oh," said Beatrix, "she was a subtle one. She'd leave a sticky note either at my home or here at the shop. On it, she'd print the tax hotline number and the sum she wanted. When next I left her an envelope with her cleaning fee, she'd expect the extra to be in it."

"She never let up?" I asked.

"Not a bit. And the money wasn't enough. From time to time, she'd fancy something in the shop or at my cottage, and instead of a sum written below the tax hotline, she'd jot down whatever it was she wanted and place a checkmark by it as the signal she'd taken it. That's how she got the teapot back after I'd had it several years. Wasn't it considerate of her to let me know, so I wouldn't think I'd misplaced it?" she asked, sarcasm dripping from her voice.

She felt wronged by Alice but didn't seem to feel remorse for her own actions. "Beatrix, I have to be honest with you—I'm shocked Alice was blackmailing you, but I think I'm more shocked that you've been breaking the law."

"Now, wait a minute, Leta. Who are you to judge me, you a rich widow who picked up and moved here without a care in the world? Bought a historic cottage, no less? What do you know about running a business and making ends meet? Don't you dare lecture me."

Okay, I hadn't worded that last bit as well as I could have, but her comment about me being a rich widow stung. As tends to happen when I'm angry or put on the defensive, I responded in a soft but stern voice. "Yes, I'm *rich*, but being a widow wasn't a choice I made. You know I'd trade it all to have Henry back."

Beatrix looked a bit abashed. I think she knew she'd crossed a line. "Alright, I'm sorry about the widow comment, but can we agree that Alice blackmailing me was wrong, no matter what I might have done?"

"Well, of course. And, Beatrix, I'm sorry I got on my high horse about the taxes. I do feel strongly about it, though, so I'd rather pay you full price for the book to make it right. Okay?"

She rolled her eyes, but she accepted the additional £10 I handed her.

I was still digesting what she'd told me, and realized I'd had no inkling there was anything like that going on between her and Alice.

"Beatrix," I asked, "How long has the blackmail been going on? Since she arrived?"

"Pretty much. It started the second month she was here. I figured out the amounts went up and down depending on how much she needed to make ends meet. Sometimes, she'd go months without making any demands, but when her car was in and out of the shop, she asked more often and for larger amounts.

"But you know, Leta, even after what she put me through, she didn't deserve to die. She was so darned likable despite the blackmail. I certainly didn't want to be exposed for tax evasion, but if someone murdered her, what must she have had on them? I can't imagine."

"I agree. It's kind of creepy thinking that someone we know in Astonbury is capable of murder. I admit I don't know everyone listed in her book, and I can only hope it isn't one of the folks I know well . . . or *think* I know well."

"Leta, please don't tell Gemma about this. I realize she needs to know, and I'll tell her myself, if you don't mind."

"Of course I don't mind."

I couldn't help myself. Just as I'd done with Toby and Peter, I suggested to Beatrix that Gemma was bound to ask her for an alibi. And her response was much like Toby's. "Right, like I have an alibi for any night. I live alone, have done my whole adult life. Where am I going to come up with an alibi?"

All I could do was throw up my hands in a "who knows" gesture and give her a hug. The door tinkled as another customer entered, so I picked up my package and waved goodbye.

I had a cup of tea at Toby's and ordered sandwiches for lunch with Wendy. When Toby brought my order to the table, he leaned down and whispered, "Thanks for lending me an ear. I feel better for having talked it out, and I'm meeting with Gemma later today." I smiled in acknowledgment and headed out the door.

At home, I started a list of things to tell Wendy and decided right away that there were some details I didn't need to share. I'd tell her that Beatrix was being blackmailed but keep the *why* among Beatrix, me, and hopefully Gemma. I'd give her a bit more detail about Toby and Rhiannon so as to set the record straight about their relationship. As for Peter and Alice, the less said on that score the better.

My snooping at the inn hadn't turned up anything about Gavin and Libby, nor had the notebook revealed any strange payments for them, but the information from Gemma would make for an interesting discussion. And Wendy would get a kick out of the note and book in Dave's room, just as I had. And, of course, I'd point out what Christie had found in the photos—only Wendy wasn't to know it was my curious cat who'd found it.

Dickens and Christie both greeted Wendy as she came in the kitchen door. "Hi there," I said. "It's turned warm, so I thought we could eat in the garden. Does that work for you?"

I could hardly hear Wendy's response over Christie's plaintive comments. "What about me? Isn't it time I get to explore the garden? I promise to stay close, scout's honor, whatever that means."

Wendy and I both looked at Christie and laughed. "It cracks me up how she changes the pitch of her meows. I'm betting that last bit means she wants to go outside with us. This will be her first outdoor adventure in England, so I'll have to keep a close eye on her," I explained to Wendy.

I uncorked a bottle of wine for our meal. "By the way,

before we dive into detective work, I've been meaning to tell you—I'm having dinner with Dave Prentiss tonight. Maybe you can help me decide what to wear."

"Dinner? Is this a date, Miz Parker?"

"I think it's more he's thinking of writing a travel article and is looking for an outsider's perspective on life in the Cotswolds, but it's an excuse for me to wear somethings beside yoga pants or jeans."

"Okey dokey, then I'm happy to be your fashion consultant."

I laughed, imagining Wendy draping me in pashminas and necklaces. "Good. Guess we need to get started, but I think we owe ourselves a glass of wine first given how hard we've been working." And then I launched into the tale of my findings. I used my phone to show Wendy the clues I'd found in the "Alice" photos, as I now referred to them.

"I can't believe she took not only your figurine but your Frog Prince book too," exclaimed Wendy. "I wonder what the attraction could have been. And the pages in the notebook are a revelation. We didn't have time to study those the other night. Have you figured out what all the extra things are on some of the pages?"

"Unfortunately, I have," I said. And I told her about my conversation with Toby and how it had caused the aha that the notations had to indicate what he was paying her to keep quiet. "And the Toby connection led me to the conclusion that Alice was blackmailing Beatrix too."

At that revelation, Wendy's mouth dropped open and she poured herself another glass of wine. "If you've got much more like this to tell me," she said, "we may need another bottle."

I made the Beatrix story as brief as possible and took that opportunity to include Gemma's information about Alice's

Manchester history. Then I broached the topic of Peter. "This is Peter's story to tell, but he said it was okay to share the broad strokes with you. He confirmed that he and Alice had been in a relationship but said it had ended not long ago. He became aware she was nicking things from her clients and thought he might be able to get her to stop by helping her financially. That's how she came by the car. Your big-hearted brother gave it to her."

"Oh for goodness' sake, the big lug," she said. "He always was naïve when it came to women. Fortunately for him, he earns a good living from his garage. You wouldn't know, but he often barters with his customers for repairs. The man never lacks for fresh vegetables or firewood. Still, giving Alice a car seems over the top."

"I got the impression he was head over heels in love, and I'm afraid he knew about the blackmail too, at least of Toby. I don't think he knew about Beatrix. "

"Was the blackmail what ended their relationship? Was that last bit the straw that broke the camel's back?" asked Wendy.

"Actually, it was when she told him she'd be stopping the blackmail soon because she had a new scheme in the offing. That ripped it for him. There's more detail on all this, but it doesn't change the basics of the story, and I'd rather let Peter fill in the blanks for you if he chooses."

"Well, what's the new scheme?" Wendy asked.

"Peter didn't know, and I don't have any idea. I have another tidbit from my cleaning spell at the Olde Mill, but let's hear what you know first. Let me take the dishes in, and I'll be right back."

Dickens was stretched out in the sun and didn't move, but Christie followed me in the kitchen. She meowed, "Hey, aren't you going to tell her about the black and white photo I found? I think that's important."

"Dear Christie," I murmured, "All in good time. And, by the way, thank you for staying in the garden today. Are you ready for a treat?"

She eagerly took her treat and dashed back to the garden. She was enjoying her taste of the outdoors.

When I returned to the garden, Wendy was busy giving Dickens a belly rub but stopped long enough to pull out a list of all the items missing from Sunshine Cottage. There were quite a few figurines missing, and when she mentioned the Peter Rabbit piggy bank, I interrupted her to tell her Peter had seen it at Alice's. Belle also had a set of Winnie-the-Pooh figurines, and Tigger was missing from it.

Christie chose that moment to leap into my lap and lick my hand. *She's reminding me to tell Wendy about the photo*, I thought. "Well, that fits," I said, "since Alice had a cat named Tigger. I don't recall seeing it in the photos we have, but it could have been buried in the mess. Is there a black and white photo on your list? I saw one of those and thought maybe it was a pic of your mum and J. M. Barrie."

"If it was in a dime store frame, you guessed right," she said, "and I'm not anywhere near the end of my list. Mum has lots and lots of books, older ones from her childhood and ours and tons of romance and mystery novels from the last forty years, so trying to figure out what books are missing is tough going."

"You checked for missing romance novels?"

"No, no," said Wendy. "I wasn't trying to see if any of those were gone, but Mum's books aren't well organized, so you never know what you'll find tucked where. To give you an idea,

I found a Daphne du Maurier hardback next to *The Cat in the Hat.*

"But here's the disturbing thing—I couldn't find her copy of *Peter and Wendy* anywhere. It's probably not in good enough shape to be a collector's item, but it's inscribed to her and Gran and signed by Uncle Jim. It's possible she tucked it away somewhere for safekeeping and I haven't yet stumbled across it. I haven't wanted to ask her because I know she'll be upset if it's really gone."

"That's awful," I said. "We're talking about a treasured childhood keepsake. There were so many books flung around Alice's flat, I guess we could have missed it, but somehow I doubt it. And given that Alice must have known a thing or two about books, I'm betting she took it because she thought it was valuable. I wonder whether she sold it to someone she knew in Manchester, maybe at the flea market. Lord, I hope not."

"Well, I'm going to keep looking," said Wendy. "And you know, after all this, I've a hankering to go through Gran's letters with Mum. I'd love to hear her reminisce as we look at them."

"Oh, that reminds me," I said. "I understand now why Dave Prentiss got so excited when he saw your mum's Winnie-the-Pooh books. Here's a photo of a notepad I saw when I was cleaning his room: Poe book, one of 50 copies, sold for $600,00 and *Winnie-the-Pooh* signed first edition--$6500. And he had this book, *Rare Books Uncovered: True Stories of Fantastic Finds.* I guess as a writer for *The New York Review of Books* and *The Strand,* he's pretty knowledgeable on the topic."

"Gee, maybe as two retirees with English degrees, we should take up book collecting," said Wendy. "With that jingle, we could hire out, dontcha think? And on that note, we're still going to Oxford, right?"

"I'm looking forward to it. It'll take our minds off all this unpleasantness. Boy, that's an understatement if I ever heard one—unpleasantness. It's so much more than that. Now, before you leave, can you come upstairs and help me decide what to wear tonight?"

"Sure. Where is Dave taking you?"

"I don't know. He was going to ask Gavin, but you know nothing is all that dressy around here. I'd just like to wear something a step above jeans or cords. I thought maybe a skirt and boots."

Wendy looked through my closet. "It's so funny," she said. "There's not a color in here that would look good on me. It's all black, white, and jewel tones. Even your gazillion scarves are in that color scheme. I mean, look at this purple next to my platinum hair. Ghastly! That's why my closet is filled with winter white, shades of taupe, and lots of pastels."

I laughed. "You're right, and not a one of those colors does a thing for my olive complexion. What do you say we start with this black skirt? It's mid-calf length, and I like the way it swirls when I walk."

It was Wendy's turn to laugh. "You crack me up. You have four black skirts, each one a slightly different style, and I see several pair of black pants and leggings. And, for goodness' sake, how many black belts do you have?"

"I don't know what's so funny. Different bottoms require different style belts. If we stick with the swirly skirt, as I call it, I can wear my black suede knee-high boots. Should I go with a white top, or maybe a red one?"

Wendy pulled out a crisp white top with thin, vertical silver stripes. "I like this one. Pair it with that wide belt and your red and purple scarf and you're set. So, are you going to put this much thought into what you pack for Oxford?"

"Already done," I said. "Cords for the drive up and the Library tour, my favorite red dress for the play, and a different sweater to pair with the cords for the return trip. And, of course, a hat or two. I'm betting you'll be in winter white, and we'll make a smashing duo."

"Right on both counts. Who's going to take care of Dickens since the hotel won't let us bring him?" she asked.

"Yikes, I meant to ask your brother if he could ride by Thursday night and again Friday morning. That's all Dickens really needs, and you know Christie will be fine on her own for an overnight trip, but it's possible I can also get Peter to give her a dab of milk while he's here. I'll ring him at the garage as soon as you leave."

Peter was happy to help me out.

My next call was to Libby to ask if she'd like my help again. "Wendy and I will be in Oxford two days," I said, "but I can come by tomorrow if that would help, and again on the weekend."

"Oh, I wish I could go with you two, but there's not a chance. I didn't realize how much work Alice did around here until I started doing it myself. I'm already going to owe you," she said, "but I could really use you tomorrow, and again on Sunday."

Now all that was left on my to-do list was to prepare for my dinner with Dave. I chose not to use the word *date*. That was too scary to contemplate.

Chapter Nine

By the time Dave arrived, I'd done a bit of light housekeeping, prepared a plate of grapes, hummus, and pita chips, and had a bottle of wine chilling. I let Dickens out the door when I heard the car pull up.

"Hey, boy," I heard him say. "How you doing?"

Dickens eyed him and barked, "Nice of you to ask. I'm doing fine."

I chuckled as the two came toward the door. "I think he just told you he was fine," I told Dave.

I admired his tweed sport coat and was glad I'd chosen dressy casual for the evening.

He handed me a small box as he came in. "I explored the village of Broadway today and couldn't pass up the chocolate shop," he said. "I hope you like chocolate."

"Fortunately or unfortunately, depending on your perspective, I like chocolate and most sweets," I replied. "Let me open some wine and I'll show you around the cottage. Would you prefer red or white?"

We settled on red, and I poured two glasses before I took

him back outside to start the tour. "I fell in love with this place when I saw the pictures online," I said, "but the fact that it had been a schoolhouse in the 1800s pretty much sealed the deal for me. Thankfully, it was in great shape and had the space I needed. The appliances have been upgraded, and the garden is a dream."

"Look, it even has a school bell," Dave observed. "And the mullioned windows are a nice touch. You're going to have to tell me the story of how you decided to move to England and the Cotswolds in particular, plus how one goes about finding a fairy-tale cottage like this one."

As we returned to the kitchen, I suggested we save that story for dinner. I gave him the indoor tour, pointing out that the two very large rooms downstairs were originally classrooms but had been turned into a sitting room and extra-large play-room when the school was converted to a cottage.

I'd added bookcases on either side of the fireplace in the sitting room and a comfy cushion to the window seat in the other room, now my office. In there, I'd positioned my desk to see out the large picture window to the garden. Slowly filling the bookcases put in by the previous owners with books and local pottery was one of my great pleasures.

Next was a quick tour of the two upstairs bedrooms, where Dave was as enchanted with the mullioned windows of leaded glass as I was. Returning to the kitchen, we grabbed the snacks and the bottle of wine and settled in the sitting room. He was admiring my collection of books when Christie made her entrance.

"Pffft," she hissed. "I'm not sure about this one. I much prefer Peter."

Dave laughed. "Uh-oh, I suspect that sound means she doesn't like me. Or does she greet all newcomers like this?"

The answer to his question was no, she didn't usually have that reaction, but I didn't want to hurt his feelings, so I told him she hadn't adjusted to her new home yet.

"Leta, you know you're lying to the poor man, don't you?" she meowed. "I'll grant you there haven't been many men around since Henry left us, but there's something about him I don't care for. For sure, he's not a cat person."

I picked her up and carried her upstairs. "Enough of that, young lady. He's my guest, so behave yourself. First Dickens judges my friends based on the food they sneak him, and now you're not giving poor Dave a chance."

Of course, when I came downstairs, Dickens was getting a belly rub from Dave. My boy was relentless when it came to demanding belly rubs.

"Well, Christie may not have taken to you, but Dickens sure has," I said. "Did he beg for a pita chip too?"

Both man and dog looked at me innocently. Dave nodded yes with a smile and Dickens barked, "How'd you know?"

Gavin had suggested a restaurant in Northleach, so I put the plate of snacks in the fridge and we headed out. Northleach was a picturesque village, not quite as large or touristy as Bourton-on-the-Water. Dave said Gavin had been able to reserve us a table by the fireplace.

We agreed on a bottle of red for dinner and skipped the appetizer course, since we'd indulged at my cottage. I chose the lamb, Dave the beef tenderloin, and we asked the waiter to hold the main course for a bit. Dave was a good conversationalist, and I enjoyed hearing tales of the authors he'd interviewed. Some had been charming and some temperamental.

He seemed genuinely interested in how I'd wound up in Astonbury, so I reflected on how to shorten the saga of my twenty-year marriage, Henry's bicycle accident, and my decision to throw caution to the wind and make a major change. He certainly didn't need to hear every step along my two-year journey.

After the accident, I was inconsolable and I'd taken a leave of absence. I'd find myself up in the middle of the night going through photo albums, standing in front of Henry's clothes in the closet, or staring unseeing at the television.

About the time I felt emotionally prepared to return to work, I sat down with our financial planner to discuss selling the house and downsizing. Ever a practical person, I couldn't see living in a five-bedroom house that had been too big even when Henry was alive, and I wanted to get some of these major decisions out of the way before returning to my demanding career.

I was taken aback when, after going over the numbers, she asked, "Have you given any thought to retiring?" I must have looked dumbfounded because she paused before continuing. "I mean, have you considered that with Henry's substantial life insurance and pension, you don't *have to* work?"

Almost speechless, possibly a first for me, I left the meeting with a list of questions to answer—questions that pretty much amounted to laying out things I'd always thought of as pipe dreams. Henry and I were similarly practical, so our dreams had never run to mega-mansions, around-the-world cruises, collecting antique cars, or owning vacation villas around the globe.

The one pipe dream that kept resurfacing was retiring to England. I was a lifelong Anglophile. I'd taken as many British Lit courses as possible while pursuing my English degrees and especially loved British mysteries by authors like Elizabeth George, Deborah Crombie, Peter Robinson, and others.

Where in England was easy—the Cotswolds. I'd fallen in love with the area on our first trip to the UK. Once I got rolling with the idea, the possibilities seemed endless.

". . . and yet, and yet, I couldn't make the leap," I told Dave. "I went back to work, I sold the house, and I continued to grieve, but it wasn't until one too many late-night calls from the boss from hell that I said, 'The heck with this, I'm outta here.' I completed my retirement paperwork in no time flat, and here I am."

"Whoa, that can't have been easy," he said. "Did you find yourself wanting to bounce ideas off Henry at every turn?"

"How did you know?" I said in surprise.

"I've never been married, and I've never lost a loved one, but I was in a long-term relationship once—ten years. When we split up, I kept wanting to run article ideas by her like I always had, even though I was in New York and she'd moved to the West Coast. I'd find myself wanting to tell her about some arrogant author or ask her opinion about a chair for my apartment. I think it's just natural."

"Yes, and it still happens, but not as frequently," I said and laughed. "Now that Dickens and Christie are here, I just talk to them. Sometimes they give me ideas for my columns." Dave had no idea how serious I was.

"You write columns?" he asked. "For what paper?"

"Oh, they're not major papers, just small weekly publications, one in Atlanta and another in North Carolina," I explained.

He smiled. "Hey, no need to be so modest. A column's a column. How long have you been a columnist?"

I had to think for a minute. "I was still working for the

bank . . . it must be seven or eight years now. It's funny, I really loved my corporate job, but writing? I think I've found my passion. My day isn't complete if I haven't written something."

Said Dave, "It's amazing, isn't it? Even though writing is a job for me, I love it. Nah, I didn't say that well. What I'm trying to say is not everything I write about is fun and exciting or inspiring, but for the most part, my job is a blast."

So, we have that in common, I thought, *even if it's on a slightly different scale.*

"So," Dave continued, "tell me more about life here. I feel like it's harder and harder to make friends the older I get, but I can tell you've made a few here, and you and Wendy especially seem to have lots in common."

"Yes, Wendy and I are both English majors and avid readers, and we both lived in the South—as in the Southern US. And I didn't teach as long as Wendy, but I taught high school English for a few years before I went into banking. So we've really hit it off. I have to admit I get lonely for my long-time friends back home, but we're pretty good about staying in touch. I'm hopeful some of them will come visit now that I have a place for them to stay."

Our talk shifted to books we'd enjoyed and eventually to the authors who'd summered near Astonbury. "Did you get a kick out of hearing Belle's story?" I asked. "I sure did. It even prompted me to pick up a Barrie biography. In fact, Beatrix had a first edition available."

"Really?" he said. "I have a few first editions, though nothing like what some of the major collectors have. My budget doesn't run to spending hundreds and thousands of dollars on a book. I read that someone had paid $600,000 for an Edgar Allan Poe book recently. Amazing."

I acted surprised and didn't let on that I'd seen the note in his room. "Why would anyone spend that much money on a book?" I asked.

"Collectors are a breed unto themselves," he said. "One reason I was so interested in Belle's *Winnie-the-Pooh* books was that I've seen first editions of A. A. Milne books offered for upwards of a $1,000. And Belle has not one but all four of the books—all signed first editions. The right collector would buy them in a heartbeat."

"How do they locate the books?" I asked. "Think about Belle. Those books have been sitting on her bookshelf for decades, and she had no idea they were valuable until you told her, so how do collectors find out? Do they wander the globe visiting little old ladies?"

Dave laughed. "That's quite an image. Can't you see a bespectacled old man in a tweed suit carrying a large black portmanteau from house to house? The reality is books like Belle's usually wind up in a used bookstore, and if the owner of the store knows his stuff, he'll put the word out."

"And what do collectors do with the books once they buy them? Sit and stare at them?" I asked.

"You know, that's a good question. Sometimes rare books disappear into a collector's private library, never to be seen again until he or his heirs donate it to a university or museum. You most often hear about the books when someone donates an entire collection to his alma mater, like the Ransom Collection at the University of Texas in Austin. An unpublished J. M. Barrie play was found there not long ago. Maybe it's all about getting your name on a building or an exhibit."

"Ah, well, this is all too rich for my blood," I said. "I'll stick to reading my mystery novels and donating them to the thrift shop when I'm done."

I took a final sip of wine and reluctantly said, "This has

been a wonderful evening, but I promised Libby I'd help her at the inn tomorrow, so I'll need to be up early."

"You really are a good friend. I want to make an early start tomorrow too. I'm checking out and driving to Plymouth and Portsmouth to do a bit more research on Arthur Conan Doyle. I'd also considered going to Edinburgh where he was born and attended university, but I can't do it all, and I've already stayed in the UK longer than I'd planned."

"I'd love to read the article when it comes out. I'm always looking for the next Sherlock Holmes variation, and I've enjoyed the Sherlock Holmes movies with Robert Downey, Jr., though I suspect a purist might not approve."

"Well, the modern novels and movies may not be true to Doyle's vision for Sherlock, but they've kept the story alive. And that means there's still interest in the character and the author, so people like me get to write about both. I bet you didn't know the first Sherlock Holmes short story—"A Scandal in Bohemia"—was published in an 1891 issue of the *Strand Magazine*. And it's the *Strand* I'm writing this article for."

By then, we'd pulled up to my cottage. Dave walked me to the door and gave me a peck on the cheek as I thanked him for a lovely night out. Dickens joined me outside as I waved goodbye, and then the inquisition began.

"Where did you go? What did you eat? Do you like him? Are you going out again?" asked my curious dog.

I was explaining that I'd had a marvelous time, but Dave was just a friend, when Christie strolled into the kitchen. "Friend, indeed," she said. "Let's invite Peter back for dinner. He's tall and slim like Henry, and he rides bicycles too. He's more your type."

"Enough, you two. Can't I have male friends without you comparing them and playing matchmaker?"

I woke up smiling Wednesday morning and knew it was because of Dave Prentiss. I hadn't enjoyed an evening that much in a long time—possibly since Henry had passed away. It seemed the perfect time to email my sisters and avoid any discussion of murder and mayhem, so I took my cup of coffee to my office, where I was joined by Christie and Dickens.

"So, who's coming to dinner tonight?" asked Dickens. "Or is someone else taking you out?"

"Yes," meowed Christie, "You've suddenly become very popular, or has it been like this the whole time you've been here?"

"Funny, funny," I said to them. "This has been an unusual week. Most nights, I'm at home reading a good book . . . by myself." I wasn't sure they were buying my story, but it was the truth.

I wrote my sisters a detailed description of my dinner date. *Yes*, I thought, *it really was a date, and the entire evening had been a delight—no uncomfortable moments, no awkward silences.* We had lots in common, but since I wasn't in the market for a boyfriend, his living in the States suited me fine.

I hit send and switched into high gear so I wouldn't be late for my morning shift at the inn. The forecast was for rain, so I decided to forgo a morning walk. Dickens hopped into the car, I latched his harness, and I drove to the Olde Mill. It appeared most of the guests had checked out, as only Dave's rental car was in the gravel drive.

Gavin was coming out of the conservatory with dirty wine glasses. "I'm herding dishes," he said. "This morning, they seem to be scattered all over the inn, and I want to get them into the dishwasher."

"Gavin, why don't you let me do that," I asked. "I'll do the rooms like I did the other day, and then I'll police the premises for all the glasses, cups, and whatever. That way you can work in the office, visit the co-op for groceries, and do everything else on your list. Dickens and I are now on duty."

At that, Gavin set down the dishes and gave me a huge hug. "You've got it. The boss has already given me a list for the co-op, so I'll go there before it gets crowded. Maybe we three —oh excuse me, Dickens we four—can have a cup of tea when I get back."

Dickens wondered aloud where Paddington was and said he should be included in tea too, and I stuck my head in the laundry room to alert Libby that Dickens and I were on the job. She was ironing napkins and tablecloths—a thankless job, in my opinion. Henry used to say I had clothes I'd never wear if it weren't for him doing the ironing, and he was right. I attributed my intense dislike and avoidance of ironing to the fact I'd had to iron sheets when I was a little girl. I still grimaced at the memory.

"Everyone checked out except Dave?" I asked Libby.

"Yes, but he plans to check out soon. He's decided to visit the coast and maybe return here for a few nights next week. That means all the linens need changing. You're a lifesaver."

Dave coming back after his trip was news to me. *I wonder whether I'll see him then,* I thought. *Maybe I can cook for him. Oh stop,* I said to myself. Dickens and I got to work, and the pile of linens in the hallway grew. Like he had last time, Paddington darted up the stairs and dove in. Dickens joined him and soon they were tussling and barking and meowing. Just like kids in a pile of leaves.

I took a load of glasses to the kitchen and returned with a

stack of fresh towels from the linen closet. When I got to the Yellow Room, I knocked and said, "Maid service."

He appeared distracted as he opened the door, a pair of glasses perched atop his head. "Oh," he said, "I'm not sure who I was expecting, but it sure wasn't my dinner date from last night."

I grinned. "You just never know where I'll turn up. Libby tells me you're checking out today, so I'll come back later to get your room ready for the next guests."

"How is it you always show up when it's in my brain to ask you out? Can you squeeze me in next Sunday or is your dance card full?" There was a twinkle in his eyes as he said that.

I had to admit I was quite tickled at a second invitation. "Hmmm, I'll find someone to bump so I can arrange a spot for you," I joked. "Dinner sounds great. Let's make it my treat this time."

"Well, we'll work that out next week," he said. "Unfortunately, right now, I'm kind of in a rush to get on the road. Can I just gather up the wet towels to give you and leave it at that?"

"Sure," I said. "I'll look forward to hearing from you when you get back. Meanwhile, I wish you the best with your research."

I headed downstairs with the last load of dirty linens and towels, Paddington and Dickens on my heels. "You two are going to be disappointed if you think I'm creating a new pile for you to play in."

I went through the downstairs gathering dirty dishes. Along the way, I found two empty wine bottles, and Paddington found a champagne cork beneath a couch in the conservatory. My last stop was the sitting room. The hearth looked in need of sweeping, so I retrieved the broom and dustpan from the broom closet.

Paddington and Dickens seemed to be having a conversation by the bookcase, but I couldn't quite make it out. "What are you two going on about?" I asked.

"This," said Paddington as he stood on his hind legs and reached for the second shelf from the bottom. He used his paw to lever a book from the shelf, and it fell to the floor with a thud. "It doesn't belong here."

Dickens said, "He claims he knows all the books on the bookcase. I'm not sure I believe him."

"Well, let's see what we have here," I said, kneeling on the oriental rug in front of the bookcase. My mouth dropped open as I picked up the book. It had a faded green cloth cover, and I saw the title *Peter and Wendy* in gold lettering on the front. Carefully, I opened the book and read "For Mary, who was my savior on many a dreadful night. May you and Belle enjoy my story." It was signed by J. M. Barrie. I sat back cross-legged, all thoughts of cleaning gone from my mind. Here it was—Belle's copy of *Peter and Wendy*—and it was signed by the author. How did it get to the inn?

Paddington nudged my elbow and meowed, "Alice put it here. I thought she would come back to get it, but she never did."

"When was that, Paddington?"

"The day of the party, Leta," Paddington mewed.

It had been published in London in 1911. I turned the pages gingerly, afraid I might tear the delicate paper in a book that was over a hundred years old. As I continued, a thin sheet of paper slid out. Across the top was the salutation "Dearest Mary" and the signature at the bottom read "Uncle Jim." *Oh my gosh,* I thought, *this is one of the letters to Gran.* I scanned it and realized it must have accompanied the book.

Dearest Mary,

I realize little Belle won't be able to read this book for some time, but when she's a bit older, I hope you'll read it to her. I think she'll enjoy the story it tells.

Much Love,
Uncle Jim

I oh-so-carefully returned the letter to the book, told Dickens to stay, and grabbed my rain jacket from the hook at the front door. I wrapped the book in my jacket and quickly went to my car and placed the bundle in the boot. Something told me it didn't belong in plain sight on one of the seats.

I almost ran into Dave as he was coming out the front door with his suitcase and computer bag. "Off to the coast," he said.

I still needed to straighten the sitting room, so I went back and finished sweeping the hearth and corralling dishes. Dickens kept asking me what was going on, but I told him he'd hear it all later. When the dishwasher was full, I added detergent and switched it on. I grabbed clean linens and ran upstairs to change the sheets and towels in Dave's room.

As I passed through the kitchen on the way to the laundry room, I found Gavin unloading groceries. "Hi," I said. "I think everything is shipshape, so Dickens and I are heading out."

I sat in my car and thought about what to do next. First, I needed to call Wendy to let her know I'd stumbled across the book, but then what? Should we talk to Gemma? Would this be an important clue in her investigation, or was I on the wrong track? Or maybe we should speak with Beatrix, who was knowledgeable about rare books and had been one of

Alice's victims. Perhaps she could shed some light on the situation.

Of course, I had to figure out a way to explain how I knew Alice had taken it. I couldn't come out and say Paddington had *seen* Alice put it on the bookshelf and had *told* me about it. Then again, Alice taking it was the only logical explanation for the book winding up at the Inn. It wasn't like Libby or Gavin ever visited Sunshine Cottage.

I rang Wendy. "Oh my gosh," I said when she answered the phone. "I've found your mum's copy of *Peter and Wendy*."

"What? How? Where was it?" Wendy gasped.

"It was at the Inn mixed in with the other books on the bookshelf. Remember Gavin telling us he and Libby had shopped estate sales for old books? Um, if it hadn't been sticking out slightly, I never would have noticed it."

"Oh my goodness," said Wendy. "Why? Who put it there?"

"Could it have been Alice? No way Libby or Gavin have anything to do with this. And Alice was here just about every day. And get this—there's a letter tucked in the book, a letter from Uncle Jim!"

"That . . . that can't be," stuttered Wendy. "That means Alice found Mum's letters. I mean, it's not like they're hidden, but it would take a lot of nerve to go through a box of someone's personal letters. Who does something like that?"

"Listen, it may be a good idea to speak with Beatrix about this. She knows rare books and can tell us what your mum's book could be worth. She might even know who Alice would have contacted if she was thinking of selling it. You know she didn't take it just for the heck of it. She had to be planning to make money on it. What do you think?"

"Do you really think we need to involve anyone else?"

"Yes, because we still don't know who killed Alice—or why.

Figuring this out could be the clue we're missing," I replied. "Can you meet me at the Book Nook in an hour?"

"OK, I'll be there," she said.

Way too much going on, I thought, *but we can't stop now*. I ran by my cottage for a protein bar to keep me going. Christie sensed something was up, but when she asked, Dickens got snippy.

"Never you mind, Christie," he barked. "We'll fill you in when we have all our ducks in a row."

"Don't you get huffy with me," hissed Christie. "Ducks in a row. Do you even know what that means?"

I apologized to Christie for Dickens's behavior and told her we were in a hurry, that I'd explain everything later. She was howling in indignation as I locked the door.

Chapter Ten

Wendy and I arrived at the Book Nook at almost the same time. It must have been obvious to Beatrix that something was up, because she came around the counter and asked, "What's wrong?"

For the moment, there were no customers in the shop, so I took the lead and tried to explain about the book. I'd transferred it to a padded computer bag and wrapped it in tissue paper when I stopped by my cottage, and now I slowly revealed it.

Wendy said, "To me, it's just a book Mum read to us when we were kids. I can't imagine it has anything to do with Alice's death."

"Let me get this straight," said Beatrix. "First, you two somehow pieced together that Alice was taking things from the three of us and possibly others when she cleaned our homes. I know that's true because she took things from me, and you told me, Leta, that she took your Frog Prince figurine—"

"And one of my Frog Prince books," I interjected.

Wendy piped up, "And once we realized she'd nicked items from Leta, I started inventorying Mum's stuff. Mum's Tigger figurine is missing from her Winnie-the-Pooh collection. Then, I couldn't find Mum's *Peter and Wendy* book anywhere, but I kept thinking it would turn up. She used to keep it with her *Winnie-the-Pooh* books in the bookcase in the sitting room, and I couldn't fathom why she would've moved it."

Beatrix picked up the story. "And now you've found Belle's book? At the inn, of all places? Surely, you don't think Libby and Gavin have something to do with this, do you?"

"No," Wendy and I said in unison.

"Think about it, Beatrix," I reasoned. "If you wanted to ensure no one found an especially valuable old book, what better hiding place for it than in with a bunch of other old books?"

"I *am* thinking," she retorted. "I just can't wrap my brain around the idea that Alice was that well informed about books. But then again, she'd recently been reading up on J. M. Barrie."

The bell over the front door tinkled, and three women wandered in loaded down with shopping bags from several shops on High Street.

"You two stay put," Beatrix whispered before greeting her customers.

I looked at Wendy. "Are we going to tell her about the letter?" I whispered.

"I'm beyond thinking clearly about this," moaned Wendy. "But the letter seems more personal to me, and I don't think we should tell anyone else until we've run it by Mum."

After Beatrix's customers left with several books about the area, she rejoined us. "Believe it or not, I managed to think about all this while I listened to those women dither about spending money on books. Books are probably the most practical purchase they've made all day. Of course, I'm biased."

Wendy asked, "And what ideas did you come up with?"

"First I'm going to look online for what signed copies of *Peter and Wendy* have gone for lately. Let's see where that leads us."

It probably would have taken me and Wendy hours to find the right websites, but in less than fifteen minutes, Beatrix had discovered that a signed first edition of the British printing had gone for $8,000 USD in the States and that there was a first edition on offer but not signed.

"Good grief," exclaimed Wendy. "That's unbelievable. Thinking back to what Thom explained to us at Book Club the other night, I suppose that copy was in much better condition than Mum's, but still. What if Mum's copy were worth even half that?"

"Ladies," murmured Beatrix, "Thom will be in shortly. I think we should run this by him. He's not an expert on rare books, per se, but he did study under an Oxford professor who, by all accounts, is pretty obsessed with all things having to do with J. M. Barrie. I bet Thom can do some digging for us and find out whether there's been chatter about this book among collectors."

I hesitated. This situation was fast becoming bigger than a breadbox, and I wasn't at all sure how to proceed. I was certain we'd uncovered clues Gemma was unaware of, but even if we went to her with them, how long would it be before she could or would follow up? Before I could answer, Wendy spoke up.

"Let's do it!" she said. "It's been four days since Leta found Alice's body, and we haven't heard word one about progress towards finding her killer. I think we're on the right path."

"OK, then," I said. "What say we grab a bite at Toby's and come back when Thom is due in. What time is that, Beatrix?"

"Come back around two. He'll be here until closing, so we should be able to grab a few minutes to huddle at some point."

Wendy and I walked across the street to the Tearoom. We agreed we owed ourselves something sinful as a snack with our tea. She chose a fudge brownie, and I went for the Manchester tart. What could be better than a pastry shell spread with raspberry jam, topped with custard filling, sprinkled with coconut flakes, and garnished with a maraschino cherry?

It was becoming the norm for me to have a stressful morning and start feeling exhausted when the adrenaline wore off. I told Wendy I might have to get ice cream next to restore my energy, but she knew me better than that. That was another thing we had in common—we were both short and vigilant about watching our calories.

We saw Thom walk into the Bookshop and gulped our tea so we could get back across the street and get started. We still had our sense of humor and joked we'd have to wrap this up quickly before our sugar highs wore off and we collapsed in a sleepy heap.

I'd thought about how to explain our involvement to Thom. I didn't want him to think we were two crazy little old ladies with too much time on our hands. Little we might be, but crazy and old we weren't.

"Thom," I said, "I know I said I wanted to speak further with you about rare books, but that was just out of curiosity. Believe it or not, Wendy and I have a real situation to run by you."

He looked intrigued. "I'm all ears, ladies."

"Okay. Before we get to what happened this morning to bring us here, let me give you the short version of what's been going on since I found Alice's body. That day, when Wendy and I realized Alice's cat was likely on its own, we rushed over to her flat and found that someone had 'tossed the place,' as they say in the crime books.

"We realized she'd been stealing from us, her clients, and that led Wendy to discover that one of her mum's books was missing. This morning, I stumbled across that book hidden in an unlikely spot. That's why we're here at the Book Nook. Beatrix did some research but thought you'd be a better resource for us. You told us at Book Club you'd studied under a professor who was a collector of Barrie's works. Well, that's what we've got." I wasn't at all sure what I'd said made any sense, but Thom seemed to be following me.

I brought out the book and opened it to reveal the inscription. Thom's face lit up, and I took that to mean this was a great find. Though the book was worn, he explained, the inscription changed the game.

"My professor would know its general value, if you will, but he might also know of a collector who would be interested above all others."

"Whoa, wait a minute," said Wendy. "We don't want to sell it. We're hoping that determining its value might be confirmation that Alice could have been involved in a larger rare book scheme, a scheme that led to her murder. Please don't give the wrong impression to your professor."

"Thom," I asked, "will your professor want to help if the book's not for sale?"

"He's a scholar first," said Thom. "He'll be interested in this for its historic value and the possibility that Belle and her family might someday want to donate or sell it to Oxford for their collection. Believe it or not, despite Barrie's affiliation with the Cotswolds, Oxford has very little in the way of Barrie manuscripts and books."

"If you'll leave the book with me, I can photograph it and send him the images," said Thom.

"Heck," said Wendy, "Leta and I are going to Oxford on Thursday. We could make an appointment and show it to him."

"He has a pretty busy schedule, so I don't think you'd be able to get in," said Thom.

"In that case," said Wendy, "I'll just take it home. No offense, Thom, but now I've got it back, I don't want to let it out of my sight. Can you take just a few photos and see what you can find out from him?"

Thom obliged and said he'd be in touch as soon as he heard something.

As we walked to our cars, I turned to Wendy. "Would you be alright with me keeping the book for a day or two? I'd love to read through it. Who knows? Maybe a lightbulb will come on in my brain as I read."

"Sure. While I don't want to lose it again, I'd feel more comfortable if it weren't at Sunshine Cottage for the time being. Like there's something about this book that attracts trouble."

"Great, then I'll be the trouble magnet? I hope not," I said.

"After all this, are we still going to Oxford?" asked Wendy.

"I'm game if you are. Do you still think we can put all this out of our minds? If I have to bite my tongue every time I start to say something about Peter Pan or books or whatever, I might just bite my tongue in two before our trip is over."

I could tell Wendy had a mental image of the health of my tongue because she giggled. "How about we just say we'll try to not obsess over this? I don't want to be on the Bodleian tour and have you whispering Peter Pan in my ear."

"OK, agreed," I said. "We'll work to keep it to a minimum. Besides, I haven't yet given you the highlights of my dinner with Dave. We'll start with that. See you tomorrow, bright and early."

Christie was none too happy to hear I was leaving for two days, though Dickens was fine, since he liked Peter. "Do you think he'll take me to see Martha and Dylan?" he asked. "So far, that's my favorite walk."

Before I could reply, Christie piped up, "Sure, it's all about you, Dickens. What about me? Does Peter know how I like my milk? Will he stay long enough for me to snuggle in his lap? Will I get to go out in the garden again?"

"Enough," I said. "No one knows how you like your milk, even me. That seems to change daily. And I don't know that Peter will have time to sit. As for the garden, I expressly told him not to let you out, young lady. Until I return, only Dickens gets to go out, and no, I don't know whether Peter will walk past Martha and Dylan."

My four-legged companions discussed the situation while I packed my suitcase and loaded it into the car. I knew they'd be well looked after, and I was looking forward to spending time in Oxford. Henry and I had enjoyed our visit there, but it had been too short. We'd tried a little bit of everything. We took the Inspector Morse walking tour and a boat ride on the River Isis and wandered the city, but there was so much more to see and do.

I called Wendy to let her know I was on the way, and she

was waiting outside when I arrived. We were leaving bright and early because we had morning tickets to tour the Bodleian. We'd do a bit of shopping, check in to our hotel later in the day, and take in a play at the Oxford Playhouse that evening. Day two we'd planned as a day of leisure. We'd stroll, shop, eat, and be back in Astonbury in time for dinner. Most importantly, we really would try *not* to talk about the happenings of the last few days. We needed a break.

Of course, before we could talk about anything else, I had to give Wendy a blow-by-blow of my evening with Dave Prentiss. "I really did enjoy myself. The conversation didn't have any of those awkward dead zones, and I think we could easily have continued a bit longer. I may have to look for his articles online. And, breaking news, he's asked me out for next week."

I laughed and continued, "I can't believe I've had dinner with three different men this week—Toby, your brother, and Dave. Of course, the first two turned into confessionals, so this one was a nice break."

"That's three more than I've had," Wendy said. "I haven't had anything approximating a date since I moved in with Mum, not that I had that many dates in Charlotte either. A trip to relive my university days will just have to do. I haven't visited in a while, but I do have fond memories of my years at Balliol College."

"And you met your husband there, right?" I asked as I maneuvered my way onto the A40.

"Yes, he was doing his Junior Year Abroad at Oxford, and we continued our relationship long-distance when we were both seniors. What do the kids call them nowadays? Starter marriages? That's the way I felt about our marriage, though it lasted for ten years. We were married in Astonbury and then moved to North Carolina where he had a banking job."

"Have you kept in touch? I know you both lived in Charlotte, but I have a vague idea that he moved around quite a bit with the bank," I said.

"No children and not much reason to stay in touch, and you're right. I had a teaching job in Charlotte and never left, but he lived all over the US, anywhere the bank asked him to go. I can't imagine I'd have retired to England if we were still married. England just wasn't his cup of tea, so to speak."

I laughed at her wording. "Well, I'm glad you're here. It's so funny to have met someone in Astonbury who lived in the South, though your accent isn't quite as pronounced as mine."

"It seems to depend on where I am. The longer I lived in Charlotte, the more Southern I got, but whenever I visited Mum in the summer, I'd immediately get my British accent back. Maybe soon, I'll be all Brit again."

"Isn't it funny that Dave thought we were both Americans the other night? There's no mistaking my accent, but yours is a bit of a hybrid."

"That reminds me," said Wendy, "I found an article on the internet last night that made me think of him because it was in the *Strand Magazine* and he told us he wrote for them. I had no idea that a previously unpublished J. M. Barrie play was discovered in 2017."

"Huh," I said, "Dave mentioned the same thing to me at dinner the other night."

"How strange. It was bundled with other letters and manuscripts by Barrie. It had all been at a university in Texas for fifty years, and I guess no one had ever looked closely at the contents. Oddly enough, it's a murder mystery."

"What a coincidence. Between the two of you, I'm eager to dive into the Barrie biography I got from Beatrix yesterday. Maybe I'll do that when I get home," I said, "but only after I'm done with the book I'm reading now. I've never been one of those people who likes to read two books at once."

We entered Oxford city limits in the midst of the morning rush hour, and I was thankful Wendy was in the car to direct me. I still wasn't all that comfortable driving on the *wrong* side of the road in traffic. We made it to the hotel without incident, parked, and walked to our tour.

We two English majors were fascinated with the facts our tour guide shared—from the architectural wonders of Christopher Wren to the tales of Oscar Wilde's days as a student. We chuckled when we heard the Divinity School, where the tour started, had served as not only the Hogwarts infirmary but also the dancing school in the Harry Potter films. It was almost too much to absorb, and I took copious notes, thinking the experience might be a good topic for one of my newspaper columns.

We wandered to Oxford's version of the Bridge of Sighs and visited Blackwell's, the oldest bookshop in Oxford. By then, it was late enough for a pint at the White Horse Pub next door. I recalled from my previous visit that it was the scene of many an Inspector Morse and Lewis adventure.

"Wendy, are you a Morse fan?" I asked. "I was so disappointed when the *Inspector Lewis* series ended, and then I got hooked on *Endeavor.*"

"Oh yes, I don't know what I'd have done without out PBA and PBS in Charlotte. In the days before streaming, that was the only way I got my British telly fix," she said.

"What do you say we wander to the river before lunch?" I asked.

She was quick to answer yes, and we strolled to the River Isis, as the Thames is called where it runs through Oxford. Then we decided to have lunch at Pieminister in the Covered

Market and do a bit of shopping before we checked into our hotel.

We each chose a different pie so we could try two kinds. I'd never attempted to make a savory pie. Well, truth be told, I hadn't made many sweet ones in my life either. I could make several Greek desserts and that was about it.

"Oh, there's The Hat Box," I said. "I've got to check it out. Henry bought me a red beret when we were here, and I still have it."

Wendy laughed. "Of course, it was red. Oh, look at the fascinators. That's what we need, except I have no idea where we'd wear them."

"Unless we get Libby to throw a Royal Wedding dress-up party, I don't either, so I guess I'll stick with wool hats and scarves for now."

By then, we were ready to check in to the Randolph. We'd chosen it because neither of us had stayed there before, and we agreed a nap was in order before the play that evening.

Wendy called home to check on Belle before we set out for the play. Peter was already there and answered the phone. She put him on speaker so we could all chat.

"Mum's fine," he said. "I brought some takeaway and she's already told me which shows we must watch on the telly tonight. And, Leta, I cycled to your cottage and took Dickens for a good long walk before that. He let me know he wanted to see Martha and Dylan, so that's where we went."

"He let you know? And how did he do that?" I asked, wondering if I'd just discovered another person who could talk to the animals.

"Well, he's a strong little fella, and he headed that way. Didn't seem any use in arguing with him," he said.

Wendy and I both laughed at that and told him about our

day. He was jealous of our visit to the pie shop but said he was fine with missing the Hat Box and the library.

"Ladies," he said, "I plan to get up early without waking Mum, ride my bike to check on Dickens and Christie, and then come back here to fix Mum's breakfast. She should be up by then. After that, I'll be at the garage unless I hear differently from you. You'll be home by dinner, right?"

"That's the plan," we said in unison.

We had a quick bite and walked to the Oxford Playhouse. Afterward, I surprised Wendy with a visit to the Varsity Club's rooftop bar. She'd never been and agreed the views of the "city of dreaming spires" were breathtaking. Leave it to two English majors to toast Matthew Arnold. After a bottle of red wine on the rooftop, there was no debate as to how we'd finish off the evening. A trip to the Morse Bar in our hotel was a must.

We closed down the bar and were so busy talking, we didn't turn out our lights until after two. With only a trip to Gloucester Green to shop the antique and arts and craft market on our Friday agenda, we were looking forward to sleeping in.

When the phone rang before 8:00 am, I groaned and thought it had to be a wrong number. I managed to locate it only after knocking over the glass of the water on the bedside table. "Hello," I whispered, trying not to wake Wendy.

"Wendy, is that you?" I heard.

"No, she's still asleep. Who's calling?" I asked.

"Leta, it's Gemma. I'm afraid there's been an accident, and I need to speak with Wendy."

I shook Wendy awake and handed her the phone. I could

hear Gemma's tinny voice coming through the phone. "Wendy, Peter's had a bicycle accident and he's been taken to Cheltenham Hospital."

Wendy's questions tumbled out. "What? Where? Who's with Mum? Has she been told? How badly is Peter hurt? Where was he?"

"He wasn't far from Leta's house when the accident occurred. Constable James and my dad are on the way to your mum. The constable will break the news to her, and Dad will drive her to the hospital. You need to get to Cheltenham as quickly as you can."

Wendy started crying, and I grabbed the phone and told Gemma we were on our way. We threw our belongings in our bags, checked out, and hit the road.

We found Belle and Gavin in the waiting room outside the emergency room. Belle was surprisingly calm, calmer than Wendy, and I guessed that was because she was a retired nurse. The only sign she was distressed was the constant wringing of her hands.

Gavin explained that Gemma would be along in an hour or so after she'd done what she could at the crime scene.

"Crime scene?" I said. "I thought Peter had an accident. It's so easy to do on these country lanes, especially when it's not full light. It only takes hitting a rock in the road or swerving to miss a partridge."

"No," said Gavin. "Gemma says there were tire tracks that make it look like he was deliberately run off the road."

I took a deep breath to calm myself. If I lost it over the

similarity to Henry's bicycle accident, I wouldn't be able to help Wendy and Belle. I couldn't go to pieces here.

"How is he, Mum?" asked Wendy in a little girl's voice. "Is he going to be all right?"

"Sweetheart, it's not good. The scrapes and broken collarbone can be easily tended to, but he hasn't regained consciousness since he was found."

"Who found him?" I asked.

Gavin told the story. "A gentleman out walking his dog before work saw the mangled bicycle on the road, and his dog took off into the brush and led him to Peter. Thank goodness for cell phones. He called 999 and told them an ambulance was needed right away. The police and the ambulance arrived fairly quickly, and when they saw the scene, they called in Gemma. She called me and then you as she was on her way there."

"Who would do this to my brother? What's he ever done to anyone to deserve this?" cried Wendy.

"Well, dear," said Belle, taking over from Gavin, "we had an unsettling occurrence at Sunshine Cottage last night. Could have something to do with this. I don't know."

"What happened at the cottage? Why didn't you or Peter call me?" asked Wendy.

"Nothing you could have done off in Oxford. I'd gone to sleep after my shows were over, and Peter had taken his book upstairs to his old room at the back of the house. Tigger had been in his lap all night, and I think he followed him to bed because that cat never did come to see me.

"Peter told me later that he heard something downstairs and thought at first it must be Tigger until he saw him curled up on the toybox at the foot of his bed." A smile crept onto Belle's face. "Funny, my little dog Tinker liked to sleep in the same spot back when that was my bedroom." She seemed lost in those more pleasant memories for a moment.

"Anyway, he knew it wasn't me because I'm dead to the world once I go to bed. He came downstairs in his bare feet and saw the front door open and a light in the sitting room. Smart boy, he positioned himself in the kitchen doorway to watch. He figured out it was a man but not who it was. The only thing easily to hand in the kitchen was the brick doorstop, the one covered in needlepoint, so that's what he grabbed.

"Whoever it was must have heard Peter because suddenly he turned and dashed out the front door, but not before Peter had hurled the brick at him. He hit him somewhere because the man cried out as he ran from the house."

"Oh my gosh, this sounds like something out of Agatha Christie," I said. "When did he tell you all this, Belle?"

"He ran after the fella but not far. Then he came back to the house to make sure I was okay. We checked my bedroom clock and saw it was midnight. Well, once he'd woken me up, I had to know what was going on, because, of course, I hadn't heard a thing. So I popped in my hearing aids and got the story. Can't hear a thing without 'em."

"What were they looking for, Mum?" asked Wendy.

"Haven't a clue, luv. Your brother didn't want me out of bed late at night, so I haven't had a chance to see what kind of mess my sitting room is in, though he said it wasn't much disturbed. A few books pulled off the bookcase and a footstool out of place. And, of course, he left to walk Dickens before I got up this morning. Instead of Peter back to fix breakfast, it was Gavin and Constable James who showed up at my door."

Gavin looked at Belle as she wrapped up her story. "Belle,

have you told Gemma or Constable James about what happened last night?"

"Haven't had a chance, have I?" Belle snapped.

"Okay, okay," I soothed. "Gavin, if you give me Gemma's cell number, maybe I can get her on the phone and let her know she's got another crime scene." *Good grief*, I thought, *I sound like Miss Marple.* I'm not that old, but if things didn't calm down, I'd soon have her head of white hair.

I plugged Gemma's number into my phone, but before I walked to the parking lot to ring her, I pulled Wendy aside. "Let's think for a minute. Do we think someone could have been looking for your mum's copy of *Peter and Wendy*? After talking to Beatrix and Thom, we know it's valuable, and we know they didn't find it because it's at my cottage."

"Oh no," Wendy cried. "Is all this about a book? Someone broke into my home and maybe ran my brother off the road over a book?"

I gave her a hug and told her I didn't know, but I'd bring Gemma up to speed and let her know how I fared.

I rang Gemma, hoping I'd be more articulate without Belle, Gavin, and Wendy chiming in. "Gemma Taylor," was the crisp answer on the other end.

"Gemma, it's Leta, and I'm at the hospital where I've heard something I'm sure you need to know."

"Give me one minute," she replied as she gave directions to someone. When she returned to the line, I heard her take a deep breath. "Now, Leta, what's up? Has Peter come around?"

"No, not yet," I said. "Belle just told us about an intruder at Sunshine Cottage last night."

"An intruder? The poor woman. She must be a basket case, an intruder and her son run off the road? What happened?"

"Amazingly, she's far from that. She may be the calmest of

us all," I said. And then I relayed Belle's story of Peter finding the intruder.

"I also need to let you know that we think whoever it was may have been after one of Belle's books, a book signed by J. M. Barrie," I said.

"Are you kidding me?" Gemma shouted.

"Um, no," I replied. "And Gavin, I mean your dad, says you think Peter was deliberately run off the road, and that makes me think the two incidents are connected. In fact, Belle wondered the same. And I know I sound like some silly mystery book, but the phrase 'another crime scene' popped to mind, and I thought you needed to know."

"Yes, you do sound like a something out of *Midsomer Murders*, but your assumption makes sense, or at least needs to be taken into consideration. I'm about to wrap up here, so I'll head to Sunshine Cottage. Any chance you can meet me there?"

I hesitated. "Sure. I'll leave Wendy here with your dad and Belle." Why did Gemma want to see me? Did she suspect me of something? Had she gotten wind of my meddling?

Chapter Eleven

In the car alone without the distraction of looking after Wendy and her mum, thoughts of Henry and his bicycle accident overwhelmed me. Peter's accident had dredged it all up, and big fat tears rolled down my cheeks. I was in danger of falling apart and decided a quick stop by my cottage to get Dickens would help me hold it together.

Dickens was happy to see me and didn't understand why I was in such a hurry. "What's up? Aren't you going upstairs to say hello to Christie? Oh, you're taking me on a ride?"

On the way, I broke it to Dickens that his friend Peter was in the hospital. I told him I'd explain everything when he, Christie, and I were all together.

Gemma was leaning on her car talking on the phone when we pulled up, so I let Dickens out of the car and told him to stay close, that Gemma and I had work to do. She quickly wrapped up her call and greeted me. "I was calming Mum down," she said. "She's worried sick about Peter and Wendy and Belle."

"I can only imagine," I said. "I've only known everyone for

a few months, but they've all been friends for years. And on top of Alice, it's just too much."

"That's why I asked you to meet me. A murder and attempted murder in the space of a week in the small village of Astonbury can't be a coincidence. Before I go any further, let me be clear that I've been furious at your meddling, but—"

"I know, I know. I'm so sorry—"

"Let me finish," interrupted Gemma. "I said I've been furious, but as more and more information came to light because of you, I began to get over it. That's right," she said with a half-smile. "First Toby came to see me. Then it was Peter, and yesterday Beatrix showed up. And every one of them said it was you who encouraged them to share what they knew."

"Yes, that's true," I said hesitantly. "Was what they had to say helpful to the investigation?"

"I'll say. Some of it was corroboration of things we suspected; some of it was altogether new information. I'd really like to know how you pieced it all together. Actually, maybe I don't. Just how long were you at Alice's flat before I arrived with Constable James?" she asked.

Whoa boy, I thought. "Not that long. Long enough to take photos with my phone, and to dig Tigger out from beneath the bed. That's all."

"And long enough to touch a vital piece of evidence, right?" she pointed out.

"If you mean the purse with the notepad in it, I guess you're right."

"So, if I set aside the fact that you along with Wendy and possibly Belle knowingly disturbed a crime scene, I can't help but be grateful for your pushing the investigation along. Let me be clear, though, I don't approve, and I'm telling you now, don't get any ideas about making this a habit."

I felt the way I had when I'd been caught reading in the dark as a child, possibly my worst transgression—until, that is, I snuck makeup to school to apply in the girls' restroom. I'd been forbidden to wear makeup and thought my mom was being utterly unfair.

"Now, that I've gotten that out of the way," said Gemma, "I'd like your help here in the cottage. You've been here before, and I'm counting on you to help me see what's out of place or suspicious. Okay?"

Phew, I thought. I'd half been waiting for the ax to fall, but it seemed I was off the hook. "Sure," I replied. "Based on what Belle told me, I guess all we need to check is the sitting room."

Tigger was curled up in Belle's chair and looked at us warily. "What now?" he meowed.

"Oh, Tigger," I murmured. "This mess is déjà vu, isn't it? But at least you're not wedged up under the bed scared to death."

"This time, the man tried to be quiet so no slamming around, no cursing. I think it was the same person." Tigger told me.

That was good information. Seeing books pulled from the bookcase and lying open on the floor reminded me of the scene at Alice's flat, but this mess was minimal in comparison. "Think it was the same person who broke into Alice's?" I asked Gemma.

"Could be, but it's certainly not as big a shambles. Could be Peter interrupted whoever it was before they could get too far."

"This makes me wonder whether someone was not only looking for Belle's book but also looking for a photo or a piece of paper or a pamphlet, something that would fit between the pages of a book. Oh no!"

"What?" asked Gemma.

"The letter in the book completely slipped my mind," I cried.

"What letter in what book?"

"Sorry. It's hard to keep it all straight. Inside the book I found was a letter from Barrie to Wendy's gran. So maybe whoever was here was also looking for letters."

"Are you purposely talking in riddles, Leta? What book?" Gemma asked again.

"*Peter and Wendy*. Wendy discovered Belle's copy was missing, and I stumbled across it at the inn. We heard all about collectors the other night at book club, how they want not only books but also correspondence and manuscripts. What do you think?"

"Bloody hell, you think this has to do with a talk at book club? Are you kidding me? Would that be worth killing someone for?"

"Gemma, my gut tells me it's all tied to Belle, her book, and maybe more. Why do we keep finding books pulled from bookcases if these break-ins don't have anything to do with books? Is it too far-fetched to think we're dealing with a deranged collector?"

Gemma looked at me in astonishment. "Of course, it's too far-fetched, Leta. Let's be practical."

"Well, we're talking about a lot of money. But look. I'm curious now. See this footstool by the corner cupboard? It's usually by Belle's easy chair. I'm thinking someone was about to use it to reach the top shelf of the cabinet. Let me see what's up there." I stood on the stool and reached up, but at 5'2", I was too short to reach the top.

"Here, let me do it," said Gemma. She reached and brought

down a wooden box decoupaged with pastel flowers. "It's only a box of letters, nothing else up there."

"Those must be Mary's letters," I said. "Belle mentioned she had tied them with a lace ribbon and stored them in a box. Could Peter have interrupted the intruder before they could climb on the stool to get them?"

Gemma again looked at me as though I'd lost my mind. "So now it's letters? Someone would break in for letters? Why on earth would anyone do that?"

In my brain, bits of information were falling into place, like puzzle pieces. Sunshine Cottage had been given to Gran by Uncle Jim, and Belle had said the treasured letters were from him. All this week, I'd been hearing random facts and anecdotes about J. M. Barrie—his visits to Stanway House, his donation of the cricket pavilion, a newly discovered play, and the gifts he'd given Belle. Were these latest incidents somehow connected to the famous author of *Peter Pan*?

I was beginning to feel defensive and just a little irritated. "I don't know," I retorted. "I'm still trying to piece it together." I didn't have it all worked out in my head and Gemma sure wasn't buying the book idea. Why was that any less believable than killing over knickknacks?

I tried again. "Another thing I haven't had a chance to tell you is that Wendy not only discovered the book was missing but also that quite a few other things were too. She planned to go through the letters next to see if they'd been disturbed. Given what you told me about Alice's flea market background, I thought at first she was supplementing her income by selling knickknacks, and beyond that, blackmailing her clients. Is it possible she had moved onto something bigger?"

"Like what? Books? You can't be serious." Gemma scoffed.

I tried to stay calm even though she was speaking to me

like I was a crazy person. "But what if we're talking rare books? I read that an Edgar Allan Poe book sold for $600,000 USD. That's what I meant by a lot of money. Could someone be looking for something rare by J. M. Barrie or one of the other authors who summered with him at Stanway House?"

"Leta, I have no idea. Let's leave it and finish doing what we came to do. Can you tell if anything is missing?"

Well, that's that, I thought. *She won't even consider me being on the right track.* I'd had about all I could take. "Fine, just fine. I can't see anything obvious missing. We'll have to wait until Belle or Wendy can look through the letters."

"You're not going to let it go, are you?" Gemma asked in exasperation. "We'll ask them, but for now, how about you go home and organize your thoughts—maybe you'll come up with something beyond books. But do *not,* and I repeat do *not*, go out and start asking questions. One person is dead, and one is seriously injured. You need to be careful."

Now she was not only irritating me but also scaring me. I couldn't think of anyone else I'd talk to anyway. Except Wendy and Belle, and we knew they were both innocent.

"I'll take another look at the suspects I have for Alice's murder to see whether they could in any way be in the frame for the break-in or the attack on Peter," continued Gemma. "Even though my gut tells me that most of them are in the clear for Alice's death, I need to consider the timeline and the evidence for all three incidents now."

"And then we'll compare notes?" I asked. I desperately wanted to know who she suspected but was afraid she'd shoot me there and then if I asked.

"Yes. Call me tomorrow so we can put our heads together," she asked. "Frankly, if I don't make headway fast, CID is going to swoop in and take over. It may already be too late. Once today's attack makes its way up the chain of command, I may be removed from the case and be out of the loop."

"Oh no," I said. "Maybe we haven't gotten all that far, but we've likely made as much headway as anyone could. I'll ring you tomorrow, then. I plan to be at home or at the hospital the rest of today."

I stopped by home long enough to take a shower and grab something to eat. I stood with my hip against the counter waiting for the coffee to brew. I surely needed coffee too. I was munching on a protein bar when I noticed the note on the kitchen table, and I teared up when I realized Peter had written it. As I read the note aloud, Dickens laughed, and Christie was, of course, indignant.

> **Leta,**
>
> **Your bicycle is propped against the wall just inside the garage door. I think I've put the seat back in the proper position for you in case you want to take it for a practice spin. If not, maybe we can take a ride together next week. What do you think about putting Christie in the basket? HA!"**

I was hesitant to tell them the details of what had happened to Peter, and when I finally did, they were visibly upset. Dickens paced the kitchen while I ate, and the fur on Christie's back stood up.

"He's a very nice man," said Christie. "He poured my milk just the right way this morning and let me sit in his lap before he took Dickens out. Why would anyone want to hurt him?"

"And, he took me to see Martha and Dylan—twice!" barked Dickens. "They like him too. Can I go see him, please?"

"Sorry, boy, they won't let you in the hospital, but if I get to see Peter, I'll tell him you asked about him. Now, you two, I hate to leave you on your own again, but I need to see how Wendy and Belle are doing."

Christie piped up, "Leta, I can't help but think all this has something to do with what happened to Alice. Since we can't go with you, maybe I can look at the photos again to see if we missed anything. I'm worried, and I want to help."

I wasn't sure there was anything more to see, but if Christie wanted to help, it couldn't hurt. I turned on my computer and once again set up the slideshow of photos, and Detective Christie leaped up and settled on the desk. I rubbed her sleek black head and kissed her goodbye on her nose before turning to Dickens to scratch his ears.

Not much had changed in the waiting room at the hospital. Gemma had come and gone and gotten the story of the break-in from Belle. She'd confirmed that the tire tracks on the soft dirt on the shoulder, or *verge* as the Brits called it, told the story of a deliberate hit-and-run. As bad as Peter's injuries were, he was lucky he'd been wearing his helmet.

Once I arrived, Gavin went home to help Libby, and I reminded him I'd be there the next day to prep the rooms for the weekend guests arriving Friday evening. Wendy looked dreadful and had little to say. Belle remained calm, but I could tell the waiting and the worry were taking their toll. I was reflecting on the scene at Sunshine Cottage when I thought of a way to distract them both from the current circumstances.

"Belle," I said, "I noticed your smile earlier when you

mentioned your toybox. Was that another gift from Uncle Jim?"

Belle's face lit up. "Yes," she said. "He was the most amazing little man. It wouldn't do for me to have a plain wooden box for my toys. He had to bring me one with the inscription 'Belle's Toybox' in gilt lettering. I filled it with stuffed animals and wooden blocks and a baby doll, and it played a major role in the stories he told me."

"It sounds as though you remember the stories, Belle. I'd love to hear one."

"Oh, there were quite a few, Leta, but the ones I remember best are those he put in the book he wrote for me. I knew I was in for a treat whenever mum said, 'Let's read *The Family at Sunshine Cottage.*'"

I squealed, "He wrote a book for you?"

"Why yes, dear, and he also had a friend draw some lovely pictures to go in it." I could tell Belle didn't think this was anything special, but even Wendy perked up at this point.

"Mum, are you talking about the storybook you used to read to Peter and me when we were small?" she asked. "I always thought it was a book Gran had found for you at a shop. It wasn't?"

"Oh no, sweetheart. I think Uncle Jim had it specially bound and printed up for me. I don't recall all the details, but every once in a while, Uncle Jim would send Mum a letter with a story in it. It seems after he accumulated several, he decided they should be in a book. He knew I adored the *Winnie-the-Pooh* books he'd given me and wanted my stories to be in a book too. Instead of *The House at Pooh Corner*, my book was *The Family at Sunshine Cottage.*"

Anyone who passed the waiting room right then would have seen two grown women with their mouths hanging open.

I think Wendy and I were equally amazed, and we could tell Belle was puzzled by our expressions.

"Mum," said Wendy, "are you telling me that you have a book of stories written by J. M. Barrie, a book written especially for you?"

"Why yes, Wendy. I read it to you and Peter any number of times, though you two were never quite as enchanted with it as I was. I adored it and still do. The stories are about me and Tinker and Gran and my magic toybox."

"Um, Mum," said Wendy, "where do you keep the book now?"

"In the toybox in Peter's old room. It's not in bad shape, considering. Once you and Peter outgrew it, I wrapped it in tissue paper and stored it with my favorite toys. Silly me—I had hoped I'd someday have grandchildren to read it to, but that didn't come to pass."

Belle teared up as she uttered the last sentence, and Wendy moved to the couch to put her arms around her mother. Just then, the doctor came to the doorway. I couldn't tell from his expression whether he was the bearer of good news or bad.

"Mrs. Davies, your son has regained consciousness, but he's understandably disoriented. He's resting comfortably and we'll move him to a room as soon as we have one available."

Wendy burst into tears, and it was Belle's turn to comfort her. I breathed a sigh of relief and sat there not knowing what to do. I wondered whether I could take them both home to freshen up.

After some back and forth, we agreed I'd run them home, and Wendy would drive them back to Cheltenham later. I was glad Sunshine Cottage wasn't in awful shape from the break-in because I didn't think either mother or daughter could take much more stress.

I helped Belle from the car as Wendy grabbed her suitcase. I purposely settled Belle in the kitchen and put the kettle on while Wendy took her bag upstairs to her bedroom. Tigger must have understood I was trying to keep his mistress from seeing the sitting room because he appeared in the kitchen and jumped to Belle's lap.

Wendy came down the stairs and walked into the sitting room, and we heard her shout, "It's not too bad, nothing like Alice's place." She continued talking, perhaps to herself, but neither of us could make out her words.

"Here we go, tea and biscuits," I said as she sat down at the kitchen table. "After we've all had a cup, I can help you straighten up, but maybe I should ask Gemma before we do that?" Then I reconsidered. Gemma hadn't said that Wendy and Belle couldn't touch anything, so why miss this opportunity to find fresh clues? "Nah, never mind," I said.

Belle, Wendy, and I took turns studying the room from the doorway to see whether anything leaped out at us, but nothing did, except for the footstool and the box of letters sitting on it. I explained that Gemma had taken it down from the top shelf. Then we entered the room and looked at the books on the floor to see if there was anything significant in the titles. Again, nothing. I offered to put the books back on the shelves while Wendy looked at the box of letters.

That's when Belle interrupted us. "Girls, I'll go through the letters. Just move my footstool back in front of my chair so I can be comfortable."

I obliged and watched as Belle removed the lid from the box. "Well I never," she said. "I can tell right off that someone's been in my letters. Just look at how the lace ribbon is tied."

Wendy and I glanced up as Belle continued in a low voice. "And they're out of order and not folded properly."

We weren't ready to tell her yet that we'd found one of her letters at the inn. We asked whether she needed our help, and she told us, a bit peevishly, to carry on straightening. We carefully replaced the books and then looked at each other. It seemed we had the same idea because when I whispered, "Let's look in the toybox," Wendy started towards the stairs.

In Peter's old room, the bed was made and his bag was on the single chair by the window. Stretched out on top of the toybox was Tigger, who was none too pleased when we moved him. Wendy carefully lifted the lid, and we peered inside. We couldn't help but smile at the array of toys that had to be at least eighty years old. Nestled in the midst of the stuffed animals lay a tissue-wrapped rectangular parcel.

"Oh my," whispered Wendy. "Can it really be . . . ?" She sat on the bed and unwrapped the yellowed tissue paper. Inside was a thin beige book titled *The Family at Sunshine Cottage*. The faded cover illustration depicted a Cotswolds cottage of golden stone with a huge sun beaming down on it. Barely visible in the doorway was a little dog.

She gasped when she saw the inscription on the title page, "For my Beautiful Belle, May this book bring you as much joy as you've brought me. Love, Uncle Jim."

With tears in her eyes, she slowly turned the pages. The illustrations inside were reminiscent of the Pooh books. Belle and her dog Tinker were the constants with occasional pictures of her mother. We looked in awe at drawings of a garden and stuffed animals drinking tea and were speechless with wonder.

"I remember it now," said Wendy. "I'm not sure whether Peter and I realized the book was about Mum and Gran and Mum's little dog Tinker. That it was by a famous author would never have registered with us at that age. I mean, we'd heard the stories about Uncle Jim, but I know I never put all that together with this book. And I'm pretty sure Peter didn't either."

"Wendy, could the break-in have been about this book, not just *Peter and Wendy?*"

"Yes . . . maybe . . . I don't know. Who would even know about it besides me and Peter and Mum? I'm sorry, Leta, there's just too much going on right now for me to begin to figure this out." She thrust the book at me. "Mum and I are leaving to go to the hospital. If this is anything to do with Alice and Peter and the break-in, we can't leave it here. Can you take it? For now?"

I was very much afraid it *did* have something to do with the happenings of the past week, and I was hesitant to have it in my possession, but I already had the *Peter and Wendy* book, and I couldn't turn Wendy down. "Yes," I said, "I'll take it and find somewhere safe to put it until we can sort everything." I found a bag in the kitchen for the book and joined Wendy in the sitting room to see how Belle was coming along.

"I've got the letters back in order," said Belle, "and I think several are missing. It's not as though I have them memorized, so I'll need to study them more carefully before I can be sure. I just have a vague feeling that things aren't right. And, of course, it's hard to focus today."

Wendy looked at me, and I could tell she didn't want to leave the letters at Sunshine Cottage either. I sighed and asked Belle whether she'd feel comfortable with me taking them away for safekeeping. I pulled Wendy aside and asked if she thought I should also take the signed *Winnie-the-Pooh* books. She agreed that was a good plan and helped me gather everything together and place it all on the floorboard of my car. I gave her a hug and made her promise to text or call me with any updates on Peter.

Now what? I thought as I pulled into my driveway. I carried everything inside and upstairs to my bedroom, where I put it all in my cedar chest, another thing I'd brought with me from the States. It had been my mother's hope chest.

Then I let Dickens out and watched him as he explored the garden and rolled in the grass. I was weary, I was worried, and I was exhausted.

Dickens and Christie peppered me with questions. "How's Peter? How're Wendy and Belle? What's all that stuff you brought in?"

Dickens wanted to go for a walk, and Christie wanted to show me what she'd discovered on the computer. "Not now," I said. "I'm going upstairs to lie down. We'll talk later."

I must have dozed off, and when I awoke, Christie was tucked by my side purring and Dickens was on his bed in the corner. "Guys," I said, "I'm starving. Let's see what I can find in the kitchen."

I decided a late afternoon snack of grapes, hummus, and pita chips would do fine. Even after that, I felt as though I was in a fog. *Duh*, I thought. *Could the events of the last twenty-four hours have something to do with that?* I knew I needed to outline everything I'd discovered—Belle's book, the letter, the information on Alice's notepad—so I could share it all with Gemma the next day. I also wanted to read through the letters, but I couldn't find the energy.

I texted Wendy for an update on Peter and got a reply that indicated there was no change. "What I need is a walk," I said. "Who wants to go?"

"Me, me!" barked Dickens. "Where to?"

"Let's head to town. We'll get in a good walk and then have a proper cup of tea at Toby's."

It was threatening rain, so I dressed accordingly in my black rain jacket with the hood. Dickens loved the rain and wouldn't mind getting soaked if it came to that. Christie was slightly miffed, and she reminded me I still hadn't looked at the computer with her. I promised that would be the first thing I did upon my return.

The bottom didn't fall out until we were inside Toby's Tearoom. "Phew," I said as I shrugged off my jacket and put my gloves in my pockets. The aroma of fresh-baked cookies drew me to the counter, where I ordered a pot of tea and two cookies—one chocolate chip and one sugar. The young girl behind the counter gave Dickens a dog biscuit as I paid for my order.

I sat and stared out the window at the pouring rain and was surprised when Toby brought my order to the table. "May I join you?" he asked.

"Sure," I replied, "though I doubt I'm very good company at the moment. I can't think straight, much less speak intelligently."

"No need to speak," he said. "I've been calling the hospital, so I'm up to date on Peter's condition, and the fact that Gemma stopped by around lunchtime to ask about my whereabouts this morning tells me she isn't treating this as an accident. Thankfully, I'm in the clear, since I was here at the usual crack of dawn baking scones and muffins. Several villagers can attest to that."

"That's good," I said. "I don't think she seriously suspected you, but she has to go by the book. Between Alice and Peter, no one knows what to think." I saw no need to share the news about the break-in at Sunshine Cottage. That would come out in good time. I sat quietly sipping my tea. Toby squeezed my shoulder and left me to my thoughts.

The rain turned to a light mist as I was finishing my tea, just in time for me to put my jacket back on and set out for home.

Dickens held his head high and pranced all the way home. "This is my kind of weather," he barked.

The walk had done me good, so after I toweled Dickens dry, I sat in front of the fire with a notepad and pen. Christie came and sat beside me and patted my pen with her paw.

"Ready to look at the computer yet?" she meowed.

"Yes. Sorry I've been neglecting you, little girl. Let's see what you've found." I hoisted myself off the couch and walked to my office. Once again, I started the slideshow and waited for Christie to point to the screen.

"There," she said. "See the book?"

I saw the book but couldn't make out the title. I zoomed in and discovered it was *Rare Books Uncovered: True Stories of Fantastic Finds.* Why did that ring a bell? "Oh my goodness," I exclaimed. "Dave Prentiss has the same book in his room at the inn."

"You mentioned that to Wendy, didn't you? Does that mean something?" asked Christie.

"I'm not sure. It seems an odd coincidence. I can under-stand Dave having a copy after our conversation the other night, and I can see Alice having a copy because she sold books at her flea market stall . . . but it strikes me as strange. I for sure need to put this on my outline to discuss with Gemma."

I returned to the couch in the sitting room, tucked my comfy throw around my legs, and picked up pen and paper. I treasured my fleece throw not only because it was warm, but also because my aunt had made it for me. This one had cats on it, and she'd made me a second one with dog images. Appropriately, Christie snuggled in my lap with the cats as if to help me think.

What if *The Family at Sunshine Cottage* had been published and sold to the masses? Wendy and I had assumed Belle's was the only copy based on what Belle had told us. Yes, the inscribed copy could have been a special gift for her, but that didn't mean it had never been published. I grabbed the Barrie biography I'd purchased, knowing there'd be a list of his works in the back.

There was no mention of Belle's book, and more random thoughts swirled through my brain. What might Barrie's letters to Gran tell us? And did the books and letters have something to do with Alice's murder and Peter's accident? Was I leaping to the wrong conclusion? *It's awfully hard to brainstorm by myself*, I thought.

I realized I hadn't heard from Thom about his conversation with his professor and wondered whether he'd left a message for Wendy. He may have decided not to bother us in the aftermath of Peter's accident, I thought, but he'd be a good person to talk to. I called Beatrix for his number.

"Oh Leta," said Beatrix when she answered, "How are you? You and Wendy and Belle have been in my thoughts."

"I don't know much more," I said. "I'm doing okay, and Wendy and Belle are hanging in there. To keep from obsessing over Peter," I fudged, "I thought I'd try to catch up with Thom to see what he's found out about Belle's book. Can you give me his number, please?"

When I got Thom, he inquired about Peter and asked how Wendy and Belle were holding up. I gave him an update and then asked what he'd discovered about the book.

"Professor Bartholomew tells me that a pristine signed copy was recently sold by an Australian bookseller for $7800 AUD. That's similar to what Beatrix found about a copy sold in the States. He thinks since Belle's copy is fairly worn, it might go for more in the neighborhood of £5,000. We're still trying to see if there's any noise about a recently found copy."

"Well, that's nothing to sneeze at. Thanks for the info, Thom," I said. "I'm wondering about something else too. We discovered there was a letter from J. M. Barrie tucked in the book. It was to Mary, Wendy's gran. Based on what you told us at book club, I'm thinking there'd be interest in it among collectors too. Am I right?"

"Wow!" he replied. "Absolutely. Would you like me to make inquiries about that too? Do you have it there with you? You could take a picture of it and text it to me. That would be helpful."

"Yes, please see what you can find out, but remember that the family has no interest in selling at the moment. This is for informational purposes only. By the way, I've heard of a book, *Rare Books Uncovered: True Stories of Fantastic Finds*. Is that something I should get Beatrix to order for Wendy, for later when she has time for all this?"

"Yes, she'd probably find it entertaining. It's not a how-to, but it's an inspiring read. If she eventually gets into collecting, I'm sure Beatrix and I can both recommend some others."

"Thanks, Thom. I'll look forward to hearing from you

about the letter, and I may pick up that book to help Wendy pass her time at the hospital."

Why didn't I tell Thom about the other book, *The Family at Sunshine Cottage*? Was the fact that Wendy felt uncomfortable keeping the books and letters at her cottage making me uncharacteristically nervous? Well, maybe with good reason. Gemma had warned me this was serious business.

I spent an hour jotting down my thoughts before my late night in Oxford and the stressful events of the day caught up with me. Though I wasn't sure my brain would slow down enough for me to sleep, I let Dickens out one last time, locked up, and went to bed.

Hopefully, when Gemma and I got around to comparing notes, we'd have a breakthrough.

Chapter Twelve

I woke bright and early, rested, but with my brain in turmoil. I reflected on what I'd written the night before and realized it wasn't as much fact as it was instinct that was making me think this series of events was driven by book collecting. Of course, master sleuth Hercule Poirot had said, "Instinct is a marvelous thing. It can neither be explained nor ignored." If it was good enough for Poirot, it was good enough for me.

What an awful thought—that someone would kill over a rare book or manuscript. Maybe I was correct about the motive, but I was still clueless as to the who. Who could it be? Was it someone I knew from the village or a local I didn't know? Or a complete stranger?

Christie was sitting by the kitchen door. I poured her milk, and she looked at me and said, "Forget the milk, I want out. I need some fresh air before you take off for days again."

"Oh, really," I said. "You *do* exaggerate. I don't have any big plans for today."

"Sure," she meowed skeptically. "You'll end up going somewhere, and Dickens will get to go, and before you know it, you'll be off on another adventure without me."

I gave in and let both her and Dickens out, then poured a cup of coffee and joined them in the garden. It was sunny and the air was crisp. Christie jumped to the garden wall and sat staring at the birds and making squeaky chirping noises. I always thought of her chirps as her special language for the birds, though she'd always been strangely secretive as to what the sounds meant. To her credit, she never chased the birds, only chirped at them.

Dickens looked up but continued checking out the corners of the garden. Corner checking had become his morning routine. *One never knew what dangers could be lurking*, I thought with a chuckle.

"Okay," I called as I finished my coffee, "Let's have a quick bite to eat before we attack the day."

Just then my cell phone rang, and I saw it was Wendy. "Peter's still a bit confused and doesn't remember anything after walking Dickens, but he's getting more coherent."

"Oh, thank goodness," I said. "Can I do anything? Come sit with your mum so you can go home and rest? Or come take her to Sunshine Cottage so she can sleep? Except neither of you may want to stay at the cottage. You can stay here. Just say the word," I babbled.

"We're good for now, Leta. And Gemma's on her way to speak with Peter, so we don't want to leave."

That told me Gemma was continuing to see all three incidents as connected and hadn't yet changed her mind. I left my two companions eating breakfast in the kitchen while I dressed for a morning walk.

"Dickens," I called as I came down the stairs, "Let's go to

the Cotswolds Way by the cricket pavilion. We never did get to walk there."

"Leta," asked Dickens. "I'd like to go back and see more sheep, but are you sure you want to go back where we found Alice?"

"No, in fact, I'm pretty sure I *don't* want to go back, but we've got to face it someday— the sooner the better. Let me get my backpack, a water bottle, and your collapsible bowl, and we should be good to go."

Dickens barked. "I love it when you mention my special bowl. That tells me we're going on an extra-long walk. Woo hoo!"

"We'll see how ready we both are," I said as I latched his harness in the car. "Neither of us have been on many long walks lately. Hmmm, could be that Bev took you on some really long ones when you stayed with her, but I sure haven't done much more than the two miles to the Inn."

Dickens barked, "Bev liked to walk for an hour or two, but we made lots of stops. As she'd say, unless it was during one of the miserable Atlanta heat waves, we hardly broke a sweat. We'd stop for questions like, 'What kind of dog is that? Does he bite? Can I pet him?' And, of course, we'd stop for the tiny humans to hug me and rub my belly."

"Let's hope you have as many admirers here," I said, "so we get plenty of rest stops along the way."

When I parked, I kept glancing at the pavilion as I unlatched Dickens and let him do his preliminary sniffing at the entrance to the Cotswolds Way. Should we go right to the building and get it over with, or should we walk first? Do we even need to go over there? Or want to? I could see the crime scene tape fluttering in the breeze. I'd thought that after a week, it'd be gone.

I knelt to ruffle Dickens fur. "Aw heck, let's just do it, as they say in the shoe commercial." I went up to the tape and wondered about ducking beneath it to get closer, and while I was wondering, Dickens beat me to it.

"Not much has changed," he said. "Except I don't smell Alice anymore."

"Probably not," I mumbled, "But I still see her lying there. What an awful sight that was. I guess I should be thankful I'm not dreaming about it the way I dream about Henry's accident. That's enough, Dickens. I've faced my fears and we can take our walk now. The real test will come when Peter next has a cricket match. Will I be able to sit through that?" I teared up as I wondered whether there'd be any cricket in Peter's future.

It was a beautiful fall morning. The air was crisp and cool but not too cold, and there wasn't a cloud in the sky. We met lots of walkers and ramblers, as long-distance walkers are called in the UK. Dickens finally got to see some sheep up close, and he could easily have gotten lost in their midst.

"Dickens," I said, "I bet you didn't know that in the Pyrenees mountains, Pyr puppies are raised with herds of sheep and blend right in with their new families. From the time they're pups, they protect their herds. All it takes is that deep, throaty bark to scare away wolves or anything else. Are you my protector?"

"You know it, Leta," barked my boy. "I've got the bark thing down, right?"

"That's for sure. I wish you weren't quite so good at it, though. You realize you sometimes make me crazy with your barking, right?"

"Sounds like a personal problem to me. Barking's part of my winning personality, right along with my love of roaming and my ability to think for myself."

"Think for yourself?" I said. "Is that how you describe your tendency to ignore my commands? Your tendency to come only when you feel like it?"

"Harrumph," he huffed. "And your point is?"

I laughed at his indignation. It was time to turn back. We'd done a brisk two to three miles out, only slowing down for Dickens to meet sheep and greet walkers who just had to hug him.

As we approached the verge where my taxi was parked, we heard someone call, "Leta, Dickens, hi there." I looked around to see Thom standing in front of the cricket pavilion with his bike. I wasn't eager to go that way a second time, so I waved and motioned him our way.

"Out for a ramble?" he asked as he scratched Dickens behind his ears.

"Hardly," I laughed. "Those long-distance walkers are hard-core. I think we may have gotten in five or six miles, which is a gracious plenty for us. I suspect they average fifteen miles a day. What are you up to? No cycling tours today?"

"No, a family canceled at the last minute. I'm sure going to miss the tip I would've gotten, but I'm making the most of a day off by getting in a ride on my own. This is one of my favorite routes. Have you done any cycling since you've moved here?"

I hesitated. "No. Maybe someday I will." I could hardly bring myself to utter the next sentence. "I haven't been back on a bike since Henry died on his; just haven't been able to bring myself to do it."

"Oh hell, Leta," Thom said, "I knew about the accident. I just never thought about how it would impact you getting on a bike. Sorry I brought it up."

"It's okay. It's been nearly two years, and I thought I might be getting closer to trying. But, with Peter's accident . . . let's just say bicycling isn't high on my list right now."

"I can only imagine. On a different topic, I've spoken with Professor Bartholomew about the letter. He's digging to see what he can come up with as far as value and whether there's any talk in the collector community about Barrie letters. And, oh, you haven't sent me a picture yet."

"Oh, it slipped my mind. Maybe later today after I go to the hospital. Have you heard Peter has regained consciousness?" I asked.

"No. That's great news. Any prognosis on his recovery?"

"Hopefully, I'll hear good news when I get there. Gemma was going to try to talk to him this morning to see what he remembered about being run off the road. When he first woke up, he couldn't remember anything about the accident."

Thom looked surprised. "Is that typical with head injuries?"

"On all the television medical dramas, it is, though I don't know if that means it's so in real life. But he may be able to give Gemma some information about the break-in the night before, even if not about the accident. All this stuff seems somehow related."

"Interesting," he said. "You know, you never did tell me where you found Belle's book. Was it just buried somewhere in her cottage?"

"Believe it or not," I said, "I found it on a bookshelf at the Olde Mill Inn."

"Blimey," exclaimed Thom. "What on earth was it doing there? Who would have put it there?"

"Heck," I said. "I can only guess. Tell me what your young Oxford-educated brain thinks? How could it have gotten there?"

He looked taken aback at my question. After a pause, he blurted, "Alice."

"Ah-ha," I said. "And what makes you think that?"

"Alice was in and out of everybody's homes and a few businesses. Who else would have access to the Sunshine Cottage and the Inn, access no one would question?" He seemed to be putting it together.

Hmmm. I never thought to ask Thom what he knew about Alice. It's not like she cleaned his rooms above his uncle's shop, and his name wasn't in her notebook. He could have run into her at the Book Nook, though. And with his knowledge of rare books . . .

"Thom, how well did you know Alice?"

"Not all that well. Mostly I saw her at the Book Nook when I worked late to change out displays or place orders. Since I've graduated and I'm available for more hours, Beatrix has made a habit of going home as soon as the book shop closes. Can't say I blame her, but it was those nights I worked late that I'd see Alice. She cleaned once a week after we closed."

"Ever discuss rare books or collecting?" I asked.

"Why do you ask?" he said.

"Like you, I think it could have been Alice who took Belle's *Peter and Wendy* book, but why? Would she know how valuable it was? I probably shouldn't be telling you this, but Alice was stealing things like knickknacks from her clients. A rare book is a horse of a different color, though."

Thom frowned. "Um, as in it's one thing to take a box of bric-a-brac to a flea market to hawk, but books are a step up?"

"Exactly!"

Thom confirmed my thoughts. "Hmmm. You know she used to sell used books in Manchester, right? Not in a shop, but in a flea market? She probably had some knowledge of books, but it's hard to say how much."

"You're right, she probably did. Good grief, I feel as though my brain is about to short-circuit. I'd best get home so we—or I—can get cleaned up and get to the hospital. I bet it would cheer Peter up to see Dickens, but that's not gonna happen.

"Thanks for listening. And again, I can't wait to hear the update from your Professor. Enjoy the rest of your ride."

I was explaining to Dickens once again why he couldn't visit Peter when my phone rang.

Wendy didn't miss a beat after I said hello. "Leta, can you feed Tigger?"

"Well, hello to you too," I said. "And sure, I can feed Tigger."

"Mum and I completely forgot about the poor thing. Guess we haven't had him long enough. And while you're there, can you grab a jumper for Mum, please? It's freezing up here."

"OK. Your timing is perfect. I was on my way out the door to drive to the hospital. See you in a bit."

Tigger was understandably happy to see me and was full of grumbles. "Where are my new humans? I'm hungry, and I'm lonely. Please tell me they're coming back."

I fed him and freshened his water bowl and told him Wendy and Belle would be back soon. He probably wasn't accustomed to being on his own overnight, and now he'd been by himself two nights, the night Alice was murdered and again last night. Poor little guy's world had been turned upside down.

I locked up and drove to the hospital and was parking when my phone rang. It was Thom. *That was quick*, I thought.

"Leta," he said. "I'm working to dig up the information you requested, but I need a bit more detail from you. I don't think I can explain to you what to look for, so is it possible for me to meet with you to look at the book again?"

"I guess so," I replied. "I'm hesitating because I'm at the hospital now and not sure when I'll get home. How flexible can you be about time?"

"Since the cycling tour was canceled, I'm free all day," he said, "So why don't you ring me when you're on your way home and I'll meet you at your cottage?"

I agreed and hung up as I spotted Wendy in the waiting room. I gave her a hug and asked for the latest.

"Peter's getting stronger but still doesn't remember the accident. He was able to tell Gemma that the intruder from the night before wore a hoodie, but how helpful can that be? Seems as though every bad guy these days wears a hoodie, along with every school kid."

"Shoot, Wendy," I said. "You're right. Even I have a hoodie. Of course, I'd be easily identifiable because mine says 'GRITS, Girls Raised in the South' in bright bold letters. I daresay it may be the only hoodie of its kind in the UK."

"Leta, it never ceases to amaze me the things we have in common. I once had a sweatshirt with the GRITS logo. I think I got it on a beach trip."

We were laughing over that coincidence when Belle returned to the waiting room. The hospital would only allow one visitor at a time in Peter's room in ICU, so Wendy and Belle were taking turns.

"His broken collarbone is pretty painful, but other than

that, he's in pretty good shape and may get to go home tomorrow," said Belle.

"Oh, that's great news," I exclaimed. "Shall I see if I can organize a schedule for a few of us to bring meals? I'm sure Toby, Rhiannon, Beatrix, and Libby will sign on."

Wendy laughed at my suggestion. "Leta, I know people do that in the States, but I've never known anyone to do it here."

"Well then, it's time our friends learned some new tricks," I replied.

Belle piped up. "Sounds like a grand idea to me. Wendy and I can certainly cook, but we've got our hands full contacting Peter's customers and trying to find someone to fill in for him at his garage. So far, the customers we've called have been understanding, but their patience will wear thin if they can't get their cars repaired soon."

"No worries," I said. "I'm on it. By the way, Tigger sends his regards and says hurry home." I showed her a photo of him curled up in her chair in the sitting room.

"Looks like he's keeping my seat warm," she chuckled. "I'll be happy to get back to him."

We chatted a bit longer and then Wendy and Belle let me take a turn with Peter. "Boy, you're a sight for sore eyes," I said as I entered his room.

His voice was weaker than usual as he replied, "I'm a lucky bloke. Could easily have been a goner. Thanks for looking out for Mum and Wendy."

"Don't mention it," I said. "They'd do the same for me. Rumor has it you may get home Sunday, and I'm pretty sure folks will be lined up to wish you well. Everyone wants to see for themselves that you're going to be fine. Think you'll be healed by cricket season?"

"Since it won't start until April, my collarbone should be

fine. It'll be getting back in shape that will be the challenge. Got to get back on my bike."

"Well, perhaps we can do that together. You can be my inspiration to face my fears. If you can get back up, surely I can," I murmured.

His eyes were at half-mast, so I took my leave. I told Belle and Wendy that Thom was coming by my house later to take a look at her copy of *Peter and Wendy* and the letter I'd found in it so that he'd have all the information he needed to continue his research.

"Ladies, I haven't told him about *The Family at Sunshine Cottage,* but do you want me to show him that book too?" I asked.

Belle and Wendy looked at each other and then back at me. Said Belle, "If learning more about the books can help us figure out what happened to Alice, then I think we should. It's kind of the lad to offer his assistance."

"Well, I'm clueless as to how exactly the books and letters connect to Alice's murder and Peter's accident, but I think they do. I just wish I knew what Alice was doing at the cricket pavilion," I said. "And I sure hope Gemma is having better luck coming up with a theory of the case than I am."

In the parking lot, I leaned against my car and called Gemma. I was eager to speak with her and find out what progress she'd made, but I got her voicemail. Next, I called Thom. He said he could be at my house in an hour. If he was lucky, I might still be coherent by then. I was fading fast.

"Finally, you're home," meowed Christie. "Can we sit in the garden, purty please?"

"Why yes, little girl," I said as I leaned down to rub her head. "Let me make a cup of tea, and we'll both sit in the sun." I'd already let Dickens out, and he was contentedly rolling in the grass.

I was carrying my cup to the garden when I heard Timmy talking loudly. He was running towards the school bell by the front door when I intercepted him. "Timmy," I exclaimed, "Would you like to meet Christie?"

"Oh, yes, yes, yes!"

"Then I'm glad I caught you before you could ring the bell. Do you know why?" I asked.

"Um, no."

"Christie's scared of loud noises, so when you want to see her, you have to knock on the door, okay?" I hoped he'd understand this new rule. I'd enjoyed hearing the bell all these months, but he was never going to meet the cat if he continued ringing it every time he came over.

He looked a bit crestfallen. "Yes, Mrs. Parker," he said. "Where is she?"

I led him around to the garden, where Christie was sprawled on the warm stone patio washing her face. I cautioned Timmy to approach her slowly so she wouldn't dart away, and I pleaded with Christie to stay put.

"Is this the rascal who rang that awful bell?" she asked.

"Yes, but give him a chance," I cajoled. "He's a sweet boy, and he and Dickens have become friends."

"Christie, he helps me feed Martha and Dylan," said Dickens. "And, if you let him, I bet he'll rub your little black belly."

Timmy sneezed and gently touched Christie with his fingertips, and when she responded by rolling and stretching, he laughed. "Oh, you're pretty," he said and sneezed again.

"Timmy, you're not allergic to cats, are you?" I asked.

"No, Mummy says I'm getting a cold. I had to be good and ask nicely so she'd let me come out today." Dickens bounded over and licked Timmy's face. Timmy quickly abandoned the cat, and soon, he and Dickens were both rolling in the grass as Christie looked on disdainfully. "Such immature behavior," she said, "but I guess boys will be boys."

Christie jumped to the patio table to check my plate for crumbs and then climbed into my lap. It wasn't long before I heard Thom call, "Hello, anybody home?" He'd followed the sounds of Timmy and Dickens around to the garden.

"Unlatch the gate and join us," I said. "Meet my neighbor Timmy." Thom greeted Timmy and gave Dickens a pat on the head.

"May I interest you in a cup of tea?"

"No thanks," he said. "I can't stay all that long. I'm putting together a new route for a bicycle tour and want to get home and finish up my notes."

"And where will this one be?" I asked.

"I'm calling it the Intermediate Windrush Valley Tour," he said. "It covers much the same area you and Henry cycled with me, but with more hills."

"More hills?" I groaned. "I couldn't have done any more. The short steep ones like to have killed me as it was. It was a beautiful route, though. Will it still begin and end in Burford?"

"Yes, same start and endpoint, but we often get groups asking for more of a challenge, so that's what they'll get," said Thom.

"Just thinking about it wears me out," I said. "Well, let's go inside and I'll get the letter."

I gave Timmy a hug and sent him home. "If you feel better tomorrow, you can come back again, but if you want to see Christie, remember not to ring the bell."

I showed Thom to my office, and I went upstairs to get the books and letters from my hope chest. He was looking at my collection of children's books when I returned. "You've got all the classics," he said. "*Beautiful Joe, Big Red, Old Yeller, Black Beauty,* and of course *The Cat in the Hat* books. I read them too. The *Tarzan* books were my favorites, though, and I haunted the flea market until I had them all. I wonder whether today's kids read these same books."

"That's a good question," I said. "I'm pretty sure *The Cat in the Hat* books are still popular, but I'm not sure about the others. Anyway, pull up a chair." I turned on the desk lamp. "Let me show you what I've been telling you about."

He studied the inscription in *Peter and Wendy* and used his phone to take a picture of it. When I handed him the letter, he handled it carefully and murmured he couldn't believe he was holding something handwritten by J. M. Barrie. He snapped a picture of it too.

I'd saved Belle's special book for last, and Thom was speechless when I showed it to him. He looked at me and said, "May I?" and opened the book when I nodded.

He looked at me in astonishment when he saw the inscription. As he slowly turned the pages, he said, "I can't be sure, but I think these drawings were done by Ernest H. Shepard, the same man who illustrated the Pooh books. His name isn't on the title page, but I'm almost positive this is his work."

"I wouldn't have any idea," I said. "See, that's why you're such an incredible resource. They are beautiful drawings, though, aren't they?"

"My God, this is an incredible find," he said. "Do you recall the term Holy Grail from the book we read, *The Bookman's Tale*? For some collector, this could be the Holy Grail, the ultimate acquisition for him or her. That would make it worth more to that one person than it would be to any other."

He took a few pictures and quietly, almost reverentially, closed the book. "I'll send these pictures off tonight, but it may be a few days before I get a response on this. I mean, if this really is a one of a kind book, someone's bound to know whether there've been rumors about its existence. What I do know is that collectors will come out of the woodwork if word gets out."

That last remark worried me, and I said, "Thom, remember please that the Davies family does *not* want to sell the book and they certainly don't want any publicity. This research is more about finding a lead to Alice's murder than stirring up demand. Can you continue to make inquiries under the radar without the book world beating a path to Belle's door?"

"I'll be discreet," he said. "Will you be available if I get some information in the next day or two?"

"Pretty much," I said. "Other than helping Libby clean the inn in the morning and going out to dinner tomorrow night, I plan to be on the home front. That reminds me, I need to come up with a place for dinner. Any suggestions? Perhaps somewhere in Chipping Camden or Bourton-on-the Water, and might any of them have live music? I'm sure you have to advise the tourists from time to time."

Thom offered several recommendations, and I thanked him for his help in that arena as I saw him to his car. We agreed he'd call or text me when he had news but that we probably wouldn't connect again until midweek. At least I'd put some things in motion, and I had plenty to share with Gemma even without an update from Thom.

Chapter Thirteen

It was getting on towards dinner time. I took Dickens for a quick walk and decided on cheese grits for dinner. I'd been craving them since I'd told Toby about them. That conversation seemed like it had taken place ages ago when it had been only last week.

Making grits isn't very involved, so I ate dinner and washed the dishes in no time. I planned to read a while, but first I wandered into the office to check my emails and catch up on the latest news online.

Anna had sent me photos of her newest kittens, Crunch and Munch. Crunch was a tiny thing and was black like Christie. Munch was a handsome longhaired gray tabby. Brothers, they were being fostered together when she found them online.

The photos of the two kittens snoozing on her desk or perched on her shoulder were adorable. In her email, she promised to send videos of them playing on the cat tree next. When I was still in the States, Anna was forever trying to get me to adopt another cat . . . or two. She was never convinced that Dickens and Christie were all the family I needed.

Christie's reaction to the pics of Crunch and Munch was predictable. "So cute when they're sleeping, but you know the rest of the time, they're way too rambunctious for my taste. We don't want any of that behavior around here."

"Christie," I said with a laugh, "I'm not planning to get any kittens, but I might one day. And you still chase Dickens's balls around the house on occasion and zoom up and down the stairs when the mood strikes, so don't act as though you're Miss Sophistication."

Next, I wrote Anna and Sophia about my long walk with Dickens and the news that I had a second date scheduled with Dave. Keeping the update lighthearted almost made me forget all the distressing things going on.

I lit a fire in the sitting room and put my feet up. I was more than ready to relax with my mystery novel. And I did relax and read a chapter or two before the events of the past week intruded. *I can't just sit here; I've got to do something to move this investigation along*, I thought.

I looked at Dickens and Christie. "What can I do on my own? What haven't I done yet? I could go through Belle's copy of *Peter and Wendy* to see if there's anything remarkable in it, like scribbles in the margins from Barrie." *Yeah, right*, I thought. *Doubtful*. On the other hand, looking through it and reading the story might tell me something. What, I wasn't sure.

Christie meowed, "Well, Detectives Dickens and Christie are here to offer support while you read if that's what you need. Are we working in the office or in the sitting room? Say the word, and we'll be there."

I chose to remain on the comfy couch in front of the fire.

The storyline in *Peter and Wendy* was similar to the play and yet different. I didn't care for the illustrations as much as I did the ones in *The Family at Sunshine Cottage*, but they suited the story in a way the whimsical ones in the other book wouldn't have. Beatrix had told me this book was darker than the play, and she was right.

"Oh my gosh," I said as I turned a page, "it's another letter."

Dickens and Christie both looked up from where they were stretched out in front of the fire, and Christie stretched and leaped to the back of the couch to peer over my shoulder. The thin paper crackled in my hand as I studied it.

The writing was faded, but I could see that this short letter was addressed only to Mary.

Dearest Mary,

Please read this tea party tale to little Belle. It seems when I think of her, stories spring to mind. Ask her who else we should invite to the tea party, and I'll add more guests to the story.

Much love,

Uncle Jim

The letter ended there, but where was the tea party tale? Now I was eager to flip through the book, but I forced myself to turn the pages slowly. Sure enough, several pages later, there was another piece of parchment entitled "The Tea Party." It was about Belle and Tinker and a hedgehog.

As I read it aloud, Christie piped up, "There needs to be a

cat. You mentioned a dog and some creature I've never heard of—a hedge what? A cat would be way cuter."

I was in awe as I read the tea party tale. This must be how *The Family at Sunshine Cottage* took shape. Barrie started by sending sweet stories to Mary to read to Belle. I had an image in my mind of Uncle Jim dipping a quill pen into an inkwell, a blank sheet of paper on his desk, and a smile on his face as he began a story for Belle.

And later, he collected the stories into a book. Just one book.

I needed to compare this handwritten tale with the one printed in the book I'd hidden safely away in my bedroom. *But first,* I thought, *I wonder whether there are more letters tucked between the pages of* Peter and Wendy.

And there was . . . one last letter.

Dearest Mary,

Here it is, finished at long last. I'm smiling as I picture you reading this book to little Belle. I hope she's as pleased with the illustrations as I am. I believe Mr. Shepard captured her blonde curls perfectly and did little Tinker justice too. You must let me know what you think of his portrait of you, sweet Mary.

I will eagerly await word that you've received this special gift for Belle. I can hardly wait to hear of her reaction to the stories she inspired.

Much love,
Uncle Jim

Oh my goodness. Thom was right. The illustrations were by Ernest H. Shepard. What an enchanting story. All it lacked was an element of magic, a character like Tinker Bell flying in Belle's bedroom window one night to place the book on the toybox. It was hard to believe Uncle Jim not only wrote a book for Belle but also went so far as to have it illustrated by the same man who'd done the Pooh books.

But it wasn't a fairy tale. It was all very real. And, if my supposition was right, Alice had snuck the very *real* letters and one book out of Sunshine Cottage, and she had to be the person who hid the book in plain sight at the inn. And if she had this letter, then she had to know Belle had another rare book somewhere.

To what end? Money. It had to be about money and the new scheme Peter had mentioned. Had she been meeting a buyer at the cricket pavilion?

I needed to add these latest discoveries to my handwritten notes. *In fact*, I thought, *typing it all up might lead to some new ahas*, so Dickens, Christie, and I trooped into my office. Christie leaped to a shelf on the built-in bookcase. Her pose, stretched out on the white shelf with the decorative red backing with one paw hanging over the edge, would make a beautiful book cover for a murder mystery. "Did you purposely choose the shelf that holds my Nancy Drew books?" I asked her.

"I see it as a perfect spot for Detective Christie, don't you?" she meowed.

"You're not dissing my perfectly good dog bed, are you?" growled Dickens. "My role as Leta's protector requires me to be as close as I can to Leta—not posing for a pretty picture."

The two traded light-hearted barbs for a bit before settling down. It was certainly helpful that they had a sense of humor no matter the circumstances. They just might keep me sane.

I typed up my notes, printed them out, and called Gemma. "Gemma," I said when she answered, "may I stop by tomorrow morning before I begin helping your mum? I've learned a lot the last two days, and I'd really like to bounce it all off of you, and hear anything you think you can tell me."

"Absolutely," she said. "Sorry I wasn't available earlier today, but we're slammed at the station even without this case. I usually run at six AM, so I should be ready by 7:30. Does that suit you?"

"That's fine," I responded. "See you then."

It was another bright sunny morning, so Dickens and I walked, feeding Martha and Dylan on the way, of course. I made a mental note that I was about out of carrots.

Gemma greeted us at the door of the guest house, and I could smell coffee brewing. "Come on in. How about a cup of coffee?"

"Sounds good," I said as Dickens started exploring. "Are you alright with Dickens checking out your home?"

"Is he trustworthy?" she asked with a chuckle. "Not going to chew on anything, is he?"

"No, not hardly. He's long since grown out of the puppy chewing phase. The behavior I can't break him of is barking, but that's only irritating, not destructive." I pulled out my notes. "Are you ready to compare findings?"

"Sure thing. Let me say upfront that while I've been able to clear some suspects of involvement, I don't feel any closer to solving this thing. I hope you've got something I can use."

Right. I'd already given her what I thought was a good lead —rare books—but she'd chosen to dismiss that idea out of hand. I handed her a copy of what I'd compiled the night before, and we began talking through it.

"Okay," I started, "we know Alice stole from her clients and blackmailed them. She dated Peter but they broke up. It's from Peter we know she sold some of what she stole, and she had some new moneymaking scheme."

"And we know she had flea market connections from her days in Manchester," added Gemma. "That way, she could probably get some money for whatever she stole."

"We know she went to the cricket pavilion Friday night and met someone there because that someone took her keys and later broke into her house and ransacked it. I don't think they found what they were looking for, do you?"

"No, I don't think so, unless all they wanted were her phone and computer. Both were missing. Keep going. It's good to review."

"You told me she was arrested in Manchester for stealing from her clients, but never charged. Things like my figurine. That still irks me, darn it. And we don't have proof, but I'd say we *know* she took Belle's copy of *Peter and Wendy*, and at least three of the Uncle Jim letters. I'd also say we *know* she hid that book at the inn, unless you suspect your parents."

Gemma chuckled at that. "Right, my parents the master criminals."

"And their daughter a Detective Sergeant! I now know from Thom Cook that Belle's book and her letters from Uncle Jim, aka J. M. Barrie, are pretty darned valuable, which makes me all but positive Alice's moneymaking scheme had something to do with rare books. Speaking of being irked, your reaction the other day to my idea about books really bothered me."

Gemma didn't respond to my last comment beyond rolling her eyes. "And we both know someone broke into Sunshine Cottage and Peter scared them off. That someone, I can't help but think, was the same person who ran Peter off the road the next day."

"And, as my husband used to say, 'it just gets curiouser and curiouser.' Belle has yet another valuable book, likely worth way more than the first one. I still can't believe she has in her possession possibly the only copy of *The Family at Sunshine Cottage*. Is this all as unbelievable to you as it is to me? Oh right, *of course it is* because you think the book angle is ridiculous."

"Wait a minute. A second book? But no one's stolen it, have they? I mean, I grew up hearing about Wendy's gran and Barrie and the cottage. Why is it all suddenly such a big deal?" asked Gemma.

It wasn't my style to yell at someone, but I was getting close. "Gemma, can't you just consider that these books are valuable, way more valuable than a knickknack here and there? And that Alice's scheme could have been about making thousands of pounds from selling rare books?"

Gemma grinned. "Could make a great movie."

I was beginning to fume. "Okay, sure. When I start thinking about who the other person at the cricket pavilion could be, it sounds straight out of Hollywood, but my gut tells me it's plausible. Was it a buyer? Or was it a middleman? Or was it someone Alice was blackmailing and nothing at all to do with books? No matter which scenario I settle on, I always come back to thinking it's all about money."

"You know, Leta, now you've got a good idea of what we

police wrestle with day in and day out. Not much is clear-cut. Okay, my turn. For starters, I've cleared the suspects I'd identified. Toby, Rhiannon, Beatrix—they don't all have hard and fast alibis for the night of Alice's murder, but close enough.

"It's the same thing for the break-in. Peter was high on my list as the angry, humiliated ex-boyfriend, but he's obviously in the clear because he was *at* Sunshine Cottage that night with his mum, and he sure didn't stage his own accident. The other three were home alone the night of Alice's murder and the night of the break-in, but are in the clear for Peter's accident. Toby was opening his shop, and we've verified Rhiannon and Beatrix were both online at the time."

She paused. "Unless, of course, there were three people involved here . . . Could Peter, Alice, and a third person have been involved in something, maybe having to do with the garage?"

It was my turn to roll my eyes. "And what, you think Peter killed Alice, and someone else attacked him? That can't be right."

"How can you be so sure? Stranger things have happened," retorted Gemma.

I crossed my arms. "I just know Peter can't have been involved in any of this. He's too good a person. Have you had a chance to consider the rare book angle at all? I mean, I don't even know how you'd follow up on that—"

"Oh, but I have, even though I consider it a stretch." Gemma interjected. "Surprised you, haven't I? I've put out feelers with used bookstores and rare book dealers in the Cotswolds and in Manchester. I called a friend from my Thames Valley days and asked her to see what she could find out in Oxford. Seems like Oxford would be a hotbed of book dealers, don't you think?"

I was excited. "What'd you find out?"

"Nothing, not a thing. No one's been looking for J. M. Barrie books, and no one's been offering any for sale. So, even with your discovery of what *you say* is a second rare and valuable book, there's nothing going on in the book world about all this. That makes coming up with a different scenario all the more critical, except I don't have one—a different scenario, that is."

"Then don't discount mine, Gemma."

I could tell she was losing patience. "You'd do well to remember who's in charge of this investigation, Leta," she warned.

I reminded myself I'd catch more flies with honey and tried to dial down my irritation. "Tell me you're kidding, and you've really got more angles you're following, or you've come up with an entirely different theory of the case."

Gemma groaned. "Much as I hate to say it, your book angle, as far-fetched as it is, is the only theory we have. I just can't get anywhere with it. Tell me more about this Sunshine Cottage book and what you've been getting from Thom Cook. How did he get involved with all this?"

I backtracked to the book club discussion about rare books and then the conversation Wendy and I'd had with Thom about the first book and my subsequent conversations. She was intrigued by his inquiries.

"So, he's got a professor who could be some help," she said. "I bet he's making inquiries online, which would go much farther afield than any feelers I'm putting out locally . . . but I don't have the resources for that. Bloody hell, now we're picturing Alice finding an online buyer for a stolen book. Can you see her doing that?"

"No, I can't," I said, "What else are you looking at? What

about the car that hit Peter? Do the police do all that stuff I see on TV, like making casts of tire tracks and finding paint flecks on Peter's bicycle?"

Gemma laughed. "You really do watch too much telly, Leta. The tire tracks showed us the car ran off the road onto the verge and back but didn't tell us much beyond that. Peter's bike is mangled more from crashing through the trees than anything else, so no forensic evidence, as you'd say. Nothing at Sunshine Cottage either."

By now, Dickens was sound asleep beneath the kitchen table, snoring as usual. If only I could fall asleep and forget about all this or better yet, wake up to Gemma having solved the case.

"Well, hell's bells," I muttered. "Where does that leave us?"

"Let's see what Thom comes up with, okay? Ring me with any little thing he uncovers for you, and I'll see if one of my computer whizzes wants to do me a favor with some online research."

Dickens woke up when I pushed my chair back from the table. "Then I guess I might as well do something productive like helping your mum and dad. I'll be sure to ring you if I come up with anything else, and I hope you'll do the same."

Several of the weekend guests were Londoners and had left right after breakfast, and the two couples who were flying out were packing up to head to Heathrow as Dickens and I arrived. I checked with Libby to find out where to start, and she told me she'd cleaned the Yellow Room herself on Saturday afternoon because Dave had called to ask if he could check back in late that evening instead of Sunday. She was happy to have him as once the weekend crowd checked out Sunday, no other guests were due until Tuesday afternoon.

"I guess it's nice to have a paying customer," I said, "But it might have been nice to have a day where you didn't have to prepare breakfast, right?"

"You know, Gavin and I are accustomed to eating a big breakfast and not having another meal until dinner, so I'm cooking anyway. Another person or two is really not a bother. What is a bother right now is trying to find someone to clean the inn," she said. "I mean, I appreciate your help, but this can't go on.

"The ironing is doing in my back, and I'm getting desperate. The girl I had Friday and Saturday was a disaster, so I've renewed my ad in several Cotswolds papers and online with the *Astonbury Aha*. If I don't get a response soon, I may have to advertise further afield. Now tell me how Peter is."

"Holding his own and improving. The doctors don't think he'll have any long-term issues, and he may be able to go home as early as today, but he'll need home help to come in for a while. Isn't it strange? When I thought of him needing meals, the first thing that came to mind was 'Call Alice.' Life changes in an instant, doesn't it?"

Libby shook her head and looked near tears. She'd taken Alice's death hard, and Peter's accident only added to her fragile state.

I gave an encouraging smile and grabbed garbage bags to take upstairs. Dickens, Paddington, and I fell quickly into our routine, as in I worked and they played.

As usual, I saved Dave's room for last. I thought I heard a muffled phone conversation before Dave hollered, "Just a minute." He looked tired and a bit frazzled this morning. Behind him, I could see papers spread on the bed.

"Hi there," I said. "Hope you had a productive trip to the coast. I've brought you fresh towels, and I'm happy to straighten up your room if it won't disturb you. Unlike in the finest hotels, you *cannot* request this maid come back later."

"Darn, I hate to ask this again, but can I give you the wet towels in exchange for clean ones? I'm in the middle of something."

"No worries," I said. I took the towels and headed downstairs to drop them off and tidy the common areas. I hoped Paddington wasn't getting ready to spring any more surprises on me, like Belle's book. I wasn't sure I could take much more.

Leaving the conservatory, I encountered Dave rushing downstairs with his briefcase. "Off to sight-see?" I asked.

"I wish. The internet connection here is slow as molasses and I've got to make this deadline. I'm headed to Toby's Tearoom. I know their internet is fast and reliable." He climbed in his car and took off in a hurry, throwing gravel as he left.

I realized Dave's room was now unoccupied, so I decided to give it a once over. It would only take a minute to empty the trash and gather any stray dishes.

"Boy," said Dickens as we walked in Dave's room. "His room's awfully messy this time."

And he was right. Dave had only been back one night, but the room was pretty much a wreck, with an overflowing trash can plus papers still spread out on the unmade bed. I thought I could pull the sheets and comforter up without disturbing the papers too much. As I went to lay the papers back out, I glimpsed something strangely familiar—one of Mary's letters, only it was a copy, not an original.

A copy? I thought. *How would Dave get a copy of a letter Belle kept in a box at Sunshine Cottage?* When I picked it up, I realized it was a copy of the one I'd found in the book downstairs on my last visit, and on the back was a message in blue ink. I read it aloud as Dickens looked at me.

Are you interested? Will sell this letter and others for 500 each. AJ

I looked more closely at the papers on the bed and saw a second handwritten note, not on an old letter, but on Inn stationery.

I've done my research. Not many Peter & Wendys around, and I've got something even better. What would a collector give for a book that's never been seen before? AJ

"Oh!" I said to Dickens. "This is from Alice. My gut was right. This is all about books . . . and letters. Libby must have a copier in the office. I need to make a copy quick." I ran downstairs and found the copier and, with my hands shaking, made two copies and ran back upstairs to replace the original where I'd found it.

Where exactly was it on the bed? I thought. *Dave can't know I've seen this.* I decided the best approach was to stack all the papers together in the center of the bed. On a piece of Inn stationery, I wrote him a note saying I hoped he'd made his deadline and that his clean room would make him smile. I signed it "The Dickens and Leta Maid Service." Surely, that would allay any suspicion he might have that I'd been snooping.

Dickens was talking a mile a minute as we went downstairs. "Leta, we've got to tell Gemma. This is scary. I thought Dave was a good guy. Didn't you?"

"It just goes to show what a poor judge of character I am," I said. "And, apparently, you're not much better."

Let's go see if Gemma's still at home."

No such luck. I knocked and even looked around back on her patio, but there was no sign of her. I dialed her cell phone, but it went to voicemail. My message was a terse "We need to talk—again." I looked at Dickens and said, "I guess there's nothing for it but to head home and try to sort through this mess on my own."

"Yes, let's go," he barked. "Though, I need to remind you you're not all by yourself. You have Detective Dickens and Christie at your service."

Breathe, I said to myself as I unlocked my kitchen door. Christie wrapped herself around my ankles, threatening to trip me before I could get to the kitchen table. "Knock it off," I yelled.

"Whoa, what's up with you," Christie hissed.

"She's scared, that's what's up," barked Dickens. "Give her a break."

Dickens nudged Christie into the sitting room and brought her up to speed. Of course, even he didn't have all the details yet. I couldn't decide whether to involve Wendy or not. She had enough on her mind with worrying about her twin. She might even be bringing him home today. *Looks like Dickens and Christie are going to be my sounding board for now*, I thought.

I put the kettle on and looked at them. "What do you think? It looks as though Dave is involved in this, doesn't it?"

"I told you I didn't care for him," meowed Christie.

"But I liked him," said Dickens.

I had tears in my eyes. "And so did I. I thought he was genuinely interested in me. But I guess it was all about the books and what I might know . . ."

I made a cup of tea and sat at the kitchen table with my chin in my hands. Christie jumped into my lap and meowed, "Are you sure? I don't like him, but do you think he's the killer?"

"I don't know," I wailed. "Whether he's a killer or somehow involved in the scheme, he hasn't been honest with me. And what about the note about the Edgar Allan Poe book? Is he the buyer or the finder for some rich collector? And he should've told me he knew Alice."

I grabbed my cell phone and dialed his number. It went to voicemail, and I hung up. I drank some tea and tried to collect my thoughts. Dave knew Wendy and I had been going to Oxford, and he'd learned all he needed to know about Belle's books and letters that day at Sunshine Cottage. He must've thought Belle would be by herself.

And where was he when Peter was run off the road? He said he was going to the coast, but did he? I didn't want to believe I'd been on a date with a killer, but the evidence all pointed that way.

When my phone rang, I was hoping it was Gemma, but it was Dave. He must have seen my number as a missed call on his phone. *Oh hell*, I thought, *just do it*. When I said hello, he seemed a bit irritated.

"Hi, did you call me? Is something up?"

"Um, no—I mean yes, I was calling to cancel on you for dinner. Something's come up."

Dave didn't respond right away. "Are you alright? You sound a little funny."

"I'm fine," I snapped. "I have a conflict, that's all."

"Okay . . . well, I'm still trying to make my deadline, so I'll call you later, alright?"

"Sure, if you want to. Bye," I said as I hung up. Oh, for goodness' sake, I could have handled that better, but at least it was over and done with. Now I needed to talk to Gemma and tell her what I'd seen and what I thought.

Why hadn't I texted her the copies of the notes I'd found in Dave's room? I rooted through my purse for the copies I'd made and scrolled through the photos on my phone for the earlier note about the $600,000 paid for the Poe book and the picture of the *Rare Finds* book.

I texted it all to Gemma with a message, "We need to talk."

I didn't hear from Gemma but instead received a text from Wendy. Peter was checking out of the hospital today, and she and Belle were taking him to his flat above the garage. My first thought was I needed to swing into action and organize his meals.

I sent an email to the group explaining the American custom of providing meals when a friend was in need and asking them to sign up for lunch and dinner slots starting Tuesday. A week of meals would probably do it. I volunteered for Monday, so I made a grocery list and drove to Sainsbury's. Perhaps shopping and cooking would take my mind off murder and mayhem.

I bought the ingredients for chicken salad, Greek salad, and baked ziti, and since desserts weren't my forte, I picked up some fresh-baked cookies. Back home, I spent the afternoon cooking. It was a good thing nothing I was making required carefully measured ingredients, as my mind kept wandering to what I'd seen in Dave's room and what it meant.

I could pretty much make a Bolognese sauce in my sleep, so the baked ziti came together without a hitch. With enough for two batches, I put one in the freezer, thinking I might invite friends for dinner one evening. I'd popped the chicken in the oven as soon as I came home, so while it cooled, I chopped celery, onion, and fresh basil for chicken salad. I'd prepare the Greek salad fresh at Peter's Monday evening.

Gemma rang as I was washing dishes. "Okay, I don't have time for a wild goose chase, so can you please explain to me what you think those notes mean? I can see some are from Alice, but where'd you find them?"

"Oops, guess I left out a few details," I said. "They were in Dave Prentiss's room at the inn, the journalist. I think he was in league with Alice somehow. Maybe he met her at the cricket pavilion; maybe he broke into Sunshine Cottage; maybe he ran Peter off the road."

"Whoa, Leta, those are a lot of *maybes*. Why are you suddenly pointing the finger at him when he wasn't even on our radar? What else do you know about him?"

I told her the little I knew about Dave's background and explained that his being a journalist who freelanced for literary magazines was a big red flag in my mind. Who better to understand the ins and outs of rare books? And who better to be able to connect with potential buyers?

"There you go again grasping at straws. We can't just make up suspects out of the blue, you know."

"What's that supposed to mean, Gemma? You asked me to ring you with any little thing I uncovered, and this is *big*. I think Dave had a motive and you can find out whether he had the opportunity. And, for your information, I consider him such a strong suspect, I canceled the date I had with him for tonight."

"What? You think he's a murderer and you accepted

another date with him? Given what you *think* you've discovered?" she asked.

"That was *before* I found the notes," I yelled. "I got scared, so I called it off."

"Well, thank goodness for that. How about staying put tonight so I don't have to worry about you? I'm trying to arrange a guard for Peter's home and don't have the manpower available to be chasing after you. So no more snooping, you hear me?"

"Oh, I hear you alright. If this is the thanks I get, I won't be bringing you anything else. I'm tired of being treated like I'm some kind of idiot." And with that, I hung up. If I'd had an old-fashioned landline, I'd have slammed down the phone for good measure.

Chapter Fourteen

I meant what I'd told Gemma. I was scared. I was lonely, and I was feeling sorry for myself. Not a good combination. I put together a plate of fruit and cheese for dinner, poured a glass of wine, and tried playing Words with Friends. I found I was making too many amateur moves and blamed my distracted state. I'm a tad competitive, so playing poorly just wouldn't do.

I tried reading my Louise Penny book but kept having to read the same paragraph over and over. In a typical week, I would have already finished it and started a new novel, but then, this had not by any means been a typical week.

I moved to my office and tried writing a column about my trip to Oxford with Wendy. It just wouldn't flow. Finally, I turned to the TV and found a rerun of Agatha Christie's Poirot. I'd seen it so many times my lack of focus didn't keep me from enjoying it.

Christie jumped in my lap and meowed, "I always love seeing stories by the lady I'm named for." I rubbed her head distractedly and she purred in contentment.

Dickens couldn't seem to settle down. "Out you go," I said. "Check the corners and be sure they're clear." Of course, he wasn't content with corner checking tonight; he had to bark.

"Give it a rest, Dickens," I yelled out the door.

"How would you know there's a couple out here taking a stroll if I didn't alert you?" he barked.

"And I need to know that because . . . ?" Clearly, I was out of sorts.

"That's it," I said as I grabbed a second glass of wine. "I'm going to take a nice long bubble bath and see if that relaxes me. Anybody coming with me?"

My two companions followed me up the stairs. Christie stretched out on my bed, and Dickens chose the bathmat. I lit some lavender candles and doused the lights. After thirty minutes of adding hot water as the tub cooled, I felt myself getting drowsy. Okay, I've turned myself into a prune. Time to see if I'm calm enough to drop off to sleep. I chose my favorite worn flannel nightgown and crawled into bed.

I must have fallen asleep because something startled me awake. I felt as though I'd been out for hours and thought maybe the sound was part of my dream. Was it the glass wind chimes tinkling, the ones on my screened porch? No, I had a porch and windchimes in Atlanta, not here. Could it be glass breaking? Then I heard a faint click. My first thought was my mischievous cat was on the kitchen counter, forbidden territory for her, but a glance told me she was at the foot of the bed. My bedside clock showed 10 pm. I hadn't been asleep long.

Then Dickens stood up and growled. He barked his alert bark and bolted downstairs, and I heard a voice trying to calm him down. "It's just me, boy, you know me. Shhh, don't want to wake the neighbors, do we?"

Wake the neighbors? What about me? Who's in my house? I crept out of bed to the top of the stairs. I could see a dim glow coming from my office and thought at first it was the bookcase lights I always left on, but there was a moving light too, like a flashlight.

I heard Dickens bark, "It's late; why are you here?" Not that whoever it was could understand him.

The voice said, "Here's a treat. Now, will you shut up?" And Dickens did—briefly.

I returned to my bedroom in search of my cell phone. That's when the floor creaked, and just like in all the suspense stories, I realized my phone wasn't there. Must be downstairs. In Atlanta, Henry had always kept a baseball bat beneath the bed for this kind of situation. He'd never had to use it, but here in England, I'd placed a cricket bat beneath my side of the bed just in case. I reached for it and was quite proud that I wasn't yet in panic mode.

Dickens resumed barking. "Hide, Leta, hide."

I heard a yelp and thud and knew my dog had been back-handed. I grabbed the cricket bat and ran down the stairs. "Leave Dickens alone! Get out of my house! The police are on the way!"

Dickens was whimpering, and I was sure I was going to see Dave in my office with him. I had my cricket bat at the ready to prevent him from hurting Dickens any more. But it wasn't Dave. It was Thom Cook. "What are you doing in my house? What have you done to Dickens?"

"Bloody hell, Leta, what are you doing here?" he yelled. "I thought you were out on a date."

"Well, I'm not, and what are you doing here?"

Thom's eyes darted from me to Dickens and back. "Calm

down. I've come for the books and letters. Just give them to me and I'll leave."

My mind was putting it all together. It had been Thom all along. It wasn't Dave in cahoots with Alice; it was Thom. All for books?

"Right," I said as I brandished the cricket bat. He stepped towards me. "Don't come any closer," I yelled. "If I give you what you came for, you'll just leave?" I didn't believe that, but I had to keep him talking. "It was you who killed Alice."

He looked angry. "It was an accident, the silly cow. We were partners. She'd found out about Belle's books and letters by chatting her up, and she mentioned them to me. She thought they were worth a good bit but didn't have the connections to sell them. Nothing beyond some used book-stores that would never pay top dollar.

"So we came up with a plan. She'd lift 'em, I'd find buyers, and we'd split the proceeds. I was able to sell a few letters, and she seemed happy with the arrangement. She was meant to bring the *Peter and Wendy* book to the party at the inn. That was going to be our first big score. She knew I had a buyer, and I had some upfront money for her, but she rang me that day to say she wanted twice what we'd agreed on. Can you believe that?

"We had to hash it out, and that was too risky to do at the Inn. We agreed to meet at the cricket pavilion so no one would see us, and she told me not to bother to come without the money."

"So, what happened? What went wrong?"

He was getting angrier as he told the story. "She had no intention of giving me the book that night even though I'd come up with the extra money. I could afford to pay her more because I'd been keeping the lion's share of the payments. But she'd decided she could find buyers on her own, and make big money, without a middleman. If it weren't for me, she wouldn't have known how to sell the books in the first place, and now she was trying to cut me out. No way."

I was getting more scared by the minute, but I had to keep him talking. "She was double-crossing you?"

"Yes, and she'd been working on her plan for a while. She'd approached Dave Prentiss, that journalist, but he kept telling her no. He knew it wasn't on the up and up and told her he wasn't interested. She'd misjudged him."

"So, who was going to purchase the book if not your buyer and not Dave? Your professor?"

"Hell no. I'd never involved Professor Bartholomew; no way he'd have anything to do with something underhanded like this. All that talk was for yours and Wendy's benefit."

"Then who was going to buy the book?"

"Can you believe Alice had advertised in a literary magazine and hooked a moneybags collector? Alice? Alice figured out how to do that?

"She was sooo agreeable! She said she'd take the money I'd brought and wait for the rest, but she wasn't giving me the goods unless I agreed to pay her what Mr. Moneybags was going to give her. Who did she think she was?"

"And the accident?" I could tell he'd kept this all pent up and was eager to unload.

"I just knew the book was in that big blue purse she carried, and I grabbed her arm and yanked the purse. I got the bag, but she went down and hit her head, and I ran."

"And you searched her flat?"

It suddenly dawned on me that he somehow knew I was lying about the police. Why else would he spend so much time talking to me? "A lot of good that did me. Her phone was in her blue bag, and I found her computer, so I was able to find the name of the collector and contact him, but I didn't have the book. I figured it had to still be at Belle's cottage, and I knew you and Wendy were in Oxford, so I broke in. Everyone knows Belle is deaf as a doorpost. She'd never have heard me."

"Except you didn't know Peter would be there, that the twins never leave their mum on her own at night, right?"

"And I just knew he'd seen me, so I was desperate and took care of him, except I didn't, did I?"

"No, you didn't. What are you going to do when his memory comes back? Go after him again?"

"Not your problem! Just get me the books—both books and the letters you showed me," he screamed.

"OK, I'm going to slowly walk into the sitting room to get them, and I'll put them in a bag and bring them back to you, okay?" I said as I began to back out of the office. I could see Dickens had recovered and was studying Thom, but I wasn't sure what he had in mind. As I backed out, I glimpsed Christie on the stairs.

And then everything happened at once. Dickens lunged at Thom and brought him down, and Christie flew past me to leap on him and rake his face with her claws. I ran to the front door, flipped the deadbolt, and jerked the door open.

I had to ring the school bell but couldn't quite reach the rope. I scrambled up on the bench, but my feet got tangled in my long gown. Down I went on the front path. Thom had regained his feet and was lurching my way, but Dickens had different plans.

"I'm coming," he barked as he sank his teeth into Thom's calf, and Thom tried desperately to shake him off. Dickens released his victim, jumped on the stone bench, and leapt up to grab the bell pull in his mouth. He swung back and forth ringing the bell before losing his grip. My protector didn't miss a beat. He shook himself and went after Thom again. By now, lights were coming on in the neighboring cottages.

When my neighbors Deborah and John arrived, Thom was bleeding and begging for mercy. Dickens was sitting on his chest snapping and snarling, Christie was screeching in the doorway, and I was walloping his legs and ribs with the cricket bat. He must have thought the hounds of hell were after him— or at the very least a vicious white dog, a petite black attack cat, and one furious woman.

When Constable James pulled up with siren going and lights flashing, I was sitting in the kitchen with Christie in my lap. Deborah had gone to check on Timmy, and John and Dickens were standing guard over Thom where he was lying tied up in the front yard. Who knew my dentist was so handy with a rope?

Mr. Morgan, my neighbor from across the street, had dialed 999 and arrived right behind Deborah and John. When he saw John had things under control, he went back and got his wife, who was now bustling around my kitchen brewing a pot of tea and putting biscuits on a plate.

Deborah returned with Timmy and a bottle of brandy. "Good for a shock," she said as she poured a generous portion into a teacup. "In fact, I think I need a bit too. Goodness, Leta, what a scare."

I seemed to be having trouble forming words, so Deborah carried on. "Timmy's sneezing turned into a stuffy nose, so I was up checking on him when I saw a light coming from your cottage. I thought at first you were getting in late, but then I saw the light was moving through the house. John was watching telly, and before I could get downstairs to tell him, the school bell started ringing to beat all get-out."

I nodded and took a slug of brandy with tea. "Whoa," I spluttered, "that's strong stuff. What do you think, Timmy, is Dickens a little hero dog?"

Timmy's eyes were big as saucers as he looked from me to his mum. Then he smiled. "Yes, a hero dog, that's what he is."

"Pffft," said Christie, "Aren't you forgetting someone?"

"And, Timmy, Christie helped too. She and Dickens are a team," I quickly amended.

Constable James came to the door to ask me if I could hold on a bit longer while he took statements from the neighbors and got my intruder into the patrol car. I pointed to the brandy bottle and told him I'd be fine. A moment later, I heard more voices outside, and Gemma appeared.

"I stayed home like you told me," I said. "No snooping."

"Thank goodness you're okay," she said as she smiled. "Looks like your theory of the case was right."

"Yes, only it wasn't Colonel Mustard in the pantry with the candlestick. I got that part wrong."

Gemma chuckled. "Ah yes, but Thom is babbling nonstop and telling all. I think he's afraid we'll sic Dickens on him if he stops talking. May have to hire your dog to assist in interrogations.

"By the way, would it make you feel any better to hear that your erstwhile dinner date is completely in the clear?"

"Yes and no," I said. "It's not like we were an item, but I doubt he'll be eager to see me after I all but accused him of murder."

"You might be surprised." She grinned as she backed out of the kitchen. In trooped Libby and Gavin.

I nodded and murmured as they alternated hugs with questions and the kitchen began to clear. Deborah said she and Timmy would check on me the next day, and Mrs. Morgan poured me another cup of tea and said goodbye. Libby added brandy to the cup, and she and Gavin slipped out too.

Dickens put his paws on my lap and licked my face. "We got him, Leta. We're okay now."

That's when Dave walked in. *Uh-oh, this is going to be awkward,* I thought as I blushed scarlet. I started to stand and before I knew it, he pulled me out of the chair and hugged me tight. "Thank goodness you're okay," he said.

I started to cry then. It was finally all too much.

"Shush, it'll be alright," he murmured. "I'll let you explain later how you came to the conclusion I was the devil incarnate. Seriously, we'll talk, but not now. Gemma tells me she's first in line."

I had a long evening ahead of me.

By the time I'd finished telling Gemma the details of what had happened at my cottage, it was after midnight. I was keyed up, but I was also exhausted. I didn't want to be by myself, but I didn't want to leave the comfort of my home.

Constable James had found a piece of cardboard to tape over the window in my mudroom, the one Thom had broken to gain entry. I was seriously peeved he'd broken the original 1840s glass. The cardboard wouldn't keep anyone out, but I doubted I'd have any additional uninvited visitors any time soon. Dickens must have read my thoughts, because he assured me he'd keep me safe. Christie had long ago retreated to the bedroom.

I was sound asleep the next morning when I heard someone pounding on my door and Dickens barking to beat the band. It was Wendy come to find out what had happened.

"Coming, coming," I yelled as I hobbled down the stairs.

Dickens dashed out, and Wendy almost knocked me down rushing in to hug me. "Look at you, you look like death warmed over. Oops, poor choice of words, I guess."

I gave a half-hearted smile and started the coffee. I did my best to give her a blow-by-blow description of the previous day. She couldn't believe I'd suspected Dave of being the killer, but then, she hadn't been there. She hadn't seen the notes from Alice.

"And you mean Thom—sweet, helpful Thom—did all this? Did he try to hurt you?"

"He didn't have a weapon, if that's what you mean. He wasn't expecting me to be here because I'd told him I'd be out to dinner. I'm not sure how he'd have done away with me if it had come to that. And it would have. He couldn't very well have left me alive to tell Gemma he'd broken into my cottage."

Wendy looked at Dickens and Christie. "And you two? How lucky is she that you were here? And so smart to boot? I mean, grabbing the bell pull to ring the bell? I hear Thom has a pretty painful dog bite on his leg and deep cat scratches on his face."

"Yup, those scratches were well done, if I do say so myself," meowed Christie. "And Dickens, you got him good."

"Yes, these two saved me. I'm not sure how much good that cricket bat would've done me in the end, but I must admit I enjoyed slugging him with it when he was down. Too bad I didn't break any bones."

"Absolutely unbelievable," said Wendy. "Every bit of this,

from the very beginning. Things like this don't happen in Astonbury. I hope you're not sorry you moved here."

"That thought never crossed my mind, though now you've mentioned it, I'm betting my sister is going to read me the riot act. I haven't told her yet. She was cross enough when I emailed her I'd found a body and we'd gone to Alice's flat. Whoa boy. I'm not looking forward to telling her the rest."

I asked about Peter and Belle, and Wendy told me Peter was doing amazingly well. He'd had no trouble getting up the stairs to his flat and was able to shower on his own this morning. She'd fixed him a hot breakfast and left him complaining about home help coming in. Of course, he didn't think he needed any help.

"Listen," I said, "I'm on the list today for his lunch and dinner, and I've got it ready to go, but I need some time to get my act together this morning. Can I get you to take the chicken salad to him and I'll deliver dinner later?"

When she heard what I'd fixed for dinner, she laughingly threatened to join us. I told her I had another pan of baked ziti in the freezer and offered to drop it by for her and Belle to have later in the week.

After another huge hug, I shooed her out and took a cup of coffee to the couch. I needed some time to myself to process yesterday's events. Time to myself with Dickens and Christie, that is. My two protectors were unusually quiet this morning, almost as though they knew I needed some quiet time to recover.

I didn't exactly swing into action, but I managed to drag myself upstairs to get a shower. And drag, or maybe limp, was the operative word. I must have fallen harder than I realized when I tripped over my nightgown, because my knee was bruised and swollen. But it could have been so much worse if not for Dickens and Christie. I was one lucky girl.

I let calls from Toby, Rhiannon, and Beatrix go to voicemail. I wasn't yet up to telling the story over and over. I'd just hung up the phone after scheduling an appointment with a glass repair shop when Dave called. I didn't ignore his call.

"Hi there," I answered.

"Hey, Nancy Drew, how ya feelin' this morning?"

"Nope, can't be Nancy Drew. She's a strawberry blonde. Maybe Tuppence?" I replied.

"Ha. Already feisty. You must be feeling alright. Are you up for a visitor, or maybe lunch out?" he asked.

"Lunch would be nice as long as it's not in Astonbury. I'm afraid by now word has spread through the village grapevine and we wouldn't get a moment's peace."

"How about the pub in Broadway? That way we can take the hero dog with us. Okay?"

I laughed. "That would be super. I can be ready in an hour." That should give me enough time to hobble upstairs and apply makeup, though I was pretty sure no amount of concealer would cover the black circles under my eyes.

"Christie," I said as I brushed my hair, "will you be nice to Dave this time? He really is a good guy, even if he's not Peter or Henry."

"Okay, okay, I'll give him the benefit of the doubt for a little while, but I still think we need to see Peter again," meowed my opinionated cat.

Dickens already considered Dave a friend after their evening sharing pita chips. When I told him it was Dave's idea to take him to the pub with us, he gave Christie an *I told you so* look.

Dave arrived and lifted me off my feet in a hug. "Wow,

you're a sight for sore eyes. The damsel in distress and her four-legged heroes."

Christie twined herself around his legs at that comment and Dickens barked in agreement. "I understand you each deserve a medal of commendation. I can see the headline now —Dickens and Christie save the day."

I laughed for the first time in several days and looked up at Dave. "I can't begin to tell you how sorry I am—"

"Not now, let's save it for lunch and a pint."

And that's what we did. We loaded Dickens into the car and drove to Broadway. He got the first of several dog biscuits and lay beneath the table as Dave fetched two pints.

I couldn't stop blushing in embarrassment as Dave told me how Gemma had approached him with questions. When she established he really had been in Dartmouth when the second and third crimes occurred, she broached the subject of the notes in his room.

"Okay, I admit I was shocked, but my note about book prices was easily explained. The notes from Alice? Not so much. I was checking on *Winnie-the-Pooh* books after our conversation with Belle, and I stumbled across the Poe sale then. I was amazed at the prices."

I had nothing to say to that. I sipped my pint and nodded for him to continue.

"But Alice? When she found out early during my stay that I was a journalist who wrote about books, she must have decided I was her guy. She intimated she had access to a first edition J. M. Barrie book, and sure, I'd have loved to see it, but buy it? No way. Even without seeing it, I knew it would be pricey. Remember I told you I had some first editions, but nothing as valuable as what Alice was talking about.

"She didn't badger me. She just left me the two notes. I

told her one morning after breakfast that I wasn't interested, and that was the end of it. I had a funny feeling about her. Can't say why. I just did."

"Is this where I get to say again how sorry I am?" I asked. "I have no excuse. I mean, how could I? I jumped to a terrible conclusion when I saw those Alice notes, and I was devastated."

"Devastated?"

"Oh hell, you're going to make me say it, aren't you? I really enjoyed our dinner out. I told Wendy you were a marvelous conversationalist. I mean, you're witty, well-read, and charming, and I was thrilled when you asked me out again. Until I wasn't. Until I thought you were a . . . criminal."

To his credit, Dave was still smiling at me. "If I was so charming, how could you think I was a stone-cold killer?"

"Aren't all psychopaths charming?" I asked. "It's like Gemma says, I read and watch too many mysteries."

He actually chuckled. "I may have to agree with her on that point. Way too much time on your hands. *But*, and this is an *important* but, you were right about all my wonderful personality traits . . . not that I'm a psychopath—"

"Well, of course, you're not. I know that now. A little late, though. I can't believe you're being so calm about this. You seem to think it's humorous."

"Here's what I choose to think, Leta. We really hit it off, and we have lots in common. I may be charming and witty and whatever else you said, but you are too, not to mention beautiful. You got all caught up in an awful situation. You found a body, for goodness' sake, of someone you knew. Your friend Peter could have died. And, yes, against your better judgment —you jumped to the wrong conclusion."

Now I had tears in my eyes. "Somehow it doesn't sound quite so bad when you put it that way."

"Of course, it doesn't. What I'm trying to say is I won't let this get in the way of our relationship if you won't. Deal?"

Relationship? I'm in a relationship with someone who isn't furious I accused him of being a killer? What is he? The world's most understanding guy? "I don't know what to say."

"How 'bout deal?"

And so I said it. "Deal."

Dickens poked his nose out from under the table and barked, "Thank goodness. I like him, and I thought you were gonna blow it."

By the time Dave and Dickens escorted me into my cottage, I was pleasantly inebriated and feeling no pain— well, except a little in my knee. Dave settled me on the couch, elevated my leg on a pillow, and made an ice pack for my knee. He gave me a for-real kiss, not a peck on the cheek, and promised to call later.

Chapter Fifteen

I'd been answering questions from my Astonbury friends as best I could, but that meant they each had different bits of the story. Even Wendy didn't have all the details. And people were still unnerved by the crime spree in our little village, even though we knew the culprit was locked away.

Then I hit upon the idea of a party, but not just any party —a Poirot-like gathering where I could reveal the ins and outs of the crimes to my friends. It was time I cooked up a Greek feast for my new friends, and a dinner party with a captive audience would allow me to answer questions, hopefully for the last time.

I dropped by Sunshine Cottage to tell Wendy and Belle my idea. I wanted my guests to come as their favorite sleuths. Barring that, they had to at least come in fancy dress. Belle and Wendy loved the idea and wanted to help with the planning.

"Wait until you hear my idea for the invitations," I said. "Picture white card stock with the pen and ink Edward Gorey characters from the opening scene of Masterpiece Mystery."

"Oh," said Belle, "I've got a great idea for some simple

decorations. Let's get some Edward Gorey notecards, and I'll create decoupaged coasters. We can ask Beatrix to bring Agatha Christie books to place throughout your cottage."

Brainstorming with these two was a treat. "I can showcase my Nancy Drew books too," I added.

"I've got it," proclaimed Wendy. "I'll be Agatha Raisin. She's blonde and retired and lives in a small village. Perfect."

Belle sighed and smiled at the same time. "I guess there's nothing for it but for me to be Miss Marple, right? I may need a frumpy hat from a thrift shop, and I'll have to bring a bag of knitting."

"This is the perfect excuse to go shopping," said Wendy. "Who will you be, Leta?"

"I'm debating whether to come as Tuppence from the Agatha Christie tales or as Harriet Vane, Peter Wimsey's wife. Both were brunettes. Either way, I think we need to shop vintage dress shops. I'm picturing something ankle-length and clingy in velvet and a long string of pearls to wrap around my neck and tie in a knot. One of those elegant cigarette holders too."

"I'm sure we'll both need fascinators to complement our dresses, don't you think?" asked Wendy. "Like the ones we admired in Oxford?"

"Sounds as though our last stop will be the Mad Hatter," I responded.

"So, will you have the affair catered?" asked Wendy.

"Not a chance," I said. "I have the menu all planned. Kalamata olives and chunks of feta cheese plus pita bread and hummus for appetizers. Then we'll sit down to Greek salad followed by pastitsio as the main course. Coffee with baklava will round out the evening. It's by no means a Downton Abbey menu, but I feel sure everyone will enjoy it."

"Yummy," exclaimed Belle. "If it's all as tasty as your Greek salad, I'll be in heaven."

It had been over two years since I'd thrown a party, so I was a bit frantic over getting the details right. I visited the farmer's market for fresh romaine lettuce, tomatoes, and green onions, the cheese shop for feta, and Sainsbury's for olives, hummus, pita bread, and the pastitsio ingredients. Olive oil and red wine vinegar were always in my pantry. Friday, I set the table and set out coasters and Nancy Drew books. Beatrix had promised to come thirty minutes early on Saturday with the Agatha Christie collection.

Doing all that ahead of time freed me up Saturday to prepare the pans of pastitsio so they'd be ready to pop in the oven as the appetizers were being served. Lettuce and onions went into a big bowl in the fridge, chopped tomatoes and olives in another. I would toss everything together with herbs and oil and vinegar right before dinner was served.

I'd hired Toby's barista Jenny and her sister Jill, Libby's new housekeeper, to pass the appetizers and pour wine. Dressed in black skirts and crisp white blouses, they came an hour ahead of the guests to help me with any last-minute things I might have forgotten. Mostly they were there early in case anyone showed up while I was upstairs getting dressed.

I was quite pleased with my dress. Wendy and I'd had a ball visiting shops all over the Cotswolds before finally finding what I'd envisioned. It looked like something Lady Mary might have worn in Downton Abbey except for the slightly risqué plunging neckline. I could picture Lord Grantham putting his foot down and Lady Grantham calming him.

The burgundy velvet dress draped beautifully, and the gleaming pearl necklace and cuff bracelet completed the 1920s look, but it was the fascinator that was the pièce de résistance. Crystal sequins sparkled on the tiny velvet headpiece, which was topped with a black peacock feather and a short net veil. I had to laugh when I thought of tossing the salad in my outfit. Heaven forbid I splatter it with olive oil.

"Leta, this is even better than your red dress. Stunning, you look stunning," meowed Christie. "Not sure about that thing on your head, though. Looks like a cat toy to me."

"Don't even think about it," I said. "That's why it's been tucked away in a box in the top of my closet. Only Agatha Christie's Tuppence can pull off this look, not Christie the cat. But I *do* have something special for you too."

"Me? Is it a toy? Or a treat?"

I could tell she didn't know what to think when I pulled out a tiny rhinestone collar, but she sat patiently while I exchanged it for her usual red elastic one. She hopped up on the dressing table to admire herself. "Ooh la la, I look like a diva."

Dickens looked askance at his sister. "Please tell me you're not dressing me in something prissy like that."

"Now, Dickens, I have a gentleman's ensemble for you—a black bowtie and satin vest to set off your white fur." I'd had quite a time finding his outfit. The bowtie wasn't so hard, but the vests had been sized for smaller dogs. It was my friend Bev who finally found one online in Dickens's size. I couldn't wait for her to see the photos.

"Okay, you two, ready to head downstairs? Beatrix is probably already here, and the rest of our guests will be close behind her."

Too bad only Jenny, Jill, and Beatrix were there to appreciate our entrance as I glided down the stairs followed by my well-dressed companions. Still, they gave us a round of applause. Beatrix had chosen to come as forensic archaeologist Dr. Ruth Galloway from the Elly Griffiths mysteries. Dressed in a white lab coat, she had what appeared to be a femur in one pocket and a skeletal hand reaching out of another.

Jenny uncorked several bottles of wine, and Jill arranged appetizers on a silver tray. I reminded them not to set any food on the side tables in the sitting room or even the kitchen table lest Dickens help himself. Beatrix and I were sipping wine as Jenny opened the door to more guests.

Belle made her grand entrance as Miss Marple, complete with knitting needles so we had a third Christie character, and as promised, Wendy came as Agatha Raisin in a beaded turquoise sheath that set off her blue eyes and blonde hair. Her fascinator featured clear crystals and a peacock feather with the blue middle. Peter, dressed in a tux, had me stumped until he put on his monocle. "It's Lord Peter Wimsey, isn't it?" I cried.

"At your service, madame," he replied as he began ferrying coats to my office.

We all hooted as Gemma, Libby, and Gavin arrived. Gemma had smudges of flour on her cheeks and was brandishing a rolling pin. The logo on her white apron and her chef's hat said The Cookie Jar, and I knew immediately she was Hannah Swensen, amateur sleuth and owner of the fictional bakery in Minnesota. She was followed by Libby, dressed as Hannah's big gold cat Moishe.

"Is that Libby?" asked Dickens. "She looks a bit like Paddington."

"I'm not sure who she's supposed to be," meowed Christie, "But I want to play with that tail."

Behind the cat was Gavin in a rumpled raincoat with a cigar in his mouth. "Columbo," we all shouted.

Next was Toby dressed in a tux with a bit of extra padding —well, lots of extra padding—to give him the round shape of Hercule Poirot. His hair was slicked back and he was sporting a curled black mustache.

It took us all a moment to recognize Deborah. We knew right away she was Sherlock Holmes, given her deerstalker hat and pipe, but she'd added a large nose that made her almost unrecognizable—until, that is, we saw her husband John in a tweed three-piece suit with a stethoscope hanging around his neck. Ah yes, it was only fitting for John Watson, our village dentist, to come dressed as Dr. Watson.

Bringing up the rear was Rhiannon in a plaid skirt and green twinset, a strand of pearls around her neck, and her hair tinted strawberry blonde. It was Belle who piped up, "Lo and behold, it's Nancy Drew!"

Christie had retreated to the bookshelf in the sitting room to hold court and was getting plenty of compliments on her sparkly collar. Dickens wasn't retreating anywhere. He was saying hello to each and every guest in the hopes he'd score a belly rub or a snack. So far, he seemed to be doing well on both counts. I put the pastitsio in the oven and kicked off the main event.

As we three had agreed, Gemma, Wendy, and I gathered in front of the fireplace and quieted the crowd. "Welcome one and all," Gemma started. "We're gathered here tonight to celebrate the end of what we hope was Astonbury's first and last crime spree. It's time for our lives to get back to normal, but before that can happen, we need to lay to rest the rumors and wild imaginings that have been circulating."

"First," I said, "No dragons were slain."

"Second," said Wendy, "No spells were cast."

"Third," concluded Gemma, "We couldn't have done it without all of you. Now, I'm not sure we can sum this up as well as Hercule Poirot would, but we'll give it our best shot. Toby, we may have to call on you for help since you've dressed the part." Toby stood and took a bow.

It was my turn. "By now, everyone knows Dickens and I found Alice's body at the cricket pavilion and that it was Thom Cook who accidentally killed her. Yes, it was an accident. They'd had a falling out over a moneymaking scheme to steal and sell rare books. And I emphasize accident because I choose to believe that Thom didn't set out to harm anyone, but once he killed Alice, it seems his inner demons got the better of him."

Continued Wendy, "You may not know that Miss Marple over there, along with Tuppence and I, went to Alice's flat to see to her cat. I'm not sure Gemma believes us, but that's really why we went—except we discovered her place had been ransacked and couldn't help but look for clues."

Miss Marple giggled and Gemma rolled her eyes. "And that's when we three amateur sleuths started our own investigation," I said. "We discovered Alice had been stealing from clients, even blackmailing a few. What led to her death, though, was her plan to get her hands on Belle's valuable books and letters from Uncle Jim—or, as most of us know him, J. M. Barrie."

Wendy picked up the story. "What we didn't know until it was almost too late was she'd hooked up with Thom to find buyers for the books—buyers who would pay unbelievable amounts for my mum's childhood treasures."

"Turns out," Gemma added, "the two knew each other from Manchester, where Thom bought used books from

Alice's flea market stall—at first to read, but later to sell as a means to help with his Oxford expenses, and to help him fit in with his peers who were better off than he was. He was the perfect middleman for the Peter Pan scheme, as I think of it, and even had a professor who was a Barrie expert."

"I hate to admit he bamboozled me and Wendy with his nice guy, 'let me help' attitude when we approached him to do some research," I said.

"Heck, he bamboozled me," interjected Beatrix. "He was one of the most knowledgeable assistants I ever had at the Book Nook. I still can't believe what he was up to."

"And what he was up to," said Wendy, "was getting Mum's books and letters at any cost. That's why he broke into our cottage, thinking Mum was on her own. He might have gotten away with it, too, if Peter hadn't been staying over."

"Even at that point," said Belle, "I don't think he planned to hurt me or anyone else. He was in over his head by the time Peter chased him out."

"Uh-huh, you all are being awfully forgiving of the lad, but I'm the one he ran off the road," said Peter. "And I'm thinking he'd have come back to finish off the job because he couldn't be sure I hadn't figured out who he was."

"Yes, I mentioned that to him when I found him in my cottage looking for the books and letters I'd so naively shown him. How was I to know it was Thom who killed Alice and tried to kill you?" I shuddered at the memory of our confrontation.

Gemma piped up. "None of us knew, but we might have gotten there sooner if someone hadn't gone off the rails thinking she'd found the 'real' killer. Tuppence, I'm talking about you."

And in walked Tommy, Tuppence's sleuthing partner in the

Tommy and Tuppence mysteries. It was Dave, looking dashing in a tux, a jaunty white silk scarf, and a top hat. "Ah, yes, dear Tuppence, you did send Gemma off on a wild goose chase. Would you care to explain to your friends how you came to believe I was evil personified? That I'd been the one to kill Alice and go after Peter?" He chuckled as he swept off his hat and bowed in front of me.

"You devil," I cried, "You told me you couldn't possibly make it back from New York." He'd returned home, where he was putting the finishing touches on his article about Belle's Barrie collection, including the only copy of *The Family at Sunshine Cottage*. Belle had given him exclusive rights to the story.

"Got to keep you on your toes, dear Tuppence."

"Enough," I said. "The short version is I found notes in Dave's room at the Inn, notes from Alice, trying to get him to buy Belle's books, and I jumped to the wrong conclusion and never saw that it was Thom all along. But all's well that ends well, right?"

"Right," said Deborah, "let's just gloss over the part where Thom broke in here and you were almost the third victim."

"Or the part where Christie and I saved you," barked Dickens. By now my four-legged protectors were standing by my side. I reached down to pick up Christie and then grabbed a glass of champagne as Jenny came through with a tray of glasses for all.

"I'd like to propose a toast or two or three," I said. "First, here's to Dickens, my little hero dog, who brought down my assailant and in a stroke of genius rang the school bell to bring Deborah and John to my rescue."

"What do you mean 'little dog'?" barked Dickens as my

friends marveled at his ingenuity. "I was big enough to grab that bell pull, wasn't I? Christie is little. I'm not."

"Second, thank you, Christie, for jumping in to claw the culprit and inflict maximum damage."

Christie preened and meowed and tried to sip my champagne.

"And here's to Gemma," said Wendy. "Thank you for listening to our ideas and putting them together with what you found through good old-fashioned police work."

I had to interrupt. "Though you do have a habit of rolling your eyes!"

"Setting that aside," continued Wendy. "Justice was done because of you."

With both hands on her cane, Belle stood and said, "Jenny, we need more champagne, please. I'd like to say a few words."

Sweet Belle. The matriarch of our group had been through a lot the past few weeks. "Leta, you've praised everyone involved in apprehending Thom, even Dickens and Christie, but what about you?

"You deserve the lion's share of the credit for solving these crimes—Alice's murder, the break-in at Sunshine Cottage, and the attempted murder of my son. Without you, Thom would have made off with my books and sooner or later come after my Peter again. You put a stop to all that." She raised her glass and said, "Here's to Leta."

I was blushing beet red and trying to deflect attention from myself by moving toward the kitchen to make the salad when Libby stopped me.

"Just a moment, please," she said. "I too would like to say a few words. All of us once knew Alice as the generous, kind-hearted, thoughtful woman who never failed to bring a basket of home-baked sweets when she cleaned our homes. We've learned she had another side, a dishonest side, but as Gemma said of Thom, I'd prefer to believe Alice's demons got the better of her. I'd like to raise a glass to the Alice I knew and loved. No matter her flaws, she was a friend."

The group took a moment to digest what Libby had said, and slowly, one by one, they stood and raised their glasses, until everyone uttered the words, "Here's to Alice."

By that time, we'd all had way too much champagne on empty stomachs. Jenny, Jill, and I plated salads and pastitsio and filled wine glasses. When we sat down to dinner, it was Toby who raised his glass and spoke as Poirot. "*Mes amis*, if happiness is to be found in an evening with good friends and good food, we are fortunate, *non*? Cheers!"

Book II

The Fall Fête isn't very festive when an illusionist is discovered dead. Can Leta and her talking pets crash the killer's party?

Read <u>Pumpkins, Paws & Murder</u> to find out.

What was Leta's life like before she retired to the Cotswolds?

How did Dickens & Christie become part of the family? Find out in ***Paws, Claws & Mischief***—the prequel to the Dickens & Christie mystery series.
Sign up for my newsletter to get your complimentary copy TODAY!

If you're a paperback reader, use this link to sign up https://bit.ly/Pennnewsletter

Visit kathymanospenn.com for Dickens & Christie news and pics, and if you're reading a paperback version, that's where you can sign up for the newsletter.

Don't miss out on the Dickens & Christie Prequel.

Psst... Please take a minute...

Dear Reader,

Writers put their hearts and souls into every book. Nothing makes it more worthwhile than reader reviews. Yes, authors appreciate reviews that provide helpful insights.

If you enjoyed this book, Kathy would love it if you could find the time to leave a good, honest review . . . because after everything is said and done, authors write to bring enjoyment to their readers.

Thank you, Dickens

*Be sure to look for the recipe at the end.
**Click here to purchase and download other books in the series. Or visit <u>Amazon</u> for the paperback.

Recipe

My sisters and I learned to make this salad by watching our father. We never measure the ingredients, but these approximations will do the trick.

Servings: 4

Ingredients:
  Salad

- 2 heads of Romaine lettuce rinsed, dried, and torn into bite-size pieces
- 1 large farm fresh tomato cut in bite-size pieces or grape or cherry tomatoes halved
- 1 bunch of green onions (scallions) thinly sliced, mostly the white part
- 1/2 cup pitted Kalamata olives
- 4 oz. crumbled Feta cheese, preferably goat or sheep's milk Feta (Note: Pre-crumbled is not as tasty but will do in a pinch.)

Dressing

- Approximately ¼ cup of extra-virgin olive oil
- Approximately 2 TBs red wine vinegar
- Garlic salt, oregano, salt, pepper to taste
- Optional: Juice of ½ lemon for a citrus kick

Directions

In a large salad bowl, toss all the salad ingredients together. Gradually add the dressing ingredients directly to the salad and toss to taste as you go.

Tips

- *Start small. Add more oil, vinegar, and herbs to taste.*
- *Three heads of romaine lettuce will easily feed ten.*

Would you like to know when the next book is on the way? Click here to sign up for my Newsletter, or visit KathyManosPenn.com to sign up there.

About the Author

Kathy at her desk when she was four years old.

As a corporate escapee, Kathy Manos Penn went from crafting change communications to plotting page-turners. Adhering to the adage to "write what you know," she populates her mysteries with well-read, witty senior women, a sassy cat, and a loyal dog. The murders and talking pets, however, exist only in her imagination.

Years ago, when she stumbled onto a side job as a columnist for a local paper, she saw the opportunity as an entertaining diversion from the corporate grind. Little did she know that her serendipitous foray into writing "whatever struck her fancy" would lead to a cozy mystery series.

How does she describe her life? "I'm living a dream I never knew I had. Picture me sitting serenely at my desk, surrounded by the four-legged office assistants who inspire the personalities of Dickens & Christie. Why is Dickens a fiend for belly rubs? Because my real-life dog is.

The same goes for Christie's finicky eating habits and penchant for lolling on top of the desk or in the file drawer. She gets it from my calico cat who right this minute is lying on the desk swishing her tail and deciding which pen or pencil to knock to the floor next."

—Kathy

Visit www.KathyManosPenn.com to contact Kathy, read her blogs, and more.

Would you like to know when the next book is on the way? Be sure to sign up up for her newsletter here or on he website. https://bit.ly/3bEjsfi

facebook.com/KathyManosPennAuthor

instagram.com/kathymanospennauthor

amazon.com/Kathy-Manos-Penn

goodreads.com/Kathy_Manos_Penn

bookbub.com/authors/Kathy-Manos-Penn

Made in the USA
Columbia, SC
05 November 2022

70520691R00152